To Susan

Distant Horizons

Best Wishes

Eric C. Bartholomew

First published in Great Britain in 2009
By KavanaghTipping Publishing,
Wingham Business Centre, Goodnestone Rd,
Wingham CT3 1AR

ISBN 978-1-906546-05-2

Copyright © 2009 Eric C. Bartholomew

All rights reserved. No part of the publication may be
reproduced, stored in a retrieval system, or transmitted
in any form or by any means, electronic, mechanical,
photocopying, recording, or otherwise, without the
prior permission of the publishers, nor be otherwise
circulated in any form of binding or cover other than
that in which it is published and without a similar
condition being imposed on the subsequent purchaser.

Cover design: CaveCeative.com

To Mary, lover, wife and friend who kept my spirits and imagination going when all else failed.

To Carol de Rose, my friend and mentor. Without her help this book would not have been forthcoming.

also on Kindle or Amazon

'Angels and Dirty Faces'
By Eric.C.Bartholomew

''Indiana Bones' out Hopefully
                              Sept 2011.

Eric is now writing the
sequeal of this Book
        ' Dark Horizons'

also you may be interested
in Eric's other Web page
  www. Slapandstipple . Co . Uk
and - www. thanekantenow . Co . Uk

distanthorizons. 7 @ googlemail .
                                com

4

Prologue

A figure pushed the bulkhead door open on its well-greased hinges, the light from behind silhouetting his dark torso. He moved silently, closing the steel door behind him, and stepped quickly to the side of the great ship. He tossed a life jacket over the side. As it hit the water, a yellow light came on, automatically flashing its mayday signal – on, off, on, off. Suddenly, he caught the sound of waterproof clothing rustling somewhere in the dark. He stood stock still, not daring to breathe. The glow from an inhaled cigarette illuminated a shape skulking in the corner of a bulkhead, and briefly lit up rusty steel walls and paint-peeled rivets. The black ship throbbed forward, the steel floor vibrating under them. He moved stealthily forward, smiling to himself. It was one of the midnight watch.

As his eyes became accustomed to the darkness, he made out the outline of the figure standing in the corner. The glow from the cigarette died and the man at the bulkhead turned, spotted the flashing light and raised his arm automatically. 'Man over—!' No other sound left his lips. The hilt of a knife stuck out from his throat; the long steel blade had severed his windpipe. Blood and mucus dribbled from his lips, splashing onto his waterproof coat. He slumped forward.

The black figure took his weight easily. Dragging the dying man towards the ship's side, he slid him over the gunnels. The body dropped like a stone, hitting the surface with a great splash. The dark figure looked around. No one had seen or heard a thing. He smiled to himself once more…

5

Chapter One

The fisherman watched the red disc of the sun rise out of the sea, as it did every morning, washed, rested, refreshed and ready for another day. He marvelled, as always, that the sea never boiled and the sun never lost its warmth. Chasing the silver moon from the sky, it lifted above the horizon, warming him now, the night's chill leaving with the cold moon. He stood up from his squat, cramped position and stretched, luxuriating in its warmth.

Joe Remerez Gonzales, whose name reflected his proud Portuguese heritage – Portuguese by name, Indian by ancestry –, stood on the Goan shore that looked across the Arabian Sea to the distant horizon, and watched his adopted village family pull and push their home made craft, some with diesel power, some, just like his own, with muscle and sail.

His feet shuffled through the sand as he walked towards his boat. A fisherman of no great distinction, every day at dawn he would heave his boat down to the sea's edge on rollers and ropes. With no engine, he had to time his launching between waves crashing onto the shore, pushing and rolling.

Sometimes, like today, his eleven-year-old son Pedro helped him. A mere child wishing for a grown man's strength, he was just able to steady the boat long enough for his father to jump in and row with all his strength over the incoming waves and out to sea. The boy would cling to the bow, bobbing up and down and side to side, a small human float, waiting until Joe, clear of the shore and covered with sweat, could drag him over the gunnels. 'Come on, son, in you come.'

Setting the ragged pieces of canvas he used as a sail, Joe, with gnarled bony fingers, would haul up the encrusted hemp ropes, mended so many times that they had more splices than the original. Then they would be out to sea and away.

At last, settled on steady feet and rolling easily with the waves, Joe would help his son unravel the fine nets with their old plastic bottles and pieces of cork roughly lashed to the top to keep them afloat. Then, panning out the net over the stern, making sure not to tangle feet or hands, they would work with the winds and currents and sail parallel to the shore according to the tides.

When the netting was finally out to sea, Joe and Pedro would sit down and watch. As they squatted in the bottom of the boat, sheltering from early morning winds, they were able to keep a practised eye on the floating bottles and corks. Reaching down into the bottom of the boat, Joe would pick up a small and heavily stained tin. Opening it, he would share with his son the meagre remains of the cold rice meal from the night before. They would then watch their nets for hours, hoping and praying the catch would yield enough to feed the two of them. Perhaps there would even be enough to sell a little at the corner of the village. This way, if Joe was lucky, perhaps he could afford biddis to smoke and maybe, just maybe, a peg or two of feni.

Sitting in the boat this way, Joe had many hours to think. He would rather think of the future but every now and again, like today, with no rhyme or reason, the past would rear its ugly head…

He is about five years old. His father, angry and stinking of coconut feni, eyes red rimmed, face bloated and flushed, sways in the moonlit doorway. He shouts abuse at Joe's

8

sobbing mother, whilst the three older children – one boy and two girls – cower around the dimly lit lamp in their hut.

'Where's my supper?' he slurs, staggering in and slamming his fist on the table.

Joe crouches under the filthy sheet in the corner of the room, praying he won't be seen. A sharp slap is heard – the eldest child has not been quick enough...

His father dies at the age of thirty-eight, choking in the middle of the night on his own vomit. Joe's mother cries and tears at her hair because, despite her former plight, she knows that times will get even harder...

Casting his eyes at the netting panned out behind the boat and glancing at his son, Joe realised he had been dreaming for two hours or more. Watching Pedro fast asleep, curled in the foetal position in the bottom of the boat, Joe's eyes softened for a moment. Reaching down, he gently stroked the boy's hair, his affection for his only son reflected in his eyes. Then, in a split second, his mind alerted him to a change on the hazy horizon. Alarm bells sounded in his brain as his experienced eye spotted a sliver of grey cloud. He looked up, noticing the sea eagle and gulls heading for the shore three miles away. In the far distance, shore-going waves with grey and white caps were forming, whilst in the opposite direction other angry waves created crosscurrents of tremendous force.

'Wake up, my son, wake up!'

'What is it, Papa?' Young Pedro jolted awake and rubbed his eyes. Trying hard to decipher the expression on his father's face, he looked back behind the boat. He saw all the other craft around them heading for the shore, their diesel engines throbbing with life, pushing them back against the tide, back to the shore in safety.

'Come my son, we must pull the net in as quickly as we can before the wind begins to strengthen.'

The sun was now at its full height and burning down relentlessly on them. There was no shade, even from the flapping sail. Hand over hand as fast as he could, ignoring the almost empty net, Joe hauled in the wet weight. The net seemed twice as long, and much heavier than usual.

Pedro curled the netting as furiously as he could in the middle of the little boat. He sensed the urgency in his father's actions, felt the tense heaving movement of his sun-blackened limbs and sweating torso. The small boy looked over the parapet of the boat and saw the strange formation of the sky rushing towards them at an alarming speed. He concentrated on the task in hand, hoping all would be well. Suddenly the netting stopped coming aboard. He looked up to see his father heaving with all his might, the ropes and netting cutting into his hands.

Blood dripped from Joe's wrists, then his shoulders slumped and he sat down heavily, catching the rudder with his hip. He did not seem to feel the impact; his eyes were almost at the point of panic. A gurgle sounded from his throat as he breathed deeply, coughing and spitting mucus over the side. Looking up, he saw the other boats, now tiny specks, moving towards the shoreline. Puffs of grey smoke rose above the distant crafts. He knew the diesel engines were working at full throttle against the current, pushing them close to the beach. He also knew that the same tide was pushing their own tiny craft further out to sea.

A small voice interrupted his worries. 'Papa, why have you stopped pulling in the net? We still have a hundred metres more to go.'

Joe looked at his son, aware that there was another life to be lost besides his own. 'The netting has wrapped itself around the tiller.'

He now knew that his two hours of daydreaming could have cost them their lives. *Fool!* he thought. *Think, Joe, think!*

He had only one choice. Pulling his gutting knife from his belt, glancing at the black and menacing racing clouds, he turned to his son. 'I'm going over the side. I'm going to have to cut the netting from the tiller. When you feel the rudder come free, steer towards the black clouds, into the waves racing towards us.'

'But, Papa, what about you? Please, Papa, don't go!'

'I have to, my son. Otherwise, I can't answer for the consequences.'

He took one more look at the rising dark clouds, scanned the sea for dark, dead-eyed devils, and then dived over the side of the boat. Swimming for the stern rudder, he came up for air, long gasping gulps of it, before diving again. He groped with his feet, down under the rudder, until he felt the netting brushing against his leg. The water in the blue deep was colder than at the surface. Tiny drops of blood from his hands dripped into the sea water.

Taking a deep breath, he dived again, feeling his way down around the rudder. He felt rather than saw where the netting had become entangled. He cut several times for what seemed like an eternity, until his lungs felt they would burst and he had to leave his task and swim up for air. As his head broke the surface again, he was shocked to see just how violent the sea had become. Waves at least ten feet high rushed towards the boat. The first wave carried him up to its crest. He felt the pull of the netting behind the boat, dragging it from the top of the wave. Gallons of sea water rushed in, soaking his son, whose eyes were concentrated with effort and fear as he tried desperately to steer the vessel into the waves. Joe knew that if he did not cut the ropes now, they would be lost within moments.

He dived once more. Cutting furiously with the knife, he felt the current pulling his legs horizontally away from the boat. Hacking with frenzied panic, he felt the ropes begin to give from the rudder. The boat rose on the crest of yet another great wave that rolled the netting and Joe free from the rudder and away from the boat. The netting and floats wrapped themselves around him, forcing him to the surface. Desperately trying to untangle himself, he saw his little boat riding away into the enormous waves crashing around the little vessel. To his relief, Pedro was still hunched over the tiller.

Joe realised there was no point struggling with this storm. He knew too that his religion could not protect him from his dilemma. No prayers to his god or deference to all the other faiths could help him. His fate was sealed. His karma lay before him. Trying to keep his arms free and above the net, he pulled all the netting and floats towards him, hoping the floats would hold, enabling him to ride the storm.

By now, it was inky black. All he could do was try and push himself as high as possible onto his nets and hope to survive. Praying he would not get too tangled as he pulled on the squares of rope, he could see fish caught in the mesh: grey tops and silver bellies, still breathing with gills opening and closing, restricted by their confinement.

About a mile from the severed netting and about one hundred and fifty feet below the surface, a dark torpedo shape rode out the storm. As it flicked its tail to remain on station, particles of some foreign blood touched the scent nodules in its mouth. Its eyes turned backwards as it sensed prey. With a flick of its tail, it started to move slowly, following the trail of the scent in the water, the smell of fish oil and the strange odours that passed through its mouth. Staying under the currents and storm, it glided effortlessly towards the source of the enticing scent. After a while it idled below the tempting tastes, taking its position under the storm and the weather, waiting, biding its time, allowing the storm to subside. Instinctively, it knew it would satisfy its curiosity and growing sense of hunger.

Chapter Two

Joe slowly began to pull at the netting, gathering it around him, knowing the dangers the sea held. Had his son been able to hold the boat into the waves? Where was he? The storm still raged about him. The squall screeched and pounded in his ears, but he thought now that with luck he may be able to ride it out. His one fear was thirst. Hunger can be forgotten, but thirst sends a man into a delirium with tongue swollen and certain death.

Tales of other fishermen came to mind: half crazed with thirst, they would feel the water around them and convince themselves that it had changed to river water. They would drink their fill while other more lucid sailors would try to tell them it was only sea water and would kill them. For the stronger mariners, attempting to keep these poor souls alive, keeping watch over them and trying not to fall asleep was almost impossible, and one by one these desperate, capsized men would drink the sea water. Survivors clinging to wreckage would find their fellow fishermen demented, choking to death on their own tongues.

Joe tried not to dwell on these dreadful stories of destruction that lingered in his mind. He set his brain to more important tasks. When he needed it, he knew he could get a certain amount of nourishment from the fishes caught in the netting. By cutting them open with his gutting knife, he could suck moisture from the creatures. But this was not his most pressing worry. The sea still lashed and screamed at him. He hoped the storm and currents were pushing him in the same direction as his son. Joe had no concern for himself, but Pedro's future was riding out there because of him. He hoped the boy could keep the boat heading into the storm.

Pedro Luis Gonzales steered the boat up the next wall of water. Reaching the crest, he felt the craft head into the valley of the waves once more. He bailed furiously with his coconut feeding-bowl, throwing as much sea water as he could over the side. Up the next wall, clinging on with ebbing strength, up and over, crashing down again into the next valley, a short respite and then again the nightmare. The howl of the wind and sea spray lashed him, turbulent gusts snatching the breath from his lungs; he felt crushed with the pressure of the storm and the roar of the waves as they fought one another. The cold foam and spray bit him as he floated up and over another wave. The next one came at him, a moving mountain high above his head, ready to crush him. Then the boat dropped over it. The minute he slid down a wave, a feeling of utter hopelessness came over him as he struggled up the next watery mountain and down deep into the next chasm, Neptune's fingers toying with him.

Pedro had been working with his father since he was six years old. All that his father had taught him in those five years was now being put severely to the test. Only God knew how long the storm would last. His fear for his father became buried in the back of his mind while he coped with the present. He missed not having his own knife. Planting his feet firmly on the decking, and wedging himself between the gunnels and the rudder, he waited for the next high.

Glancing sideways, not losing concentration on his task, Pedro saw silver flapping in the remaining netting. When the storm abated a little, he knew that the fish would be very important for his survival.

Something in his subconscious was speaking to him – primeval instincts taking hold, sharpened through generations of fishing. It was as if his ancestors had awoken and were guiding his every thought and movement.

Pedro knew this little boat was more precious than anything else that the family possessed, or for that matter, did not possess. He had heard the story often enough of how his father and his father's brother had made the boat. In his head he could hear, even now, his father's words as he fondly and proudly recounted the tale:

'First, we made the ribs – the heart and strength of any craft. We laid long planks of mango wood on the sand and drew the shape of the ribs on them with charcoal. Jorge, the village carpenter, a really skilful chap, hacked and shaped the ribs for us. We watched him with admiration as he handled his ancient metal tools, blackened with toil and sweat, sharpened and re-sharpened. When he had finished, we helped fasten the ribs onto the shaped keel of the boat. Then we burnt holes into thinner planks of mango wood with sharpened metal rods, which we took from a small brick oven built on the beach and kept white-hot with bellows. We had to protect our hands, of course, so we wrapped hessian, torn from old grain sacks, and strips of leather around the hot metal rods, as we pushed and twisted with all our strength to force holes through the planking. When the blackened holes had cooled, we threaded wet hemp rope through, pulling it as tight as possible. I used a simple piece of wood as a tourniquet, and I had to pull it as tight as I could, while your Uncle Tony made a slipknot to secure the rope as I held it in position. As the ropes dried in the hot sun and began to shrink, people said that you could hear the planking groaning as it was pulled tighter to the ribbing. We listened hard but could hear nothing.

When all that was done, we ladled on hot pitch.

Next, we split a bamboo cane that we'd hammered at one end to create fibres. We had to make sure to cut these straight, the idea being that we could use it as a makeshift brush, running it over the drying pitch until all was as smooth as possible over the threaded ropes. When we'd finished all this shaping, threading, pulling and pitching, the boat looked like an upturned banana with the top section hollowed out.

Our next task was to erect the mast, about ten feet high, spliced into the bottom of the vessel. That was hard work, I can tell you. Then we had to sort out the last pieces to stabilise the boat: the part between the ribs. For this we had two pieces of round timber jutting out across the boat and running level with the keel. I suppose these were about ten feet long and slightly thicker than a man's arm. We lashed these across the gunnels down to the water's edge. Then we added another longer timber, carved and shaped to run horizontally along the length of the vessel. This would touch the water, allowing the boat to ride the waves steadied by two protruding arms.

Imagine what it was like seeing that boat taking shape. I wish you could have seen us, my son. We fitted the rudder and bolted it to the exterior, and then put the tiller in its place. Last, but by no means least, we fastened the oar with sprogget cleat to the back of the boat, so that it could be pulled out very quickly and stored in the bottom.

When we'd finished, we just stood back and looked at it. We were so proud. It had taken us the whole of the monsoon season to make it, and at last the job was done. We hoped we would be able to earn a little money for our mother, to save her doing the jobs she slaved over seven days a week to keep us all fed.'

This had all happened years ago, long before Pedro's time. Now, he knew if he lost this boat he was too young to help build another and doubted whether his father would even have the will to start again. This

17

meant his father would be left to fish from the beach, along with all the other fishermen who had lost their boats or were too old and weary to go to sea. These old men would cast the netting out, letting it float with the tide. The net would reach a distance of three or four hundred yards into the waves. Then ten or more of these men, feet braced apart, heaving and chanting, would begin to pull in the rope, hand over hand, with all their might, edging the netting towards the shore. Still chanting and heaving, they would take turns at dragging the heaviest ends of the nets out of the sea, with the more agile running into the sea and diving into the waves. Slapping the water hard as they swam round the nets, they would try to stun the fish, hoping none would escape.

All would make a superhuman effort to bring in the nets. Once on shore they would open the tangled mess to see what they had caught. Sometimes there would be a couple of larger fish and perhaps a crab or two. Mostly though, it would consist of a few measly sprats – maybe a dozen or so, but virtually all worthless. The old women with their small pans would start to haggle with the fishermen, screaming and shouting at each other. The same old banter, day in and day out – and hope: perhaps tomorrow they would be lucky.

This was not the life Pedro wanted for himself and his father. His pride would not let them lose the boat – the only means they had of keeping their independence.

Chapter Three

Joe drifted with the storm. He pulled the netting up from beneath him so that he could reach down with his knife and sever some of the broken tiles and bricks he had used as weights, allowing him to draw the net even tighter around himself. Light was just cracking the horizon, fighting back the blackness and slowly chasing the night into dawn. He could tell by the cut of the skyline that the weather would improve in an hour or two. Feeling the first pangs of hunger, he reached round the netting until he came across a snapper. He cut into the fish, put the body to his salt-encrusted lips and sucked the moisture with relish from its flesh.

The torpedo shape below him felt the change in the weather through its instincts, sharply honed over thousands of years. It also felt the vibration from the floating mass above it and smelt the snapper. A tinge of excitement ran through its body, but it could wait for the sea to calm a bit more. This was its territory and its natural habitat.

Joe started to take stock of his situation and position. He realised that he should have taken a land fix the day before, and now made one last effort before the dawn killed the night sky. Trying to get a fix on where he was by the fast-fading stars, he looked for the brightest one in his constellation, the Northern Star. Just making out the last twinkling lights, he knew enough to realise that he had drifted many miles out to sea.

With dawn's approach the sea currents were

lessening and as the raging sea began to calm, Joe felt himself being taken over more by exhaustion than just tiredness. Slowly, through the dawn with all its colours – reds, pinks, yellows lightening to misty gold – blue began to dominate the morning sky.

Joe slept.

Gliding closer to the surface, the menacing shape flicked its tail fin pointing upwards like an elegant plane. The dorsal fin broke the surface, turning it white; ripples formed in front of the fin and left a slight whirlpool in its wake. This shark had been around some years, honing its hunting skills with every kill, looking for easier prey as it grew older; it sensed that this was an easy food supply. With muscular movement of its tail, guided by its fins, it circled the mass of netting, seeking its victim. This mako shark was about four metres in length and over a metre in circumference, with expressionless eyes like black holes. Its business end was all mouth and teeth: its jaws, when fully open, could bite a man in half; the teeth lay in two rows, one behind the other, serrated, as sharp as Joe's cutting knife

Joe slept deeply, held still by the netting, the motion of the sea rocking him backwards and forwards as if in a moving cradle. The mako could not distinguish its intended victim from the massive jumble bobbing on the surface. Circling clockwise, even closer to the netting, the shark's powerful thrust slowly began to turn the mass. Joe, completely unaware of his situation, was dreaming. It was the same dream he had had on many occasions: the ugly fate of his family…

His mother works three jobs, wearing herself to the bone until that is all that is left of her. Joe, waking before his brother and sisters one morning, wonders why the cooking

fire is cold. His mother is always awake before dawn and the fire lit. The smell of chai, chapattis, fried dahl or maybe vegetable masala usually assails his nostrils. Today, there is no sound except his siblings' gentle breathing.

Crawling towards his mother's cot, Joe reaches to shake her shoulder. He feels the coldness of her skin through her dirty sari. Jumping back with shock, he cries out, waking his brother and sisters. Scrambling for a candle and match, their only source of light, they hold it close to her. She lies dead in her bed, staring back at them with lifeless eyes. His sisters begin to scream and wail, his brother, wide-eyed with shock, gapes as his mother lies there like a baby, curled up as she was when she came into this world. She is forty-two.

They cremate her the next day. The whole village turns out to pay its respects. Joe cannot cry. The grief is too deep, the loss too shocking to bear. Joe knows that his mother's death will mean the end of the family. He can foresee the life ahead that is likely for his older siblings. His sisters, two and four years older than him, will follow a life of servitude, going to an uncle and aunt either in Bombay or Delhi, their education limited to a year or two in primary school. They will learn to plant the paddy fields in the monsoon season and from dawn to dusk they will toil, backs bent, water above their knees, for twenty five rupees a day.

And what of Tony? At seventeen, Joe's older brother will work on one of the big deep sea fishing smacks owned by a Delhi businessman. He will be part of a crew of seven or eight in the twenty-strong fleet, away on a trip for ten days at a time. He will be paid a pittance, his life at risk every minute, nourished only by water and a handful of rice.

Joe has heard of the dangers of these big vessels; he worries for his brother. He knows, too, about the betel nut – the fishermen's favourite numbing agent for the harsh conditions. He has seen the way the heart of the nut is wrapped in a tobacco leaf with chilli masala and lime – the *same lime that is used to paint walls. Sometimes they add a little loose tobacco and occasionally some dried fruit. He has seen the fishermen carefully wrap all the contents together to make a mouth-sized bite. He has watched them put this into their mouths and begin to chew, their saliva slowly mixing with the contents of the leaf parcel. He has been amazed at the vivid red that comes from the resulting mixture and how it permanently stains lips, teeth and tongue. After a few weeks of continually chewing these leaf parcels, the fishermen look as if they have a severe case of bleeding mouth. Joe has seen it in their smiles. He has learnt the word 'addict' and he knows that once you become addicted there is no turning back. This is the desperate future for his brother, Tony.*

His own future lies in the lap of the gods.

Joe's brother and sisters send home a few rupees whenever they can but this is a meagre offering and over the years it slowly peters out. He finds himself being pushed from pillar to post, first to one neighbour and then another. He is never settled; there is never a home, just a place in a corner of some kindly neighbour's hut.

Chapter Four

Pedro lay asleep at the bottom of the boat, half in water, his head resting on one of the bottom ribs. The gentle rocking to and fro made his head move from side to side. The sun, not yet above the gunnels, left him in shade for the moment. Breathing evenly, his chest rose and fell, making the water in the vessel slosh gently backwards and forwards. Complete exhaustion had shut him down for the last hour or so. His dream, nestling against his mother's breast, was safe for the moment.

He woke from his slumbers, wrenching his head from his mother's bosom as reality rapidly took hold. Shuddering, he realised his body and face were half submerged in sea water at the bottom of the boat. He jerked up, remembered where he was and peered over the gunnels of the boat, looking around in all directions. Undulating waves and a flat horizon of never-ending sea surrounded him.

Recalling the horrors of the night before, he speculated about what had become of his father. He knew that he himself could not have survived had Joe not cut the netting away from the tiller. With the optimism of youth came hope, with hope came strength, with strength came determination. Pedro knew his father could possibly be dead by now but he had to try and find him, and the vast Arabian Sea did not deter him. Pointing the prow of the boat in what he prayed was the opposite direction, he set a sea-bleached sail. Catching a strong breeze, the boat jolted forward, a slight bow wave forming as it cut through the water.

Hunger and a dreadful thirst were starting to

announce their presence. Looking at the remainder of netting in the bottom of the boat, he spotted a few small fish floating in the salt water, trapped but still alive. Grabbing a fat one, wriggling in its pitiful state, he smashed its head on the gunnels, put the fish between his teeth and chewed, discovering this quenched his thirst as well as quelled his hunger. Staring into the distance, Pedro settled down at the aft of the boat, steering the craft, studying the far horizon, hoping against hope that somehow he could rescue his father.

As he floated at the whim of the waves, unaware of his circling predator, Joe, remembering all the childhood memories in his dreams, recalled the sights, sounds and smells of his kindly neighbours as he tried to sleep in his corner of a hut...

Waking one morning at dawn, he rises and meanders around the village. Lonely and lost in thought, he wanders down to the beach, his feet carrying him involuntarily towards the seashore. Crows wing their way above him, heading out to their feeding grounds, crying to each other.

He sees that a new small hut has appeared between two sand dunes. His curiosity getting the better of him, he squats and watches close to the entrance of the newly erected hut. It is only about four feet high and about the same in width but probably six or seven feet long. Made simply of thin round poles, cut easily from trees with a long knife and driven into the sand with a casually picked up stone, the hut has been lashed together with hemp rope to form the frame of a tent. Blue plastic sheeting has been thrown over the wooden ribs and it seems very strong and durable. Coconut palm leaves have been cut and secured over the whole structure, making the makeshift hut into a waterproof home.

Joe watches the front of this new den, not close

enough to be rude, but near enough to observe the black rectangular entrance. The sun rising behind the tent makes it impossible to see the interior. He wonders who it is that has appeared from nowhere and made this familiar style of nomadic tent. He does not have to wait long before sensing movement at the entrance. A head appears and then the whole skinny body of an old man. Beetle-brown from toiling in the sun, with not one ounce of fat on his scrawny frame, his wizened knuckles clutch a stick as he crawls from the doorway of his makeshift home. As he stands up, Joe can see he is dressed only in a simple loincloth wrapped around his waist. Stretching himself to loosen his sinewy frame, he relaxes and stands there taking in the view and the boy squatting nearby. No taller than four feet six inches, he probably weighs no more than six or seven stone. Joe estimates he could be anything from sixty to ninety years old.

He looks straight into Joe's eyes. The young boy sits back on his rump, startled by the piercing emerald green stare. The old man nods at the child and beckons him over. Joe hesitates only a second, then abruptly stands up and walks towards him. As he draws near, he subconsciously realises that he is practically the same height. Clasping his hands together, Joe points his fingers upward towards the sky in a praying position and brings them against his chest, then lowers his head in deference to the older man.

Unknown to the boy, the newcomer has been studying Joe for several days now. He has watched him drifting aimlessly through the village, kicking stones or chasing butterflies. He motions the boy to come closer, and Joe does so, tentatively. The man reaches out and cuffs his head affectionately, then leads him up the sand behind his makeshift hut. Taking a long sharp knife from his loincloth, the man approaches a dwarf palm tree, reaches up, grabs the lowest branch and deftly cuts off the lowest leaf at the very base where the trunk meets the branch. The leaf, when placed on the ground base up, stands at least four feet above his head. *Gradually cutting through the greenery, he severs it from the stalk, leaving the stalk intact and thus forming the perfect fishing rod. He then places the cut stalk next to his hut in the sun, letting the scorching heat bleach and blacken his new fishing pole.*

He takes his own much-used, dry, black rod from the hut; the sweat from his palms has made it shiny and supple. It is about nine feet in length and at the tip, tied into a small groove, there is a fishing line about three feet long made of strong catgut. Tied to the end of this is a three-pronged hook baited with mussels. He shows Joe how to pierce the bait onto the hooks to get the maximum effect and efficiency for catching fish. He then wades out into the sea up to his armpits, beckoning Joe to follow and showing him how to cast for maximum length of rod.

He stands still, rock-like, in the water. As the waves kick all around him, he points to the tip of the rod with his gnarled finger and waits. Patience is a virtue Joe does not possess. His stomach rumbles in protest. His body sways to the beat of the waves. Suddenly the tip of the rod shoots forwards and the old man strikes sideways, muscles tensing. The line goes taut and the fisherman flips the rod out of the water over his head and onto the beach. A snapper about six inches long slaps down onto the sand. The old man repeats this performance with self-assurance for about an hour and a half, at which time the sun's proximity in the sky indicates that it is time to eat.

Joe follows him out of the sea back to the hut. In all the hours they have spent together, not one word has passed between them. The eyes and body language say more than words. One small fish each is taken from the pile of life, strung together by their gills, flapping on the wet sand. Taking these back to the small fire already kindled and glowing, the stranger takes two long slivers of bamboo and threads them through the fishes' mouths, down their bodies and out of their tails. He places them between two stones hanging over the fire and wedges them well in. The fish soon begin to crackle and brown. After turning slowly for about five minutes they are ready. Steam emanates from the fish as the old man passes one to Joe. The boy begins to tear the flesh from the bone, its juices dripping. Eyes gleaming and mouth salivating with pleasure, Joe has never tasted such a delicious morsel in his young life.

He goes down to the hut every day. His mentor sits cross-legged outside his home, staring with his piercing green eyes at the boy running enthusiastically towards him. Standing up, he beckons to the boy to fetch their fishing gear and motions to the shoreline. They then march down to the sea.

The old man teaches Joe everything he knows about fishing, including long line fishing – the method in which one hundred feet of strong catgut is wrapped around an old medicine bottle. Every yard of the line is spiked with a vicious hook which can impale small fish that try and wriggle for their freedom. With the cap rusted onto the neck of the bottle, it is virtually impossible to unscrew it, and the two of them walk out into the sea holding onto the bottle, the line of baited hooks trailing out behind – multiple fishing. Sometimes, a great many fish are caught, or some larger fish reward them on bigger hooks baited with bigger prey, but always there are at least a few – enough to quell their hunger.

Inshore fishing is a different game. They use a large circular net weighted down with small lead weights and wade out into the sea with the water just above their thighs. Then they cast the net away from them with a flick of the wrist so the netting opens out to a full circle, landing on the sea with a mighty splash. The lead weights plunge to the seabed, closing the net on its way down and trapping anything within its grasp.

Bamboo fishing is another method little Joe learns; the silent teacher imparts all the tricks of his trade. He shows Joe where to look for the shallow shoals of fish; in fact, everything the old man knows he teaches his young *prodigy. The bond between them is mutual and Joe learns the tricks of using any means at his disposal for survival.*

He sleeps in his corner of whichever hut he is in, dreaming of fishing, waking at the crack of dawn and running down to the beach with a smile on his face, anticipating the day ahead and watching the sun climb above the horizon. But one particular day is different: the hut is not there. Perhaps in his haste he has run past it. Backtracking, he searches every sand dune, to no avail. The old man has gone. Joe drops to his knees, the first cry deep inside him. No sound. Great sobs wrack his body as he convulses with sorrow. The first lungful of air sucks in his grief. He is not just crying for the loss of his new friend, he is crying for his mother, his lost family, the hard times he has been through and the fear of things to come. The first frantic sound from his lips is that of a wounded animal. The cries, ever louder, the sobs, ever deeper, shake his whole body. Tears flow freely down his cheeks as he collapses on the sand, rocking backwards and forwards on his hunkers with his hands over his ears. Eventually, the exhausted boy closes his eyes and rocks himself to sleep.

Many hours later as the sun moves somewhere else and the dark chases away the light, the night's chill pervades everything and Joe wakes. He slowly drags himself up off the beach and back to his village. He slips into his temporary home and sleeps the exhausted sleep of the innocent.

Waking next morning, he drags himself towards the spot on the beach where the old man had made his makeshift home only a few weeks before. Looking at the spot, Joe can still make out the footprints. He realises the old man has left him his fishing rod. Picking it up, he notices something buried in the sand underneath. He pulls the rod towards him and sees that, attached to the fishing line, hidden in the sand, are the long line with bottle and hooks, the circular net with its weights and all the other fishing gear he has become so familiar with. He knows this is the old man's goodbye to him: a parting gift to help him survive in this harsh environment. From that moment on, standing alone in the sun, Joe knows he has his means of independence. He has turned himself from a boy at sunset to a man at dawn.

Chapter Five

Joe awoke suspended in his watery bed. Sensing movement in the water, he realised the netting and floats supporting him were turning slowly clockwise. Swivelling his head from side to side, he could not see anything. His head and upper torso were up and out of the water and as he pushed himself up from the bunched netting, he could see everything around him: the sea had calmed; the sky was bright blue; a few puffs of wispy white cloud floated on the horizon; indiscernible hues of cobalt made it almost impossible to tell where sea finished and sky began. Joe noticed all of this with the practised eye of a seafarer.

Out of the corner of his eye he caught a movement. Snapping his head round in that direction, the colour drained from his face and his hands automatically gripped the netting around him; he recognised the fin circling him no more than three metres away.

The mako felt the movement in the netting. It was the only stimulus the instinctive creature needed. Homing in on the netting with powerful thrusts of its giant tail, it charged towards Joe, its mouth opening as it came on, its teeth protruding forward as it went into attack mode. One last flick of the tail and it was in the mesh. A white membrane, evolved over centuries for protection, slid over its dead black eyes, and the jaws closed over the netting. The momentum of the charge pushed the whole jumble forward, causing a wave to form over Joe's head. The force as it struck sent shivers of horror through his entire body. He screamed. The water shut off the scream in mid-flow. He instinctively lashed out.

Sensing this through the receptive nodules at the front of its head, the creature of the sea began thrusting backwards and forwards, and side to side, the muscles of its whole body shaking Joe's hiding place. The sea began to boil with the turmoil. Joe hung on desperately. The head of the mighty creature was inches away from his upper torso. A stench came from the gaping jaws: putrid smells of dead fish still fermenting in the hunter's stomach wafted up and out of it in nauseating waves, making Joe retch. He hung on with superhuman strength, his whole body in shock. The adrenaline made his joints stiff. His hands became immovable hooks tangled in the netting. Time seemed suspended.

He did not know how long this went on – an eternity. Then, suddenly, all was quiet. The shark seemed to disappear under the netting. The sea and netting around Joe ironed itself out. He twisted round, knowing this could not be the end of the nightmare; he knew makos did not give up this easily. He prayed this could be so but in his heart he knew differently. His mind began to numb with more shock as his body twitched and shook with the exertion of the fight. He tried to stay very still, wondering where the creature was.

The shark twitched below him, deciding on his next mode of attack. The tastes of the netting still lingered.

Joe wondered how much netting was underneath him. He remembered the night before. Was it really only twelve hours ago? He gathered all the meshed netting as close as he could to make him buoyant. He could only trust this would be enough. His joints slowly relaxed but the pain of his blood pumping back through the muscles was excruciating. As the convulsive jerking and twitching slowly subsided, Joe gradually brought his legs up to his chest and held his hands out in front of him, realising just how long he had been in the water: the skin was wrinkled like an old man's hands. The smell of salt filled his nostrils and he touched the crystals of salt clinging to his hair, his eyebrows and lashes, making his eyes red and swollen. He must resemble, he knew, a creature of the sea himself: the hunter becoming the hunted.

The monster started circling below the bobbing mass on the surface. Instinctively, its next move was to thrust upwards but slightly to the side, hitting the netting with such a force that its head was pitched slightly through the mass of hemp, nearly reaching Joe's back. The fact that Joe had brought his legs up saved his life for a second time; otherwise, the force of the charge would have broken his back. This explosion of power forced Joe's mouth open in a silent scream, the pain caused by the charge being almost beyond endurance. His head snapped back, his eyes popped, there was no air left in his lungs and he blacked out; his body, for the moment, could take no more. He never saw the raging shark pushing, pulling and battering with his enormous strength, shaking him in his nest like a rag doll.

Pedro followed his instincts, pointing the small craft towards the distant horizon, trying to retrace the harrowing night's outward journey. Holding onto the tiller, he started to bail the sea water overboard with his coconut shell. Always looking towards the horizon, he saw nothing but sea and sky as he realised it was becoming very still and calm; the wind carrying the small vessel slowly faded and the sail became limp, nestling up against the mast. The silence was deafening; the storm had vanished. The boat had died:

it lay sleeping in the endless ocean. Looking up at the sun beating down relentlessly, Pedro stood up at the stern and suddenly it dawned just how weak he had become as a dizzy spell overtook him and he swayed dangerously. Stepping forward, he managed to grab the mast and he stood for a moment, steadying himself.

He took stock of his situation. Examining himself carefully, he explored the damage that the violent storm had vented on his small body in only a few short hours. The battering he had taken from the pounding of the huge waves endlessly throwing him around had cut and bruised his ribcage as he had hung onto the tiller. His concentration on keeping the boat faced into the wind had left no room for him to recognise the pain he had suffered. His body, still lithe and supple, had stopped his ribs from cracking, but the bruising was visible: angry-looking, purple centres with yellowing edges were getting blacker by the minute in front of his eyes. The smarting under his right arm made him wince. He lifted it and saw that the skin, rubbed raw with the exertion of holding the tiller hour after hour, had broken open and been pushed back like that of over-ripe fruit. The salt from the seawater aggravated his wounds; his hands were raw, the palms blistered. His whole body throbbed and he slowly slid down the mast.

Sitting in the sea water in the bottom of the boat, he mournfully studied his position: his only sources of sustenance now were the few fish captured in the net the day before; a small tin of water his father always carried, tied to the mast so that it could not be washed overboard, was still there; the oar lashed to the side of the boat was also miraculously still there. Looking down into the bottom of the boat, he noticed that his absent-minded bailing with the coconut shell had exposed some of the netting and the trapped fish captured there had dried out. Exposed as they were, they had begun to putrefy in the heat of the sun. His only supply of strength and nourishment was rotting before his eyes. This jolted him from his stupor. With a mighty effort, he pushed himself forward towards the drying nets and nudged everything back into the water at the bottom of the boat. Trying to get his limbs and body to function was a supreme effort for one so young, but this action only made his resolve stronger as he focused on thoughts of his father, stranded out there in that vast ocean. It spurred him on. He knew what he had to do. Taking one of his precious store of fishes, he tore the small morsel apart with his teeth. He chewed slowly, every mouthful making him feel slightly stronger.

Getting the pain from his small body under control, he stood up. He knew his salt-encrusted wounds would ulcerate, so he tore a small strip of material from his loincloth, opened the tin, dipped the rag into the water and used a little of his meagre stock to clean his injuries. Taking care not to spill any, he squeezed the cloth out and dabbed on his torn flesh with the precious liquid, gently rubbing the wet cloth over the open sores and removing as much salt as he could. Letting his arm drop to his side, he felt blood from his wound drip down his arm onto his hand, making it sticky. He ignored this and unstrapped the oar, placing it in the cleat at the stern of the boat, then began to rotate the paddle. His hips swayed from side to side as he stood there, pushing the oar through the sea water; the little vessel began to move slowly through the now calm sea.

The sun beat down on him but his eyes did not leave the horizon. He took refuge in warm thoughts of his mother as he worked. She had been just sixteen years old, her young eyes still innocent of the world, when she had had her first son, Pedro Luis Gonzales. He remembered her laughing and playing with him; he remembered going with her to the local market, straddling her hip, her colourful sari billowing out around her...

The basket on her head balances precariously and yet it appears to be at one with her. After years of practice, it is part of her, the whole shape swaying and moving gracefully with her. Back from the market, she cooks local dishes that she knows her husband Joe enjoys, always accompanied by rice and chapattis. Together they squat down to eat with their right hands, laughing and enjoying their meal.

Later, with the dying embers glowing on their writhing bodies, their lovemaking is intense. Rivulets of perspiration run between them, a mutual pleasure forcing a gap between their lips as they reach the pinnacle of their passion. Collapsing, they fall asleep in each other's arms, the fire still glowing, dancing on their entwined bodies; they sleep the slumber of the young and innocent.

Little Pedro watches from his cot. He is not aware of his parents' love life, but he sees their happiness and their eyes shining brightly as they chat about a forthcoming birth. His father tenderly runs his hand over the rotund shape forming on the front of Pedro's mother and gently places the side of his face against it, listening for the new life within. Pedro sees his father's surprise and laughter when he jumps up with surprise as the new baby kicks out.

He also hears the cries of pain and anguish emanating from his mother in the night, when her time comes. There is a rush to get the midwife. The cries of terror seem to go on forever. Through the next day and night, the whimpers get weaker. His father paces backwards and forwards for hours, tears of anger and frustration showing in the deep scars of life etched in his face. For three days, the midwife and other village women try to help his mother give birth, but to no avail. The midwife explains to his father that the only way left is to cut the baby free. There is no doctor available for over a hundred miles. His father slowly nods his head with resignation. Sitting back on his heels and rocking, Joe waits with grief-stricken eyes.

The scream that is forced from his mother, followed by the hauntingly eerie silence, will stay with Pedro all his life. The midwife rushes out with the baby, her fingers in its tiny mouth. The baby is blue as it desperately tries to clear its airways, struggling to take its first breath. His father turns towards his home, ducking into the entrance, dimly seeing by the firelight the village women attending his wife. The blood on the sheets is fresh, staining the mattress a vivid red beneath her. Joe's eyes are drawn to his lovely wife's lower body, her legs streaked with her own blood, all dignity vanished in her battle for life. The women try to stem the flow of blood pumping from between her thighs. Their brows are covered in sweat, their hands and arms smeared by the sticky rag that has been used to try and staunch the life's blood. All to no avail.

Joe's wife turns her once lovely, now tortured face towards the door and sees her husband standing there, wringing his hands helplessly. He staggers forward and holds out a trembling hand. The hurt is etched in his face; his eyes are brimming with tears as his wife focuses on him, her sweat-soaked hair stuck to her forehead. The rest of her hair lies dishevelled around her. Her ashen face and dark eyes call to him. She holds out a delicate shaky hand towards him. Rushing over, Joe kneels beside his once beautiful wife, his tears freely falling onto her hand as he places his trembling lips to her palm. Their eyes lock in a form of ghastly embrace. She smiles at him, her face frozen in a faraway look as her strength ebbs. Life leaves her eyes as she journeys elsewhere. The women cover her spent body with blood-soaked sheets and gently creep from the hut. Joe rigidly clings to the spot, while little Pedro cries in his cot, wondering who will feed him; he is hungry.

The midwife cleans the new baby's windpipe, turns it upside down, grasps it by its ankles then slaps the tiny new bottom. No sound escapes but ... it is breathing. Turning the baby over, the midwife looks at it carefully: still bluish and blotchy, its limbs are motionless; the lifeless eyes move but are strangely dull. During her long experience, the midwife has seen this before. The baby's now rhythmic breathing makes its small chest rise and fall. The inert body has no other movement; it just lies there in her arms. She knows those first breaths have arrived too late; the spirit has moved on, gone to another house. The child has missed its chance. If it survives, it will be a burden to its family – a body with an empty spirit. The midwife places the palm of her hand over the tiny girl's mouth, putting her thumb and finger over its nose and pressing firmly down. In a very short while, the breathing stops, the infant relaxes and is still. The tiny bundle, wrapped in an old cloth, looks no bigger than a loaf of bread. The midwife steps out of her hut carrying the parcel in front of her.

Pedro's tears stream down his cheeks; he still seeks attention from his mother.

Chapter Six

Joe floated unconscious, his mind travelling back to even more painful times...

He is kneeling on the floor of the hut beside his beautiful child bride, now completely cold. Her eyes have melted back into her body, and her young life has faded away with the shadows. He rises stiffly to his feet, cramp setting his every movement. Glancing habitually into the corner of the hut, he realises that Pedro is not in his cot. Someone must have crept in and removed the boy for feeding and changing. He steps outside into the sunlight, not feeling the heat on his body, but the brightness of the sun in his eyes makes him raise his hand as a shield. The village elders are already making plans for the body of his wife to be removed. In this heat it will rapidly decay.

Joe looks around for the midwife with his precious new offspring. He goes to her hut, calls out and enters when he gets no reply. He waits the few seconds for his eyes to accustom to the gloom to see that neither woman nor baby is there. Rushing outside he runs through the village. Seeing an elder's startled look Joe starts to babble. The elder knows the situation and points to the river. Gathering speed, Joe races down, bursts through the thicket at the edge of the fast flowing water and takes in the scene at once: the midwife is kneeling on the riverbank watching a little bundle of rags bobbing just offshore. The current picks up the colourful bundle, taking it faster and faster beyond their reach, until finally it is out of sight. Joe falls to his knees and begins to scream. The sobbing forces its way from his breaking heart; giant howls come from the depth of his being; he cries as he has done only once before as a small boy on a beach. This time, however, his mind cannot endure the magnitude of his grief. He blacks out, collapsing by the riverbank, his body inert as in death.

Joe's battered body forced him through the haze of pain and shock back to the surface and consciousness. Reality dawned, making him open his eyes, aware of where he was and with whom he shared his watery prison. His wary eyes searched for the creature of the deep, wanting to locate it yet at the same time dreading the moment of truth. As he twisted round, he became aware of something wrong with his left leg. Feeling with his hand, he touched the upper thigh, then down to his calf and finally his ankle and feet: all still attached. Puzzled, he could not understand why he could not move his leg. Feeling further up and around with his hand, he touched shreds of hanging flesh. With dawning horror, comprehension set in: his left buttock was missing – completely gone, bitten off by that remorseless monster.

Tentatively, he gingerly felt round the rest of his body for more wounds. He found none. The area of the bite was quite numb. There did not seem to be much blood in the water. The bite must be too deep to bleed. Perhaps the salt in the water had cauterised the wound. The shark must have forced its way through the netting to reach that part of his anatomy. Joe realised this must have happened while he was unconscious and was grateful that the net had saved him from further damage and, undoubtedly, certain death. His whole body was now in a state of complete shock. His left leg dangled uselessly in the netting. His body screamed out for water. He reached out for the nearest ensnared fish and biting into it, he glanced around. Where was that terrible creature?

Deathly silence wrapped an eerie blanket round the netting. Sky and sea were one. The sun beat down remorselessly on his salt-covered head and

39

upper torso, and the spray from the nets splashed onto his head and body, adding more layers of salt. Joe felt panic rising, as he realised his vision was becoming impaired. He forced it down, knowing that if he did not all would be lost. He did not hold out much hope of surviving but instinct pushed him on. Momentarily, he wondered if his eyesight would hold out.

Where was that terrible creature lurking? Joe knew enough of the mako to know that it would have withdrawn for a second charge, its deadly jaws capable of clamping down on its victim and snapping clean off whatever it connected with.

He did not have long to wait: a movement to his right confirmed his fears almost immediately. The creature's instincts had awakened as soon as Joe had moved in his netting. Its taste buds remembered the last little morsel and made it want more, much more. The smells in the water tantalised him; he circled furiously, enraged by the netting. He smelt the human in the centre of the barrier and swam round faster and faster with powerful strokes of his tail, looking for an opening. What was stopping him quenching his lust for torn flesh? With the circling, once more the knitted tangle of netting began to turn.

Joe saw all this happening in front of his eyes. He stiffened with terror. How could he survive with this deadly adversary so close and so ferocious? To Joe's surprise, anger took hold of him, overriding his abject fear, turning it to sheer fury. He began to rage, hitting the water with his hands, violently screaming, 'Come on you bastard! Come on!'

The noise took the shark by surprise. Faltering slightly, it listened to get the sense of where the splashing was coming from, and then changed direction, heading straight for the scrambled netting, charging over it instead of into it. Joe saw the creature coming towards him. Its terrible mouth was gaping wide, rows of needle-sharp teeth flashing in the sunlight as the shark searched for the human. The thrash of his tail made the water boil behind him. The speed of the creature had created a wave of sea water which moved the whole jumbled mess through the sea.

Joe saw it happening as though it were in slow motion. The disjointed horror of what he was witnessing made him feel like a spectator: all this was happening to someone else. Sheer terror shut off his mind and instinct took over. The will to survive coursed through his veins. Natural impulses made him pick up his gutting knife and in a split second he raised his right arm, his knife, sharp after many years of honing, clutched in his curled fist. Twelve inches of sharpened steel gleamed in the sunlight.

The shark bore down on him with a ferocious intensity. Joe moved to the side and ducked instinctively, his knife flashing as the shark missed him by inches. The gaping mouth passed him by, so close he could see right down the devil's throat. He brought the knife down heavily on the shark's head again and again; blood spurted from wide, gaping wounds. As momentum pushed the shark across the netting, Joe knew that the penetrating knife would force the mako to try and move sideways away from the plunging blade, but he could not move further away. He was restricted and hampered by the netting, and the sideways twisting shark had trapped him. The force of the animal's body passing him grazed his cheek, rasping away skin with a hide as tough as sandpaper, rubbing away the side of Joe's face and ear, ripping his flesh as easily as tissue paper. The last thrust of the immense tail caught Joe full on the side of his face and left shoulder. He felt his eye explode in his head. The creature disappeared and the sea settled once more.

The calm around Joe belied the experience of the last minute or two. Breathing heavily, he looked down at himself lying in a pool of blood, his and the shark's mingling together in the sea around him. He felt no pain, only numbness as he reached up to feel his torn face. Tentatively he touched the ragged shreds of flesh with his fingertips, and his anger returned with the realisation of the extent of his wounds. He turned, forcing himself round in the netting to look at the last place he had seen his enemy. Lying there in his watery fortress, he waited for the creature's inevitable return. He felt the throbbing nerve-endings turn to excruciating pain. Blackness welled up inside him. He fought back, knowing that if he passed out, the huge fish would have him at its mercy.

Chapter Seven

Pedro looked out at the vast ocean as he swayed from side to side, the oar resting between his hip and arm as he pushed the small fishing craft through the waters. With the sea still calm, there was not a ripple in sight – such a contrast from the day and night before. Just to the right of the mast, the boy caught a glint of movement on the horizon – nothing discernible, just a ripple. He was sure it was not of the sea's making. Again, a flicker and then it was gone – a slight flash of light in the distance, then nothing. The sea was completely tranquil. Pedro stood on tiptoe at the stern of the boat and looked again, his hand shading his eyes. But all movement had ceased. There was no flash of light or ripple of water, just the relentless sun beating down on the boy in his boat.

He sat down, measuring with his hand the distance from the horizon where he thought he had seen the flash. He estimated it must be several miles to the spot. Pushing harder on the starboard side, he headed the boat forward.

The creature of the deep was very agitated. The knife wounds meant nothing to it; they were mere surface wounds; no vital organs had been damaged. But tantalising smells came from the human in the water. The fish rested for a while. The need to feed grew stronger as it kept its station just beneath the surface. Making small adjustments with its fins and slight movements with its tail, it held its position. The shark knew instinctively how to get at the man in the net: it had learnt to go over instead of into the puzzle.

Joe waited. His breathing calmed to a relatively normal level. Holding onto the netting, his gutting knife held firmly in his right hand, he stared at the surface of the sea, his good eye trying to penetrate the depths, his mind and senses digging, searching for that terrible creature, knowing with frightening clarity that the shark would come again.

The dorsal fin surfaced several metres in front of him, heading straight for him, getting faster as it approached. Forcing its way over the netting, the creature's dead eyes looked straight at Joe. Its jaws were open in anticipation, certain this time of a kill. At the last moment the white membrane closed over the dead lack-lustre eyes. Joe's self-preservation took over. Ducking under the water, he held the knife just above the surface. The force of the charging mako propelled it over Joe's hiding place. Joe felt the knife enter the soft underbelly of the shark, its deadly point running down the length of the torso. The force snapped Joe's wrist back and smashed him against the netting. His right arm felt as though it had been ripped from its socket. He held on. The force of the charge sent the shark right over the netting, alarm registering throughout the huge body as the knife thrust deeper into the blubbery flesh. The tail flicked as it left the battlefield. A trailing piece of rope with a float and balancing weight attached to it caught the tail as the fish swam away, its thrusting tail flicking at the rope float, trying to dislodge it.

The combination of the knife wounds and the tightening rope caused the mako to thrash around with frenzied agitation, pulling the whole untidy heap of nets, human and dead fish behind it as it tried to get away from this baffling situation. Straightening its fins and flicking its hampered tail, it writhed and with great effort dived. Joe felt his temporary refuge being pulled through the water. The whole mass tightened. Despite his ordeal, he managed to grasp that somehow the creature had become entangled as it strove to reach him. Feeling himself being pulled through the water, he knew, from the angle of the rope, that the mako was diving. Taking great long pulls of air, he filled himself to capacity.

Living and playing in the sea all his life, Joe felt at home in water. His ability to hold his breath for long periods of time gave him a far greater chance than average of staying down – he had managed three minutes in the past. But this was different. Badly injured, with no proper food or water for nearly twenty-four hours, he went under, keeping his one good eye open as he dived. He could make out the outline of the torpedo shark just in front of him. Down and down they went. Joe could feel the currents of the water pushing past his torn face as they both descended. The shark was so close, yet so far. Joe felt the fish slowing, the netting weights and floats dragging it to a standstill. Abruptly stopping, Joe looked up. The sun shone on the ceiling so far above. He felt his heart beginning to pump faster searching for more oxygen in his blood; his inner ears popped with the pressures of the depth. The whole mess became stationary.

He knew he could not hang on much longer. His eye began to bulge in its socket with the tremendous effort his body was making. Willing himself not to suck in great mouthfuls of sea water, Joe saw the creature, still and exhausted by the effort of escape. He could see the surrounding netting and floats rising above the motionless monster. The whole entangled mess moved upwards, the buoyancy of the trapped air inside the bottles and other flotsam forcing everything to rise. Joe began to fight for his life.

Pushing with his one good leg and thrusting with both arms, he tried with all his might to reach the surface. With the natural laws of flotation, the whole bizarre menagerie inexorably rose with him towards the roof of the sea, the shark too shattered to struggle against it. With his lungs screaming for air and struggling desperately, Joe did not think he would make it. Still looking at the sunlight beaming through the water, he made one final effort; kicking with his remaining strength and willpower, he broke the surface. Great gasps of air filled his lungs. Spluttering and coughing, he looked at the monster just yards away. A pink mist surrounded it. Linked together as they were, ropes attaching them both from different worlds, both hunters by nature, they were now joined as if by an umbilical cord.

The shark lay quiet for some minutes, the diluted blood seeping from its ghastly wounds, the pink mist spreading around and away from it. Feeling the rope around its tail, the mako knew there was no escape. With a flick of its side fins, it turned to face its enemy. The eyes of both man and shark met in a deadly embrace. The face of death confronted them both.

Pedro despondently leant on the oar, half-heartedly pushing the boat through the water, his eyes drooping with the effort of fighting the sun's reflection. Through hooded eyes, he saw something in the distance. He rubbed his eyes and looked hard. Straining against the glare of water and sun, he could make out a bobbing mass of netting and he could just make out the floats, minute in the distance, recognisable because he had handled them so many times before. His enthusiasm returned. Adrenaline started pumping through his body. He frantically forced the boat through the sea towards the muddled mass. He cried out, his lungs automatically filling with air as he tried to shout. Nothing came out, just a croak and grunt. Tension and the rigours of the fight had closed his throat. He renewed his efforts, willing the little craft through the waters, onwards towards the floating netting. His hopes rose. Was his father still alive? Would he be in time? Tears of anticipation ran down his face. Sobs involuntarily escaped his lips and great rivulets of salty juices ran down his face.

They looked at each other, only a few yards apart, Joe and the big fish. The great shark's strength had returned, not quite as it should, the knife wounds taking care of that. But Joe's spirits were low. If the monster attacked again, he did not know whether he had the strength to defend himself, although he was still gripping the knife tightly by its hilt. He rested his arm on the top of the netting, watching and waiting, his good eye never leaving the formidable creature, his poor bloodshot eye never blinking. He tried to think like a shark in anticipation of the mako's next move.

With the flexing of the beast's torso, agitation spilling from it, Joe knew another horrific attack was about to begin. This time, the shark was hampered in its attempt to charge straight for him by the netting and its entangled tail; it could not get a clear run at the man. In its frustration, it grabbed mouthfuls of rope, champing it in its teeth. Raising its head with insurmountable anger, it started to shake the whole structure. Chewing and slashing, chewing and slashing, the ghoulish head moved towards its foe. Supreme strength and size forced its great jaw with those needle sharp teeth through the ropes, shearing it all, the mako's sole aim to get the human in the centre.

The great belly pumped blood into the water with every thrash. The sea rose around them and Joe hung on for dear life as the boiling waters tossed him around like a puppet. The creature came within his reach, the same putrid smell wafting from those terrible jaws. With a mighty effort – no fear now, only loathing and the will to survive – he leaned in and started to slash and stab. Blood spurted, covering him with a sweet sickly smell. He made one last effort, stabbing at a membrane-closed eye. Surprisingly easily, the knife went deep into the socket, bursting the eyeball and enraging the fish into a last frantic maniacal attack. With one convulsion of its powerful body, it reached Joe. In desperation he grasped the upper lip with one hand and with the other somehow held the head of the thing. Frantically he pushed himself out of the makeshift life raft, thrusting himself away from the netting. With a final burst of strength, he felt himself float free, nothing but clear waters around him.

In his effort to escape the thrashing animal and those terrible jaws, Joe had pushed on the shark's head. As he had propelled himself away, he had felt his right hand slip into its mouth. His faithful knife had slipped from his grasp as he struggled free, and the handle, slimy with the creature's blood and mucus, had fallen sideways, slowly down into the deep dark depths. Joe had instinctively withdrawn his hand, catching it on the lower serrated teeth, sharp as broken glass. His hand had been shredded from palm to fingertip. Now he shuddered, knowing he was finished. All strength had gone. There was no food or water to sustain him. Blood oozed from his jagged wounds. If he did not drown soon, something else was bound to get him; he understood the laws of the sea. Joe swam, or rather splashed feebly away from the netting, watching the deadly creature now inextricably tangled in it. As he drifted away, aware of blood seeping from all his wounds, he fainted from shock.

The mako's momentum propelled it into the vacant hole. Down it went and stopped thrashing in the ensuing confusion. It could smell the man-thing. The pain in its eye was excruciating. The wounds in its underbelly throbbed. The rope around its tail continuously tightened, cutting circulation. It felt the need to get away to rest and it started to push through Joe's netting, but the more it struggled, the more entangled it became. Fighting against its unknown captor with all its great bodily strength only trapped the creature even more. It was completely incapacitated by the sheer force of the struggle. The netting around the shark clung completely, like some nightmarish lover's embrace.

Chapter Eight

About one and a half miles away from this epic battle and about fifty metres below the surface, another large torpedo shark held its station. Adjusting its position with a flick of its tail, the thing picked up the particles of blood drifting in the currents towards it. Analysing these with its nodules, hunger began to penetrate the brain of this primeval predator. It slowly started to swim towards the source of these tempting tastes.

Pedro continued to push his craft forwards with the stern oar. The sea remained calm and there was no wind. The waters were like a mercury mirror. The wake of the boat left behind it a fluorescent trail. The sun still beat down. Glancing up quickly and squinting into the sun, Pedro realised he had been rowing since dawn. The position of the sun overhead told him it was almost noon.

The indiscernible shape ahead moved backwards and forwards. He rowed on, trying to make the small boat go faster. The sweat dripped down his whole body, his torso glistening with the effort. He leaned forward, peering into the distance, never stopping, his head thrust outward, every muscle in his young body straining. A glint, as if from a mirror or something shiny, flashed across his eyes. Suddenly, Pedro made out the flip of a large tail. He swallowed. Trying to make his throat work, he rowed closer to the jumbled mass. Shapes were now forming. The netting had become clearer.

He stopped rowing in amazement at what he saw. The ferocious shark had just entered the centre of the netting. As it became ensnared in the whole sorry mess, the frantic thrashing made the netting move around with a life of its own. The trapped creature, with its blood oozing into the sea and out between the holes in the netting, made Pedro's heart stop. He knew his father must have made a heroic effort to survive, but he knew he was too late. The realisation sent spasms of shock through his frail body. Pedro stood there as the creature thrashed about in its watery tomb.Eyes bulging and one hand involuntarily raised, as if he could reach out and save his father, tears coursed down the broken boy's face. Pedro sat down in the stern of the boat not knowing what to do. The thought of saving his father had driven and sustained him. Now all was lost.

With these negative thoughts, his body took over: all the aches and pains, the smarting of his underarm, the bruising – his entire being throbbed with pain. Now, sitting there, he was completely alone, stranded in this vast ocean. He gamely fought down rising panic. Breathing heavily, body stiffening, he closed his eyes. What could he do?

He told himself not to panic. He heard and felt a slight bump on the side of the boat. Was the shark now after *him*, he wondered? Grabbing both sides of the boat and holding onto the gunnels he opened his eyes. Casting around him, his heart in his mouth, Pedro did not even dare to breathe. Nothing. Only silence. He made the sign of the cross. 'May God protect me.'

Looking over the side in the general direction of the netting, he saw something floating alongside his boat. He gave an involuntary gasp and puzzlement turned to horror as he recognised the floating mess. He stumbled backwards in disbelief at the full abhorrence of what he saw. Pedro could not believe his eyes. There, floating before him was his father, his face half rubbed away, the empty eye socket staring up at him, only one leg floating on the surface, his hand, completely shredded, pumping blood into the water.

'Papa!' The shock of it all galvanised Pedro out of his lethargy. Standing up, he reached over and tugged at his father's loincloth, not knowing whether the inert body was dead or alive. He tried to heave his father out of the water but he was too heavy; the dead weight nearly pulled the boy over the side. The little craft tilted alarmingly. 'Help me, Papa!' Pedro screamed at the inert body.

He had to let his father go. The boat righted itself. He went to the stern and took the oar from its cleat, his breathing laboured with the effort. He went back to the side of the boat where Joe floated, deciding to pull him to the stern. He knew if he could try again from there, he would not put either of them in jeopardy. Taking a rope from the bottom of the boat, he reached over the stern and tried to get the hemp around his father's torso. 'Wake up, Papa, wake up!' He was not going to lose him again. His efforts made him groan as he lashed the rope attached to his father to the oar's cleat.

Pedro picked up the rag torn from his loincloth, opened the meagre supply of water still lashed to the mast, and soaked the rag. Running back to the stern, he leaned over. 'Papa, have some water.' He squeezed the water into his father's parched mouth. The cracked and swollen lips parted and Pedro watched his father's throat move as he swallowed the life-giving liquid. Pedro repeated this several times, trying not to let any of the fluid drip through his fingers. 'Hold on, Papa, I will get you home.'

As the water dripped into Joe's body, his one good eye flicked open, a spark of life appearing. He

52

tried to focus his mind, wondering where he was. How dare someone disturb him when he was playing in the fields with his lovely wife and daughter. He coughed and spluttered. His eye began to focus on his son's face hovering above him haloed by the blue sky and the dream of his wife. His son stared down at him.

Is this heaven? Joe asked himself. He saw his son's lips moving, his hands holding him. Joe's ears were submerged in water and only muffled sounds reached his consciousness. Snatching himself back to reality hurt. But his son had found him! 'Pedro!' he managed to croak. Startled, he struggled in the water, tried to sit up and went under. He saw Pedro pull on the rope, steadying him as he came to the surface. Registering the horrors of the day before, everything came back with a rush. Joe's animal cunning made him look around. He knew that his son could not pull him out. He felt for the gunnels and tried to pull himself up and over. 'I will try to help you, my son.' His strength sapped. With his body half out of the water, he could not get any further. Out of the corner of his eye, in the distance, another dorsal fin stroked the crest of a wave. It was moving at alarming speed towards them. 'Quick, boy!' There was panic in Joe's voice. The trail of blood led the creature on. Joe saw Pedro follow the direction of his gaze.

'Shark!' Pedro cried. 'Hold on, Papa!'

As the involuntary cry left the boy's lips he instinctively went into action. Untying the rope from around the cleat, he ran it round the mast and back towards his father. Holding onto it tightly, he braced his legs apart, feet firmly planted on the bottom of the boat, ran the rope around his body and over his shoulder and started to lean backwards. The rope snapped taut.

Joe felt it tighten around his waist. He grunted, understanding what his son was up to. He tried to help. It was a feeble effort; he knew all his strength had ebbed away, flowing out with the trail of blood. 'God give me strength,' he prayed. 'Pull, boy, pull!' he urged, his voice little more than a whisper and his poor emaciated body trembling with fatigue.

The shark bore down on them, getting closer by the second. Pedro looked behind him. Seeing his father half in and half out of the water, he knew Joe was losing the battle, knew they were not going to make it, at least not without a miracle.

Keeping the rope taut, hand over hand, muscles in his little legs straining with every move, he retreated, placing the rope around the masthead, which held his father half out of the water. He ran back to the stern. Standing on the edge of the gunnels, balancing with his feet astride his exhausted father, he bent down and grabbed Joe's torn loincloth with both hands. It tightened between his buttocks and Pedro saw the torn flesh and the useless dangling leg. He felt sick.

'Help me, Papa.' He gave a mighty heave, his brow creased with this final desperate exertion. He felt his father slide over the stern. But this final lunge took Pedro off balance and with his arms flailing and his scream cut off as he entered the water, he plunged headfirst into the sea. As he surfaced, his head bobbed out of the water. Swivelling rapidly round, he saw the dorsal fin heading straight for him. Taking a deep breath, he ducked under the water, the dim outline of the torpedo shape just visible in the murky distance. The speed of the thing was breathtaking.

With presence of mind unusual in one so young, Pedro pushed himself around to the stern of the craft, kicking with his legs and feet. Hanging on with fingers and nails to the tar-covered ropes that kept the watertight planks together, Pedro let his legs float level with the underside of the boat. Peering round the stern, he saw the great fish appear right in front of him. It flashed past, searching for its prey, its wake making the boat rock up and down. Pedro watched the tail flick out of sight.

'Papa!' he cried out, quickly pushing himself around the stern again reaching up for the edge of the boat. Flinging himself upwards he just managed to curl the fingertips of one hand around the top of the stern, which automatically twisted his body, scraping his back on the side of the boat. As he desperately hung on, his eyes travelled out to sea. With shock, registered fear. The great shark was almost upon him. He screamed, the sound carrying to the shark. Dark, dead eyes came straight for him. The large mouth began to open and the membranes began to close over the eyes. Pedro felt fingers curling in his hair and he was swiftly hauled upwards and over the stern. Father and son collapsed in the bottom of the boat. The shark missed its prey and slid under the boat. With frustration mounting, the great fish turned towards the netting, attracted by the smells and struggles.

Turning round in the bottom of the boat, Pedro looked at his father lying in the bilge water, his terrible wounds festering in the heat. 'Can you hear me, Papa? Hold on.'

Joe's shallow breathing made his chest rise and fall and Pedro knew he was in a bad way, much worse than he had at first realised. His dead weight and wounds made it impossible to move him. Pedro knew that shade was the next priority. Grabbing the redundant sail, he covered his father. Tying the sail halfway up the mast and pushing the remainder of the canvas over each side of the vessel, he made a makeshift tent. Ducking under the canvas, he untied the tin of precious water and, kneeling next to Joe's head, he ladled a few drops at a time into his mouth. 'Drink, Papa.'

Watching him swallow, Pedro felt there was a spark of life remaining. He took off his loincloth and tore it into strips, trying his best to bandage his father's lacerated head. When he had finished, he bound the shredded hand, trying to separate the fingers and bind them one by one. Because Joe was lying on his back, Pedro could not get to his torn rump. Curiously no blood seeped from this violent gape. Turning, he reached once more for the tin of water and tried to steady Joe's head as he ladled more nourishing drops of liquid down his father's throat.

A few hours passed hazily. Pedro stood up, completely naked and exhausted. He took a few drops of water for himself. Grabbing one of the remaining fish, he chewed absentmindedly. He looked ahead and tried to estimate which direction he should take. As they drifted aimlessly with the current, Pedro knew they had to reach land as quickly as possible. The next twenty-four hours would see the end one way or another. They could not go on much longer.

Turning towards his father, talking to him all the while, hoping somehow this would help him, he felt a slight breeze rising – not much, just a whisper, but enough to cool his skin. He felt the droplets of sweat drying on his body, like a refreshing dip in the river back home. As the light breeze grew stronger, the sea began to react: it rose, undulating once more, and the boat began to sway. Pedro stood in the stern, peering at the glowing embers of the dying sun, feet firmly planted against the starting swell. He watched as the translucent reds, yellows and indigos melted together, dancing across the constellations. The first flitter of stars began to appear. No clouds tonight. He looked down at his father, whose one good eye was open, staring at him.

'You're awake.' Pedro watched him struggling up on one elbow, the effort exhausting him as he tried to move out of the sea water, pain showing all too starkly on his face. 'Lie down, take things easy,' he said, stooping behind his father and placing both hands under his armpits to help lever him backwards.

'Oh my God!' Joe cried out in excruciating pain. A smeared trail of blood was immediately visible from his torn buttock. Propping him up as best he could, Pedro tried to make him as comfortable as possible.

'Would you like some water?'

'Yes,' pleaded Joe.

The small boy again began to ladle a few drops past his father's lips. Taking a dead fish from the netting, he tried to coax him to eat. The stiffening encrusted side of Joe's face prevented him from opening his mouth very wide and he painfully shook his head. Instead he pointed to the oncoming night sky, indicating a bright star. Pedro followed his father's pointing finger and began to follow the implications of his actions. Working with his father over the last few years, a form of telepathy had developed. Body movements were interpreted without explanation; actions were understood without words. Pedro understood his father wanted him to follow that particular star. 'I understand, Papa.'

Gathering the sail from its makeshift tent shape, Pedro unravelled it from its lashing halfway up the mast and retied it properly, pulling the single patchwork triangle upwards. He felt the slight breeze take it and puff the sail out slightly, pushing the little boat through the sea.

Pedro went back to the tiller, the single oar now stowed away. He steered towards the bright star. Looking at his father whose head was lolling ominously to one side, Pedro knew he was unconscious. He watched his shallow breathing anxiously. Leaving the tiller, he gently pushed his father sideways, lowering him flat and trying desperately to ignore the terrible wound. 'Sleep, Papa, sleep.' He left him as comfortable as he could.

The heat from the sun had now gone. In his nakedness, Pedro began to feel the chill of the night air, and the wind was no longer so welcome. Hunching over trying to protect himself, with the tiller held steadfastly against his body, his eyes did not leave the bright star. Exhausted as he was by the day's events, he crouched low over the tiller, his body relaxing a little as the gunnels protected him slightly from the wind. He fell into an uneasy, dreamless sleep.

Chapter Nine

The night sky descended slowly over the little vessel, covering everything in a blanket of darkness. Above them, millions of stars appeared. Joe stirred and moaned. He could not move. Casting his eye around, he saw Pedro crouched over the tiller, fast asleep. Thirst was gnawing at him, but still he could not move, try as he might. He grunted out to Pedro, but, lost in the sleep of exhaustion, his son did not stir. Joe tried to raise himself again, thirst nagging at him. The effort was too much for his emaciated body and he blacked out once more.

Neither of them saw the large container ship bearing down on them, diesel engines throbbing, propellers thrashing, turning the water white behind it. The brightness of the ship's lights illuminated the darkness enveloping them. They did not feel the waves created by the ship as it passed two hundred yards starboard, tossing them up and down like a small cork. The throbbing engines faded and the dimming lights disappeared. The waves flattened and the sea subsided, as the noisy ship was once more swallowed by the darkness. Joe and Pedro did not stir. The only sign of the ship's passing was the long white wake foaming into the distance.

Pedro awoke as the sun climbed over the horizon. His young body, replenished by sleep, found the return of some energy. Rubbing his eyes and stretching, he looked down at his father, concern etched on his face. He saw his father's shallow breathing and noticed he had not moved his position. Reaching for the tin of water, Pedro realised they only had enough for that day, no more. Taking extra care, he ladled a few drops into his father's mouth. He filled his own mouth and gargled with the water, feeling it soak into his tongue and rinsing his teeth and gums. Then he swallowed. Picking up a fish, he ate heartily.

As he chewed, he realised his slumbers had taken him from dusk to dawn. A worried frown creased his face. He had no idea whether his course had remained true and the bright star was no longer visible. He looked at the masthead and sail, registering that the winds had filled the canvas and the craft was being pushed at a steady few knots. A slight spume lifted over the bow as the boat ploughed through the sea. Doubts crept into the boy's mind: were they heading out to sea or towards land? Now he would have to wait until sunset again to get another sighting of the stars. He made the brave decision to stay on course, knowing this was a life or death decision.

He worried for his father, whether or not he would survive another day at sea consumed his mind. Tears ran down his young cheeks as he looked down at Joe. They were still in the shaded portion of the gunnels, protected from the prevailing winds, but when the sun rose higher he would have to shield him from the relentless heat.

Feeling the call of nature rumbling in his bowels, he left the tiller but kept an eye on it as he positioned his bottom over the stern and relieved himself. Cupping his left hand, he scooped up some sea water and washed himself. As he finished, he saw his father roll over, murmuring incoherently, exposing his shattered face, the eye socket staring sightlessly up at him, but there were signs of consciousness. The torn half of his face was blackened with dried blood; no pus or seeping cracks were evident. The other side of his face seemed strangely alive. As he rolled over, his useless leg stayed where it was and his right hand was cradled to his chest as if he held something precious.

Pedro gave his father a few drops of water before lashing the tin to the mast once more. Looking out to sea, nothing but emptiness faced him, except for a few birds flapping in the distance. Birds! Pedro shaded his eyes with his upturned hand. 'We are heading towards land, Papa!'

There in the distance a slight greyness coloured the horizon. Leaving the stern, he fashioned a piece of rope around the tiller and lashed it down, leaving himself free. Ducking under the sail, he climbed the mast right to the top. The little boat swayed from side to side. Pedro hung on. Gripping tightly, he looked in the direction of the birds where distant puffs of clouds hovered above a mist of grey. He knew this must be land. Excitement flowed into him. A slight smile touched his lips and then he laughed out loud as he realised they were only a few hours from shore.

He shimmied down the mast onto the deck, watching his father's shallow breathing as he came. 'Hang on, Papa, hang on!' He unlashed the tiller, sat down at the stern of the boat and, staring ahead, willed the little craft through the water.

He sat there, the sun now climbing high in the sky, every minute bringing them closer to the shore. As he peered intently forward, ploughing through the waves, he spotted a thin line of blue-black smoke trailing just above the skyline. It seemed to be heading towards them. Then the faint outline of a funnel appeared just above the horizon. As the distance between the two crafts closed, Pedro's heart hammered in his chest with hope.

'Boat ahead, Captain! Two points off the starboard bow.'

61

Peering through the wheelhouse window, the captain of the fishing vessel saw the little craft riding the waves. Thrusting the throttle back, he slowed his boat, gliding it towards the open craft. He could just make out the naked figure of a boy standing by the mast.

Pedro made out tiny figures standing in the bow looking across the sea straight at him. He recognised the boat from the fishing fleet. He could just make out the noise of the throbbing diesel engine. The sound travelled the distance between them and the ship grew larger as he watched.

His father was now fully exposed to the glare of the sun. Pedro stood up and positioned himself between the sun and his father, using his body as a shield as he waited for the oncoming ship. When the vessel was close enough, the men in the bow started shouting at him, cupping their hands around their mouths. The sounds were muffled. He watched the ship throb towards him.

Waves of fatigue pulsing through him showed that the last forty-eight hours had started to catch up with him. He had been too concerned about his father to notice his own weariness. Not now, he told himself, so near to the end, or was it just the beginning? Fighting off fatigue, hunger and thirst, Pedro lowered the patched sail, making the approach of the big ship easier. Then he stood waiting, the morning sun casting long shadows to the side of him, shading his father's inert body.

'Bosun, throw the lifeline to the other craft.' The captain reversed the engines as he spoke. Turning the wheel expertly, he felt his vessel nudge the small craft below him. Pedro heard the reverse thrust as the engine of the boat pulled alongside.

'Are you all right?' shouted the bosun to the

boy.

'Yes, but my father's gravely ill.'

'What happened?'

'Attacked by a shark. He's been badly mauled. I don't know how long he'll survive. Please hurry.'

'What do you need?'

'Can you spare a cover and some water?'

Throwing down the rope, the bosun ran back to the wheelhouse, his sense of urgency making the captain realise the seriousness of the situation. The words 'shark attack' were enough to make him act quickly.

'Fetch what you need. I'll hold the boat steady and radio ahead.'

The bosun went to the store, grabbed what was required, returned to the little craft and threw the blanket and water container down into the stern of the boat. 'Hold on, boy, the captain's radioing ahead for assistance. We'll tow you ashore. Make the rope fast to the bow, then hold on tight. We'll be travelling pretty fast!'

By now the whole crew had run to the side and looked down into the small boat. When they saw the body lying near the stern and the boy unconsciously naked beside it, no further explanation was necessary. The state of the man lying there told them the situation was dire.

The captain watched as the child caught the rope and tied it to the front of his craft, glad that as his ship had approached the lad had had all his wits about him and lowered the sail. The large ship reversed away with an almighty roar and manoeuvred in front of the little boat. With rope secured between the two vessels, the captain thrust the throttle slowly forwards, keeping an eye through the cabin window. The bosun raised his arm, indicating the rope was taut. Forward with the throttle once more, the captain kept the helm straight. The powerful diesel engine picked up tempo. A further glance back to the bosun told the captain all was well. He pushed again, full ahead. Everything was in order. He radioed ahead, the age-old maritime signal for distressed vessels:

Mayday. Mayday. Injured party coming ashore. Mayday. Missing vessel rescued. Repeat, missing vessel rescued. One badly injured man aboard. Estimated time of arrival two hours. Repeat, ETA two hours. Emergency hospitalisation urgently needed. Arriving dock number 2. Repeat, dock number 2. Have vehicle ready for immediate transfer. Repeat, immediate transfer. Over and out.

Pedro made a makeshift cover over his father, which he lashed to the masthead and gunnels. The old blanket flapped in the wind just above Joe's emaciated body, the breeze fanning him as they floated along. The powerful ship pushed through the sea as the little craft bobbed up and down following in its wake. Pedro looked beyond the stern of their little vessel and marvelled at the white wake left behind them. He had never travelled so fast.

Taking the container of water the bosun had supplied, he crawled under the blanket, cradled his father's torn head between his knees and ladled water down between the salt-encrusted lips before taking a drink himself. A little hope for his father had taken the place of fear. He stroked Joe's face as he waited. An involuntary tear left his cheek and splashed down onto the injured man. 'Please hold on, Papa, I need you so much. Hold on.'

As the boat rounded the headland, coming into

view of the dock, it slowed. Entering the estuary, they glided up to the jetty on quarter power. At the last minute, they wheeled hard over, the boat was put into reverse thrust and kissed the quayside. Two seamen threw ropes to the waiting sailors below and tied the boat to the jetty. The engine stopped.

The little craft was secured at the same time as an ambulance reversed to the water's edge. Its crew leapt out and jumped down into the craft, immediately pulling back the blanket to examine the inert body lying there. Calling for the stretcher, they carefully placed the unconscious Joe onto it, securing him so he could not fall. They carried him to the waiting ambulance with Pedro beside them. Placing the stretcher carefully inside, they slammed the doors, rushed around each side of the vehicle, jumped in and drove away, leaving little Pedro standing there forgotten.

The crowd jabbering in his ears was deafening after the quiet of the ocean. He felt himself spiralling and collapsed onto the concrete quayside, blackness closing over him, cradling him in comfortable oblivion even before he hit the ground.

Chapter Ten

Pedro awoke covered in a warm blanket, with a fire in the hearth. He rubbed his eyes and began to take in his new surroundings. Looking down, he saw his wounds had been bandaged and as he sat up, he recognised the kindly face of the sea captain who was squatting by the fire looking at him.

'Hello, are you feeling better?'

'Yes, thank you.'

'What's your name?' asked the captain.

'Pedro.' There was a slight quiver in his voice. 'Where are we? What is this place? Where's my father?'

'Calm down, son, calm down. All your questions will be answered in due course. You're safe now.' The captain reassured the boy and explained to him where he was.

Looking around once more, Pedro noticed the spacious hut, so different from his own sparse home. Light and airy, it was clean and there was no smell of left over food or dead fires. Bright sunlight shone through the windows. Fresh cooking aromas – the wonderful familiar smells of chapattis, dahl and home baked nan – drifted out from another room. His taste buds salivating, his tummy rumbling, Pedro realised just how hungry he was.

A woman entered through the open door and he stood up to make the customary greeting. A girl and two boys ran after her, the younger boy coming to clutch at his mother's colourful sari while the older boy and girl stood slightly apart. Pedro suddenly realised he was still naked and quickly reached down to grab the blanket. Pulling this in front of him, he blushed profusely and the three children laughed.

Catching the eye of the girl, about the same age as himself, he noticed she was tall for her age but her woman's shape had still to come. The warmth in her eyes shone as she smiled radiantly at him. His embarrassment evident, he ran out of the open door.

The sea captain ruffled his children's heads as he followed Pedro out, taking the clothes his wife handed to him. Standing in the yard and looking out to sea, Pedro heard the man approach and felt a hand on his shoulder turning him around.

'Don't be embarrassed, my little man,' he said. 'Your bravery has been recognised by everyone in the village. Get dressed. Food awaits you.'

Pedro took the proffered clothes, dropped the blanket and slipped into a pair of red shorts. He flung a T-shirt over his head and slid his feet into rubber flip-flops. Walking side by side, they went back into the house. Pedro's awkwardness had vanished and he smiled as the man introduced his wife and children. Sitting down together, the brothers ate with their father, beckoning the shy Pedro to join them.

The food tasted so good and Pedro was ravenous. He looked around to see everyone staring at him and realised he was scoffing his food. 'Please forgive me. I was taught better manners than this.' He wiped his mouth and started again. After the meal he turned to the captain's wife, salaaming and bowing. 'Thank you for the meal. It was wonderful. I feel much better now.' Again he caught the eye of the girl. Pedro smiled.

They were only a few miles from his own village and he knew the entrance to the Mandovi estuary; he had seen it each time he and his father had put out to sea, but he had never actually been to that spot before. The captain explained to him that the elders of the village wanted to know all that had happened to him in the last few days.

'Do you feel strong enough to meet everybody?'

Pedro nodded his consent. 'Yes. I would like to explain what happened.'

He turned to thank the woman once more for the food and as the girl helped her clear the remnants of the meal away, the captain beckoned Pedro to follow him out of the hut.

'Come on then, my boy, let's go.'

Pedro noticed that the captain commanded much respect. Men stopped as he passed, hands held in front, dipping their heads at the same time and greeting him with, 'Salaam, good Captain.' The captain replied in return but his hand always went back on Pedro's shoulder, steering him towards the meeting place at the centre of the village.

Several men – the elders of the village – sat patiently waiting for them, smoking cob pipes. The smoke mingled above them. The captain introduced the boy and when all formalities and greetings were completed, their spokesman drew Pedro towards him.

'In your own time, tell us your story.'

Pedro looked up into his kindly eyes and taking a deep breath he began. Trembling, he told the saga from his viewpoint; his father's tale would have to wait. The elders listened intently, politely nodding when the boy paused. Pedro missed out nothing. As the child relived the trauma of those two terrible days, the captain encouraged him by squeezing his shoulder, and the tension gradually left Pedro's body with each word he spoke.

When he had finished, the spokesman of the elders placed a reassuring hand on his shoulder. 'Thank you. The village will do everything possible to help you.'

The captain rose and shook the head man's hand. 'The boy will be staying with me and my family until his father recovers.'

'How far is the hospital?' Pedro tentatively looked up at the captain.

'About twenty miles.'

'Can I see my father?'

The captain looked at the elders. A nod told him that he could speak for them all. He turned back to Pedro. 'Everybody is busy harvesting the sea while the waters are calm. Every man is needed. Perhaps in a couple of days someone can take you.'

Pedro lowered his eyes.

Thanking the elders, the captain indicated they should leave. As they walked back through the village, he tried to reassure Pedro. 'Don't worry, all will be well. We'll receive news of your father soon enough. In the meantime, you must relax with my family and get your strength back.'

Pedro said nothing. He merely walked along despondently. Back at the family home he knew they were welcoming but his worries persisted. Chai simmered over the open fire. He watched the captain's wife dip a cup into the steaming pot. Smiling, she offered him the nourishing brew. Motioning to the corner of the hut, she pointed out Pedro's makeshift cot already made up. He had no notion of the irony of the situation and joined the family round the fire until he felt himself growing sleepy. Wishing them goodnight and thanking them again for their kindness, the child then climbed into the bed and fell instantly asleep. The other children were also sent to bed.

The captain held his wife's hand as they sat and talked, whispering so as not to disturb the sleeping child.

'An extra mouth will be hard to feed.'

'I know, but we will manage somehow,' replied her husband. The captain owned his own boat and in their small world they were comfortable.

'What will happen if his father dies?' she asked in hushed tones, glancing across at the cot. 'Will he become part of our family?'

Leaning across to his wife he murmured, 'The poor man's torn to pieces. I don't hold out much hope. I'll make enquiries in his village and try to find his family – if he has any. By now, they'll be really worried.'

Dampening down the fire, knocking out his pipe on the hearth, he beckoned his wife to bed. He had an early start the next day, but sleep did not come easily. As his beloved wife, Rosa, lay sleeping beside him, Rodriguez Diaz found himself thinking of another eleven year old boy who had gone to sea with his father…

Their first born son, Michael, is the image of his mother, and Rodriguez's only worry is that he is a little slow in his mannerisms and his thinking. Perhaps the time at sea will strengthen him and straighten him out; only time will tell. He smiles as he watches his son standing at the stern, looking at the wake of the churning propeller trailing into the distance, the men panning out the netting either side of his boat. Then he sees his son trying to help with the weight of the outbound nets, which is beginning to pull the remaining rope's floats and netting ever quicker over the side.

Rodriguez steadies the boat from the wheelhouse, looking out towards the horizon, checking his instruments. The noise of the engines in the wheelhouse throbs in his ears, so when he glances back and sees the men urgently waving and flailing their arms at him, the shock propels him

*forward and out of the cabin. His son is nowhere in sight.
The men are shouting at him, shock registered in their faces.
He rushes astern.*

'What's happened?' he demands.

*They look at him pityingly. 'Michael has gone
overboard,' they cry as one, 'tangled in the outgoing netting
still panning out over the stern.'*

'Which side?' the captain cries.

'Starboard, Captain,' comes the reply.

*Running quickly back to the wheelhouse, he slams
the throttle back. The drag of the netting slows but the
forward motion does not stop. Running back, he orders his
men to help him haul the nets back over the gunnels. They
toil with all their strength, but in vain: the forward motion
of the boat makes the task impossible. Rushing to the port
side, picking up an axe on his way, he hacks at the ropes
holding the netting in place. The port netting floats away
with the tidal pull. Running back to the wheelhouse he
thrusts the throttle into reverse, shouting to the men who
are riveted to the spot. 'Start hauling the netting back over
the side,' he screams. 'Mind the boat's screw and rudder.'*

*He locks the wheel and steering into a fixed position
with rope and rushes outside to help his men haul the whole
mess, hand over hand, back over the gunnels. Time stands
still. His son's feet appear first. The men, hauling
frantically with their remaining strength, sweat pouring
down their bodies with the effort, at last heave the inert
tangled body back over the side. The boy's lips are blue, the
wrists and one ankle rubbed raw from the chafing of the
netting holding them tightly.*

*Cutting the mesh holding his son also releases the
many fish. They flap around as Rodriguez turns his son
over onto his front, straddles him and pushes down on his
back with both hands, pumping water from his boy's lungs.
As he watches the water pouring from his nose and mouth,
spreading across the decking, he cries 'Mikey! Mikey!
Mikey!'*

He keeps working on his son while the men stand around motionless, panting and staring, bent double with exhaustion, their eyes never leaving the desperate first aid scene being enacted in front of them.

Flipping the boy over, Rodriguez looks into his son's eyes. There is no sign of life, no movement in his limbs. Closing his son's eyes with his fingers and lifting him towards him, he cradles him in his arms and begins to rock him backwards and forwards. Squatting on the deck, cuddling his cold dead son just gone to sleep in God's embrace, he murmurs, 'Say hello to your grandfather. Take all my love with you. I have no more to offer.'

Rodriguez lowers his son gently to the deck and covers the boy with a blanket handed to him by one of the crew. Leaving him, he walks back to the wheelhouse and shuts the cabin door behind him.

The sun moves one notch lower in the sky. The whole tragedy has taken just twenty minutes…

The captain looked down at Pedro, fast asleep in his cot, aware of how much he reminded him of his own long-dead son.

Pedro awoke and stared into the dying embers glowing in the fireplace, his only source of light. It was not quite dawn. He rose, put on his clothes and crept out of the house. His tired body still cried out for more sleep as he walked into the dim early morning.

Chapter Eleven

The ambulance crew went as fast as they dared. The roads were full of potholes and there was always the odd bicycle to contend with. A cow or oncoming traffic slowed them frequently.

An hour and a half later, they arrived at the hospital and hurried into the building with their stretcher case. A doctor and two nurses were waiting. They wheeled Joe into theatre, where the surgeons worked on him for several hours, stitching and repairing wherever they could. After surgery, they wheeled him out of theatre with tubes and upturned bottles, needles and pins attached all round him; he looked like a horizontal porcupine. He had been pumped full of drugs and water was dripping steadily into his system, but dehydration, shock and loss of blood were all factors stacked against him. They wheeled him into the intensive care unit and a nurse was stationed to monitor his progress or to call out the emergency team if necessary.

Joe lay as if lifeless, completely still, his legs in traction, swathed in bandages, his breathing irregular. The doctors did not hold out much hope and the next thirty-six hours were the most critical. Monitors bleeped, the automatic machines flashed green on and off as they tried to regulate him. Tomorrow someone would be sent to find the village Joe came from. Someone would be sure to have recognised the boat and alerted his family.

An eleven-year-old boy, left behind by the ambulance men, could have told them all they needed to know.

Pedro walked along in the general direction that the ambulance had taken the day before. When daybreak came, he would ask the way. Someone would know where they had taken his father. As he trudged on, the grey mist broke and dawn crept over the horizon. Men and women emerged into the early morning, some walking, some riding to work on rusty old bikes. Pedro stopped several strangers to ask directions, got lost several times, backtracked and started his journey again, all the time worrying about his injured father.

Shinning up a papaya tree, he plucked a wild ripe fruit and squatted by the roadside, quenching his thirst, the juices running down his chin. He noticed the toddy man swaying above him as he ate. Normally he was fascinated by the man's scimitar-shaped cutting knife and his ability to shin thirty or forty feet up a king coconut palm with just a hemp rope looped between bare feet and nothing else supporting him between the ground and his god. Today Pedro barely acknowledged his presence. His thoughts were elsewhere.

With hunger and thirst sated and with sticky hands, he threw the skin into the jungle and moved on, intent on getting closer to his father. The intense heat of the noon sun beating down on the baked red earth beneath his feet made the road surface dance and shimmer, while tufts of sage grass bent in the wind. Tiredness overwhelmed him once more. Finding a shady spot, surrounded by the heady, sweet scents of bougainvillaea, jasmine, temple flowers and water lilies, he dozed fitfully for a while.

Up again, on he trudged. His weary legs carried him forward and the light began to fade. He saw in front of him, in the distance, the building he was seeking.

At long last he reached the hospital. He stood

74

gazing in awe at this imposing structure. Compared to his village's tiny dwellings, this was gigantic. Walking up the steps, he entered. The smell of bleach and disinfectant in the building assailed his nostrils. The general cleanliness was all new to him. Walking down one corridor after another in total bewilderment, he felt uneasy at the general hustle and bustle of doctors, nurses and orderlies. Stretchers wheeled prostrate bodies in all directions. Some were distressed, others silent. Blue-skirted nurses, white-coated doctors – Pedro was over-whelmed, but one small boy caused them not the slightest interest. He peered into rooms, not chancing to ask anyone in case he was thrown out.

He walked slowly down yet another corridor and noticed a nurse leaving a room. Pedro glanced inside. There, lying on an iron bed, covered with a pure white blanket, lay his father. Entering the room with its unfamiliar scents, he touched him with love and affection. Tiredness once more overtook him and he crawled under the bed, asleep before his head touched the vinyl flooring. When the nurse returned, she could not believe the sight before her. She rang for assistance and a doctor arrived. He told the nurse to leave the boy where he was and cover him with a blanket. They would uncover his story in the morning.

As father and son slept, the man unconscious, the boy in deep slumber, Rodriguez Diaz screeched to a halt in his battered old jeep. Rushing into reception, he breathlessly blurted out his story: 'Joe Remerez Gonzales … badly mauled … his son …' He was aware that he was not making much sense.

'Would you like to go and sit down over there. We'll get someone to attend to you.' The receptionist's tone was calm in response to his frantic questioning.

Not long after, the surgeon arrived and Diaz, with time to collect his thoughts, introduced himself, now able to tell all he knew of Joe and Pedro at a more sedate pace. With growing admiration, the doctor listened to the captain's tale of the lad's bravery.

'I'll give him a mild sedative when he wakes up and see that a small bed is put in the same room as his father.'

'What are his chances?' The captain's concern was genuine and the doctor knew he should be honest with him.

'He's putting up a real fight for his life, but there's going to be a long struggle ahead.'

The captain had no doubt that he was right. 'May I have your permission to take one brief look in on them before I leave?'

The doctor nodded in agreement. 'I don't see why not.' Rodriguez Diaz followed him from the reception area and walked with him down the corridor to the hospital room, a journey that brought memories from his subconscious, forcing them to the surface of his mind.

As he stared down at the emaciated brown figure lying in the bed before him, swathed in bandages, hovering between life and death, he smiled tenderly at the sleeping child beneath the bed. He hoped for the boy's sake that his father would pull through. He knew only too well what it meant to lose a father...

On his days off from school he watches his father put to sea. The son of a sea captain – in their world, a privileged position – he has no thought in his head other than to follow in his father's footsteps, the generations before him having travelled the same path. The sea! It runs through his veins, calling to him, the impulse to sail so strong in him. He sees his father waving to him from the deck of his ship, the steady chugging of the engines throbbing out to the open ocean, grey smoke puffing from the exhaust poking above the wheelhouse.

The crew are busy on deck preparing the boat for the open sea, a mountain of netting towering above them in the stern of the boat. The wake, stirred up by the whirling propeller, leaves behind a trail like an umbilical cord attached to the land – a magical trail helping them to find their way home. The sun rises above the horizon, turning the ship into a black silhouette. Then his mother breaks the spellbound moment, calling him home and bringing him back to earth.

When he is eleven years old his father takes him to sea. The smells and sounds live up to all that he has dreamed of. Never sick in the roughest of seas, born to ride the waves, he is a jockey of the ocean. The permanently blood-red betel nut-stained mouths of the men on board smile at him. As they spit over the side of the boat, Rodriguez is fascinated as the red goblets float up and over the waves and into the distance.

Although he is just a boy, the hardened sailors show deference to him, the captain's son. He watches everything the sailors and his father do. His eyes miss nothing and he learns quickly, copying time after time until he does things instinctively without thinking. By the time he is sixteen, the hardened fisherman-cum-sailor-cum-future captain stands on deck, balanced on steady legs and swaying hips, staring with practised eyes out to the far horizon.

He is eighteen and far out to sea when his father, standing next to him on the foredeck, suddenly lurches onto his knees with a mighty thump. He pitches forward, dead of a massive heart attack before hitting the deck. He is only fifty-two years old.

Command comes easy to Rodriguez as he remembers his father's words: 'Lead by example, son. Never lose your temper. The men will look to you for leadership. If you show fear or panic so will they.'

Following his father's example, never raising his

voice, authority present in his already rumbling baritone, he makes the long voyage home, his father packed in ice meant for the fish of the sea and the crew worrying what their future will hold.

They cremate his father with all the respect the man deserved, honouring the right gods to send him into the next world on an easy passage.

Snapping out of his reverie with moist eyes, Rodriguez realised where he was. He stepped back and mentally shook himself, the terrible past pushed back once more into the dark depths of his mind.

Turning to the doctor, relieved that both Joe and Pedro were now in good hands, he thanked him. 'I'll be back as soon as I can after my fishing trip,' he promised.

Chapter Twelve

Pedro awoke the next morning and, startled by his surroundings, hit his head on the bed above as he sat up. He rolled himself from underneath straight into the nurse's feet. He looked up at her smiling face as, amused, she helped him stand upright.

'What's your name?' She looked at him enquiringly as she pressed her buzzer; she knew the doctor would want to know the minute the boy awoke.

The boy liked the look of this lady in blue and instinctively knew he could trust her. 'Pedro Luis Gonzales,' he said proudly.

A doctor rushed into the intensive care unit in response to the buzzer, and Pedro's look turned to one of caution at the sight of the white-coated figure. The doctor squatted on his haunches to be at the same level as the child and Pedro found himself looking into caring eyes.

'Hello, young man. My name is Doctor Datta. Now you just sit down here and tell me everything that's happened.' He steered the boy towards a chair. 'Take your time.'

'How is my father?' Pedro's sole concern was for Joe and he could not think beyond his father's condition.

'Well, he's got some nasty injuries but we think he's going to be fine.' The doctor's words, carefully chosen so as not to alarm the lad more than necessary, reassured him. The doctor handed him a plastic cup. Drinking down the whitish fluid quickly, Pedro felt the mild sedative working almost immediately. It calmed him down and he felt more able to cope with Doctor Datta's questions.

As the boy's story unravelled, the doctor and nurse sat amazed by the horror of it all. Slowly, the boy's eyelids began to close and before he slid sideways from the chair, the doctor gently lowered him onto the cot now in place. They knew that sleep was the best healer in the world and, no doubt, when he awoke next time, he would be well on the way to recovery.

Meanwhile, Joe lay in the hospital bed, hovering between life and death. The latter was inviting, the former, uncomfortable. He seemed to be looking at a bright light in the distance. The blackness around him was very comforting and warm. His mind decided to stay where it was for the moment. He felt very secure and his dreams were pleasant...

He is fishing with the old man, his green eyes laughing, the sea lapping round their waists, the fish piling up beside them on the damp sands. His wife and his little daughter are waving at him as they play on the beach. In the distance, the small figure of a boy is faintly outlined in the sky, hand out-stretched, beckoning him to come forward. Joe wonders what he wants and who he is. He carries on fishing with the old man. He feels content.

Pedro stayed with his father for eight days, hardly moving from his side. He stroked his hair and talked to him, but not a flicker came from the older man's face. There was just the rise and fall of the respirator, the buzz of the machines, the little green lights flashing on and off. Nurses and doctors came and went, different people at different times. Pedro saw them all.

His only moments of happiness were when the

captain came to visit and brought a release of tension. The man cuffed his head and laughed with him. Sometimes he brought his wife, Rosa, with him and once his children. The girl, Maria, looked at him in the most peculiar way – a look Pedro could not make out. The older boy, Cristiano, gave him a small toy to play with. Antonio, his brother, hiding behind his mother's sari and peeking around at the members of his family, shied away from the doctors and nurses.

Before they left one day, Pedro watched as the captain spoke to the doctor out in the corridor, concern on his face. When Pedro saw the doctor shake his head with resignation, the tears came running down his cheeks and he pleaded in his mind, willing his father to recover. 'Show the doctors how wrong they are, Papa! Fight, Papa, fight!'

The boy did not know about his father's past; he was too young for that. Would the gods laugh at him, make him relive his father's life of loneliness with no family? To his people the importance of family was everything. To be alone was the nightmare of an Indian soul.

Joe walks out of the surf, watching the old man fish contentedly in the sea. Walking towards to his wife and child, who it seems have retreated further away, Joe looks over to the boy silhouetted against the sky, still beckoning him. Puzzled, Joe hesitates and then his feet begin to shuffle slowly towards the shadow that is calling to him, coaxing him forward. A strange light behind the boy appears to be pulling him towards it. Joe looks back. His wife, child and the old man wave at him. The pull of the light becomes stronger. The boy heads for the light, holding Joe's hand. They pass through.

Pedro, sitting by his father's side, suddenly saw his

good hand twitch. Startled, he prayed to all the gods in heaven, held his breath and watched as his father opened his good eye. Tears brimmed over and fell onto the pillow below.

The doctors were as happy as Pedro was ecstatic. From that moment on, Joe became stronger with each day that passed. One week later, he was sitting up. His strength mounted slowly every day. The drugs helped ease his pain and he took food through a tube, not yet able to manage solids, his face making it impossible to chew. He was moved out of intensive care and into an ordinary ward, his wounds concealed by bandages.

When Rodriguez Diaz arrived, Joe looked uncomprehendingly from his son to the older man and back again, until between them they explained his part in the story. With every word he heard, Joe's pleasure and gratitude grew.

The captain waved away all expressions of thanks. 'Now, I should like to invite you and your son to stay with my family as guests until you feel strong enough to be back home. The elders have set aside a small cabin in my village, and my wife and daughter will attend to your needs daily. The whole village is looking forward to hearing your tale first hand.'

Rodriguez Diaz paused to see the reaction of father and son. Joe looked into Pedro's pleading eyes and agreed.

Chapter Thirteen

Joe looked out to sea knowing he could never venture into deep water again. The scars to his mind had eased but the scars on his body were another matter. His face had healed well over the last year since the accident but, as it healed, it had pulled the corner of his mouth upwards, giving it the appearance of a permanent, lop-sided smile. His right hand looked normal except for the angry red lines where his lacerated skin had healed. It was still slightly stiff, however, which made it difficult to hold and grip. He shuffled slightly, adjusting his balance. He could just manage to hobble round, but not unaided: the crutch he carried counterbalanced his leg.

His hand rested on his son's shoulder. Pedro, always faithful, had helped Rosa Diaz nurse him back to life. After he had spent six weeks in hospital and was weaned off medication, Joe was taken back to their village. He lay in the hut for many days trying to come to terms with his terrible injuries. Pedro fished for both of them and a little money trickled in from his surplus catch. There was never much but they managed a frugal existence.

Rodriguez popped in when he had time, encouraging Joe back to health. Sometimes he would bring tobacco. Filling their pipes, Joe propped up on his elbow, they would swap stories of fishing and the sea. Rodriguez told one of his favourite stories, about the first time he took his boat out.

'I knew there would be confrontation,' he began, as he took a long draw on his pipe. 'My number two was a big burly man from the village. Everyone knew he was a bully. He was a surly, reticent sort of chap. Whenever I gave him orders he would carry them out in a slovenly manner and with contempt in his voice. The men kept their heads down; they knew there would be a showdown sooner or later. It made the atmosphere on the craft really uncomfortable; the tension permeated everything. I knew I was going to have to do something to put a stop to it.'

Diaz glanced across at Joe to make sure he was still listening. He didn't want to tire his friend but knew that the stimulation of his sea stories was just what he needed.

'I walked up behind this surly individual and tapped him on the shoulder. He stood up and turned round to confront me. I wish I could say it was eyeball to eyeball, but he was a good foot taller than me! Still, he gave me a good hard stare, and then I hit him! I was so quick that he didn't even see it coming. It caught him straight between his eyes.'

Diaz smiled as he remembered his prowess with his fist, and then his expression darkened momentarily as he thought of the years of hard labour and the fury of losing his father which had flowed through his arm. The anger had propelled a blow to the man's skull with the hardness of a sledgehammer.

'He was out cold before his head cracked on the ground. I shouted to someone to throw him over the side. I had been angry, but striking that man had turned my fury to a calmer, more controlled rage. Of course the crew protested at my order to throw him overboard. "Captain, we're many miles from shore!" they said. "Then tie him up and put him in the hold with the fish," I told them. "Feed him and water him and throw him off when we reach the shore. I do not wish to set eyes on that man again. If he comes into my sight before we land, I won't answer for the consequences." And with that I turned on my heels and went back to the wheelhouse. No one ever bothered me again.'

Joe loved that story. He loved all Rodriguez's stories; they helped him and gave him a purpose to go on. He recognised a firmness but fairness in the man who had given him a home and done so much to help restore his health and spirit, and he could see that he never had any trouble filling his boat with willing hands. He made this observation to Diaz.

'True,' replied the captain, 'but they work for me on my terms. There is no betel nut chewing on my ship. What they do on shore is their own affair, but on board they follow my rules. God help anyone missing the tide, too; they get left behind.'

Joe, remembering the fate of his brother Tony, nodded and smiled with admiration at Rodriguez Diaz. This, more than anything else, sealed the bond between them.

The villagers began to pop in to visit, asking what he needed. They learned from Rodriguez's example and began contributing stories of their own, knowing that Joe needed all the encouragement they could give him. Pedro understood and began telling his father of his fishing trips, where he had fished and what he had managed to sell at the market place.

'When you get better, Papa, we will go out together. Everyone wants to see you well.'

He woke one morning to find his father silhouetted in the doorway, standing looking out to sea. Then he collapsed. Pedro rushed over and helped him back to his cot.

'Who made the hut spin?' Joe asked.

They laughed together. Joe was on the mend.

Every day, Pedro went down to their little boat, pulled up on the beach. He would check on the contents, reassuring himself that all was well. His father became stronger by the day, until Pedro found himself, one day, standing on the sands next to him, looking out to sea.

The following day, Joe approached his friend the captain. 'I need your help,' he began hesitantly. He was still a proud man and asking for help did not come easily to him. Besides, Rodriguez Diaz had already done him kindness beyond his wildest imagination. Diaz saw his hesitancy and nodded in encouragement for him to go on.

'Would you please intercede with the village elders on my behalf for permission to moor my boat alongside one of the jetties? I am in no position to pull my craft across the beach and into the waves, and Pedro is still too young to do it by himself. Naturally, I am willing to pay my portion for the privilege.

'I've been talking this over with Pedro for quite a while. We've thought about returning home, but we truly feel that we have more kinship with these people of the river than with those in our own village. We have no family back home and if we go back, I will not be able to earn a living. We promise that we will not be a burden to anyone. Tell me what you think, my friend.'

Rodriguez Diaz pulled hard on his pipe, his eyes smiling. He would love to have Joe Gonzales to remain permanently in his community, but of course the decision was out of his hands. 'I'll see what I can do,' he promised and left straight away to put this deposition to the elders.

Man and boy waited all night to hear the wise ones' decision. The next day, the captain approached them with a smile on his face. No explanation was necessary. They laughed and patted each other on the back. Pedro jumped up and down with delight. Now he would not have to leave his new found friends, especially the captain's two eldest children, to whom he had formed a special attachment.

The men of the village went down with Joe and Pedro to the boat and pushed the craft into the sea. The young men sang as they went two abreast, pulling a runner behind them. With a rope attached to the front of the craft, some would pull while others retrieved another runner from behind.

Joe stood proudly in the boat giving orders. The men laughed. Rosa Diaz had fashioned a leather patch with string either side, and Joe now stood, patch over his dead eye, crutch under his arm, looking like a pirate of old. Pedro looked up at his father in the stern of the boat. He felt so very proud of him.

The boat slid into the sea. Pedro hopped on as the men, now waist deep in water, gave one final push. The boy and his father showed their thanks with a smile and a wave as they unfurled the sail. Pedro pulled on the hemp ropes and watched as the patched canvas caught the wind. It knocked them back slightly as the craft lurched forwards, but Joe was safely seated in the stern steering the boat, his eye burning brightly as the sea air coursed through him.

They steered for the estuary. Rounding the headland, they sailed towards the mooring they had been allotted on the jetty. After securing the ropes, they left the boat, Joe shuffling along beside Pedro. Villagers smiled as they went, father and son, back to their new home. They would fish tomorrow at dawn.

Joe and Rodriguez had by now settled into a comfortable friendship, completely at ease with each other, and the sea captain knew instinctively when the time was right to approach the delicate subject of fishing in the estuary. Keeping the conversation casual, he asked if Joe would like to trade his remaining sea netting for a finer net. 'Better suited to river and estuary fishing,' the captain commented. 'I have no use for it and I could do with your nets. It would be a fair exchange!'

Once more Joe's pride began to surface and he glanced sideways at Rodriguez, looking for signs of charity. Feeling none, he agreed. His friend's tone and expression reassured him that there was no need for concern on that score. The swap could take place that day, before a planned fishing trip.

Lying in his bed that night, Pedro could not sleep. He remembered how, earlier, they had talked on a while and then, as the captain was taking his leave he had looked over at Pedro and, taking great care that Joe could not see him, he had winked. Pedro swore that day that he would repay the kind man in the future. The excitement awaiting them at first light kept him awake. He felt his father's restless tossing and turning, knowing that he also was anxious for the coming morning. Jumping up at dawn, Pedro prodded the bedded-down fire and prepared a hasty breakfast. He took a cup of steaming chai over to his father who sat up immediately.

Making their way down to the river, they saw many men heading in the same direction. Watching the deep-sea trawlers putting to sea, Pedro recognised the longing look in his father's eye. They made ready, waiting until all the other sea-faring boats had left, then the pair headed out to the mouth of the Mandovi estuary. As they set out to fish, the sun brimming over the headland, the birds screaming in the night-to-dawn sky, the freshness of the breeze ruffling their hair, Joe looked at Pedro and smiled. The excitement was tangible between them, as the sail of the boat caught the wind and glided them out into the Mandovi. They panned out the finer nets, trying to catch smaller fish or eels, throwing lobster and crab pots as they went, their floats bobbing on the surface.

Day after day, they fished until sunset, returning before the big fleet. Manhandling their catch onto the jetty, they would then sell their wares to small restaurants or women along the beach. They made a steady living this way. A large lobster or crab would bring enough rupees for tobacco or the occasional feni. They were happy.

They went on like this month by month, completely integrated into village life. Accepted though they were, Joe nonetheless still had his pride for he saw himself as half a man. Pedro grew tall and strong, soft fluff appearing on his chin for the first time. Joe knew his son longed to go to sea with the fleet and this worried him, not because he feared Pedro would desert him, but because he knew he never would, and he wanted Pedro to be free and independent. Sitting in the church of St. Joseph, Joe offered gifts to his god and prayed to be shown a way.

Chapter Fourteen

Standing on the jetty, Pedro watched the fleet heading out to sea. The young man never flinched from his perceived duty. He put his loyalty to his father before his own personal desires and tried to suppress his fierce passion for the sea, stoically remaining by his father's side.

Sitting in the stern of the boat, Joe watched him, feeling the boy's longings. The sun was rising in the distance and the sea was calm as they set sail, heading as usual for the mouth of the estuary. In an attempt to keep Pedro's interest alive, Joe decided to make for a little place they rarely fished. The cove was not a great distance from the village and the crystal clear waters were very deep. Panning their net out in a semicircle and squatting on the deck, they waited.

As they ate some rice and curried fish, looking and watching over the side, they noticed small fish jumping out of the water and fleeing out to sea. In the depths of water below, a dark mass was visible. They looked at each other in surprise. The shape was not clearly discernible, just a huge bulk of moving, living creatures. They both stood up at the same time, watching the netting bobbing behind them. They saw the floats slowly sink beneath the surface. The stern of the boat felt heavy and started to tilt downwards. Heaving together on the suspended lines holding the unravelled nets, they hauled in.

As the heavy nets landed on board, they could not believe their eyes. They had stumbled across a swarm of prawns. Not just any prawns, but enormous king prawns, grey and wriggling in their plumpness. Joe forgot his encumbrances as, hand over hand, he and Pedro pulled together, struggling to haul the heavy netting on board. They laughed together with joy, still not quite able to believe their eyes as the last of the netting fell in the bottom of the boat. The small craft, full to the gunnels with the wriggling creatures nearly up to their knees, rode low in the water with its bounty.

They set the sail and headed back up the estuary. Sitting in the stern steering, Joe watched as his son worked fervently, relieving the catch from the nets. The creatures all around him made a strange clicking noise in their death throes. Nearing the jetty, Joe shouted to the men and women working there. Turning as one, they watched the small craft until it bumped the jetty. As they looked down into the boat, the expression on their faces was of absolute incredulity.

With the whole fleet still at sea, there were many dockhands to help. Grabbing wicker baskets, two men carefully jumped down into the boat and scooped the prawns into them. They handed the baskets to the waiting women, now forming a line on the quay, who took them to the holding sheds. The baskets soon began to pile up and when the boat was empty, Joe scanned the eager and curious faces thronging the boat.

'I need two volunteers. There is far more work than Pedro and I can manage on our own. I'll pay two days' wages to whoever is willing to help us.'

A buzz of excitement rang round the gathered crowd, and willing hands were raised.

'I'll come!'

'Choose me.'

'Let me help.'

The buzz became a clamour and Joe was overwhelmed by the response. He looked around the sea of faces, and recognising two of the village's poorest men he remembered his own days as a struggling fisherman. 'Jaime, Juan, I'd like you to help me.'

Joe put his hand on the shoulders of the men he had chosen and steadied them as they jumped aboard. Once more they set sail for the cove. Pedro took command, leading by example. Joe watched as the young man gave out his orders kindly but firmly. They reset the net, trimmed the sail and he noticed his son's whole body was alive with excitement.

They reached the cove once more. Looking down into the water, the swarm was still there. They made the trip four more times. The mass of spawning prawns did not seem to lessen. On their last journey back, exhausted but elated, they reached the jetty to find that the word had gone out and buyers from all the surrounding districts were there to greet them. As they bid against each other, the prices rose. Joe and Pedro sat there in amazement, speechless as they watched the monies change hands, the dealers waving fistfuls of rupees. Never had such a thing happened before. The fisherman of no great distinction and his son were rich beyond their wildest dreams.

Joe and Pedro were in shock after the day's events. With the realisation of their new-found wealth taking its own time to sink in, and the kindness of their neighbours overwhelming them, they took sanctuary in the church of St Joseph standing majestically on the edge of the village. Opening the door and entering, Joe and Pedro were awed as always by the vastness of the centuries-old baroque building. They crossed themselves as they knelt in the aisle between the pews.

'Holy Mary, Mother of God,' Joe whispered.

Standing up, they walked towards the altar,

the sound of their feet echoing around the walls and disappearing up into the rafters. Wrapped in serenity and tranquillity, the feeling of their religious beliefs calmed them. Taking a candle each and placing them into the rack of holders next to the altar, they lit each other's and, inclining their heads, backed away from the altar. Prostrating themselves on the cool polished floor, arms outstretched, their thoughts their own, they prayed.

Father Alphonso walked from the vestry around the font towards the altar. Seeing Joe's and Pedro's prostrate figures, he glided towards them, white cassock billowing out around him.

Pedro sensed his presence. 'Bless me, Father.' He stood up and bowed his head to the priest.

'Bless you, Pedro.' The priest crossed him as he spoke. Joe had not moved. Both looked down at him. Father Alphonso smiled. Joe lay there in the prostate position, fast asleep.

'Forgive him, Father, he's exhausted.' Pedro reached down and shook Joe's shoulder.

Joe, startled, looked up blearily. Scrambling up as best he could, he looked at the priest. 'Forgive me, Father, I don't know what came over me.'

'Bless you, Joe.' He made the sign of the cross before him. 'Congratulations both of you. With God's help I believe you had a little luck today.'

'Thank you, Father.' Pedro looked up and Joe nodded. 'When all that has happened today settles and sinks in, we feel it's only fitting to make a donation to the church and our little village school.'

Father Alphonso smiled once more. 'That will be very generous of you, my sons, but I will still expect to see you for early morning Mass, six-thirty sharp.' Making the sign of the cross once more, he he walked back to the vestry.

Joe and Pedro bowed before the altar and the statue of the Holy Mother, then turned and left. Pedro promised himself that he would say the rosary and be there for Mass – six thirty sharp. Handed down from father to son, their religion was the mainstay of their lives, their faith a strength and comfort to them throughout every hardship. Even after independence the Portuguese influence of Catholicism had remained, the brush strokes of religion reaching into many corners.

When the fleet docked that night and the hard work of unloading the fish, cleaning the ships and battening down the holds had been done, the news of Joe's and Pedro's luck brightened the village. In their excitement, they lit a hastily assembled giant bonfire in the centre and everybody came to celebrate. Joe and Pedro had to tell their tale over and over again. People sang and danced the night away.

Pedro noticed Antonio Diaz slumped forward, not enjoying the revelry going on all around him. Antonio the silent one. Pedro knew that he relished his family's status in the village; it made him feel superior. He would not be impressed by the Gonzales' good fortune. Pedro watched as the sullen boy slunk away from the firelight, out of the village and into the darkenss.

Cristiano ran up to Pedro, slapping him on the back. 'Congratulations!' A smile split his face and then disappeared as he followed Pedro's gaze. He could just make out the diminishing form of his younger brother walking away. 'Antonio being his usual self, I see,' he remarked.

Running up to Pedro, Maria sought to gain his attention, touching him on the arm. He turned and glanced down at her as she looked up into his eyes. He felt something strange stirring inside him and his expression turned to one of puzzlement.

Her voice was full of animation when she spoke to him. 'Oh, Pedro, how proud I am of you! How clever of you and Mr Joe!'

He looked down at his feet, embarrassed. 'Really, it was nothing, just a lot of hard work.'

Despite the hustle and merriment, the joys of laughter and singing going on around them, the firelight dancing on their faces, her hand, still resting on his arm, seemed to be burning through his sleeve. The magic touch of her made something stir in his loins. He felt himself begin to blush, his uncontrollable body taking hold. Excusing himself he hurried away, his body embarrassing him. As he rushed through the throng of people he glanced back. She had not moved. Her eyes followed him through the crowd, a hurt look on her face.

He saw his father sitting with a group of older men, glasses full of feni, toasting each other, his father's lop-sided grin exaggerated even more by the laughter escaping from his lips. Rushing through the crowd, his protruding manhood beginning to show, Pedro disappeared between two huts away from the probing firelight. Leaning on one of the mud walls he waited for his body to subside.

Meanwhile the party went on, the laughter and singing reaching him. A makeshift group of musicians began to play, striking up the favourite tunes of the village, the bellows of the lap organ sucking and blowing, the musicians' nimble fingers dancing over the ivory keys, tabla drums joining in. The throb-throb bass notes vibrated along the ground and violins hummed into life, the plucked strings of the vina rounding off the group. Feet began to tap, women began to sway. Pedro, now standing outside the firelight, watched the villagers dance. Bright saris billowed out as the women twirled and swirled to the music. Greens, reds and yellows blurred with purples and blues as they gyrated. Now the men danced around the women, their tunics sticking to their bodies as the sweat ran freely, dust rising as they swayed with the rhythm. The wind whistled through the palm trees, the swish of the leaves rubbing together, the trunk and the branches swaying to the tune of the wind.

A sigh and a grunt caught Pedro's attention somewhere in the darkness behind him. He turned quickly. He saw nothing as the firelight momentarily blinded him, but still he could hear the constant murmurings and grunts coming from deeper between the mud huts. Slowly his eyes became accustomed to the darkness. He moved forward, closer to the sounds, the noises quite mesmerising. As his eyes adjusted to the gloom he saw movement ahead and there, right in front of him, were two people he recognised as husband and wife who lived a few huts away from his new home. What were they doing? The woman was half naked, her breasts thrusting upwards to the man. As Pedro peered through the gloom, he was transfixed by the sight of her nipples fully erect, perspiration running between her breasts, her arms around the man's neck, her hands tugging at his hair. A momentary flicker of light on her face showed him that her eyes were bulging, her lips parted. The moans coming from her were like nothing Pedro had heard before. Her legs were wrapped around the man as he held her off the ground, her back pressed against the mud wall, her sari covering their lower bodies. Pedro watched as the man's lower body moved backwards and forwards. They seemed to be thrusting towards each other faster and faster until they each gave a final cry and fell together to the ground. They rolled in the dust, chests heaving in unison. Pedro felt himself become erect again as the recognition of what he had just witnessed dawned on him. He slowly stepped backwards, creeping around another hut before he turned and ran.

Children slept around the campfire, oblivious to the antics of their parents. Pedro could not join them; he knew now he was no longer a child. Men became drunk; women danced on. That night, the swarm in the cove moved away, dispersing into the vast ocean. The gods of the sea had paid their dues.

As dawn approached, everyone slept where they lay; there would be no fishing today. Pedro woke early. Dressing, he looked over to his father's cot. Joe was turned to the wall, snoring. Pedro crept out of the hut into the dawn. He looked at the dying embers of the big fire of the night before; an occasional spark leapt up causing smoke to billow. Bodies, fast asleep, were lying all around, their mouths open, snoring – fly-catching, he thought. He turned, glanced up at the baroque edifice of the church casting shadows over the sleeping bodies, and sent up a silent prayer to the Holy Father, all idea of Mass forgotten in his state of confusion, the only thought in his head for Maria.

He walked through the village and on down to the river. He sat on the bank, his troubled thoughts persisting in his head. His puzzlement at Maria's knowing looks clicked into place. A shadow interrupted his reverie and looking up he saw her standing there. Their eyes locked together as they reached into one another's hearts, the spark of desire kindling in their souls. At only fourteen years old, they felt the first pangs of love; in their gaze, joys, enchantment and agonies were all rolled into one.

Chapter Fifteen

A week or two after the party, bank accounts in order, set up by Rodriguez, Joe approached the captain. 'I would like to discuss something with you. Could we meet tomorrow?'

Rodriguez tried not to show surprise at the urgency in Joe's voice. 'Of course. Is everything all right, Joe?'

'Everything's fine. I'd just like to talk an idea through with you. Could we meet somewhere neutral, say down by the river at about noon?' Joe spoke hesitantly, not wanting to appear too dominating to the man to whom he owed so much.

'That's fine by me.' Rodriguez wondered what could be pressing enough for Joe to insist on meeting away from the village. They said goodbye and went their separate ways.

The next day, Joe sat waiting for his friend on the riverbank, idly throwing stones and watching the ripples form circles and race away across the water. Birds' shadows winged over the mirrored surface as he heard Rodriguez approaching.

'Hello, Joe.' Rodriguez sat down next to him, looking across the landscape at a dozen water buffalo emerging from the jungle followed by a small boy, a cane held high above his head. Swishing the cane menacingly, he drove the beasts forward and into the river. Bulls, cows and calves milled about, their skin turning darker and the dust disappearing the wetter they became. The boy squatted on a rock watching them.

'God is great,' remarked Rodriguez, observing the natural scene and waiting for Joe to speak. He did not. They eased into a comfortable silence, watching the cattle and the wild life surrounding them. Pied kingfishers and egrets called to their respective mates, fish jumped and they could hear the busy sound of insects buzzing around them.

Finally, Joe spoke. 'I've had many hours to think about what I want to say and to ask you. But now I'm finding it quite difficult.'

'Just say what you have to say. I promise there will be no interruption on my part.'

Hesitantly Joe began. 'I have never been in this position before … monies and all. But now Pedro and the Lord have put us in this position.' He took a deep breath. 'Would you consider a partnership – you and me?' He paused. There came no reply from Rodriguez, so Joe fumbled on, absentmindedly throwing another stone across the water. 'I thought – if you are in agreement – of buying another boat the same as yours, not for me, for Pedro, and – if you consent – you could train him, as well as your own two sons; then, when they're older, perhaps another boat, each son to captain their own vessel and maybe form a company. Not that I know much of these things, but perhaps an office for us all and —'

'Hold on! Hold on!' Rodriguez put a restraining but friendly hand on Joe's arm. 'Not so fast. One step at a time. First, the partnership: what have you in mind?'

'I can't fish in deep water anymore, but with training I could organise the land side of things and you could handle the offshore side. When the boys are trained, you can, if you wish, step back and run the office. You and I would go fifty-fifty, your boat and expertise and my money. Let's learn as we go. Hopefully the company will grow with us.'

There, it had been said. Silence followed, both

men deep in their own thoughts. They watched the boy on the opposite bank stand up. Walking down to the water's edge, he entered, waded out beyond the cattle, raised his cane, brought it down onto the surface and drove the water buffalo out of the river and back into the jungle. Only the trail of wet ground showed that they had ever been there.

'I need time to think on this,' Rodriguez suddenly offered. 'I normally make my own decisions, as all men do in our community, but I would like time to think and as this would be such a big step, I would like also to put it to my wife. I know this is unusual but this is my decision.'

A log drifted past and then a pied kingfisher, with a fish flapping in its beak, perched itself on a protruding branch. Standing up, Rodriguez placed his hand on Joe's shoulder, squeezed it, turned and left Joe watching the moving river.

Chapter Sixteen

Pedro and Maria looked out for each other whenever they could. Sometimes, while Maria was helping her mother do the family washing – kneeling by the river, smashing the garments against a flat rock, rubbing carbolic soap over the clothes, vigorously scrubbing them on the rock and rinsing them in the river water – she would see Pedro floating past them in his little craft. They would stare at each other and she would follow him with her eyes until he was completely out of sight. This did not go unnoticed by her mother who recognised the telltale signs of attraction and would later speak with her husband. The rumours, nudges and winks gathered pace as the village gossips went to work. Everybody watched this couple swooning around each other. The touch of a hand, a glance at each other was enough to get the most silent tongues wagging.

One day, summoning Pedro, still so young, Rodriguez sat him down. 'Tell me, have you any intentions towards my daughter?'

Pedro looked up in surprise. How did he know? Who had told him? 'I love your daughter, sir,' he replied.

'Nonsense!' came the harsh reply. 'You're only fourteen years old. But time will tell. Come to me in four years time with good intentions and we'll see. I will have words with your father about this and other matters. In my day, young man, we had arranged marriages formulated in our youth by our families. We had to hope that the partnership would turn to love. In my case it did, and I thank God for a loving wife and children. Treat my daughter with due respect. If anything happens between you before then

I will seek redemption from you and your father. In the meantime heed my words and make your father proud of you.'

Pedro's bubble burst. Four years! That was almost forever. Bowing to the captain, he left, head down, and bumped straight into Maria outside.

'I'm sorry.' He avoided her gaze. She just made out two words as he rushed past her: 'four years ...'

Puzzled she entered her home. 'Father?' she said.

'Come here, my child, I need to have words with you.' Closing the door she walked towards him.

The following day Rodriguez met Joe at noon at the same spot on the bank of the Mandovi. Joe was already there, squatting down, throwing stones into the fast flowing water.

'Hello, Joe.'

He looked up. 'Hello.'

Both men squatted in silence, neither one wanting to break the magic spell cast by the river's tranquillity. The silence was only broken by the screeching of buzzards and vultures winging overhead, gliding around in circles searching for carrion. White egrets looked at their reflection on the water's surface, hunting for fish. Joe put his hand on his friend's shoulder, nodding his head towards the far bank of the river. Rodriguez looked in the general direction of Joe's gaze. There, just emerging from the dense undergrowth, a deer's head appeared, hanging below magnificent antlers. Forcing himself from the green foliage he cautiously stepped onto the open plain between the trees and the riverbed and took a few hesitant steps, his great head sniffing the air. He was now fully exposed. Joe and Rodriguez sat absolutely still, only the sounds of the river disturbing the peace.

'Jambuck,' whispered Joe. The male deer moved to the water's edge, sniffed once more, glanced back and barked. Out of the jungle emerged three does and two tiny foals. Rushing down to the water's edge they spread their forelegs, inclined their heads and drank deeply. The stag stayed on guard, his stately head raised high, looking from side to side and sniffing the air for danger. When the does and foals had drunk their fill they turned and disappeared back into the dense darkness of the jungle. The stag lowered his head, drank, turned and followed.

'A good sign for our families; the gods are hopefully with us,' said Rodriguez, the superstitious nature of the fisherman ever present. Joe's hand left his shoulder as they both digested the privileged moment they had just witnessed.

'The proposition you put to me yesterday: I have discussed it with my wife and we both agree on one thing.'

Joe stiffened with expectation, waiting for Rodriguez to continue, his eyes fixed on the ground, the tension crackling around them. The dark green smells of bulrushes, river-weed and grasses permeated the air.

'We both agree it is a good idea.'

Joe relaxed, tension leaving his body in waves. He knew now that his son's future was secure.

'We have many things to discuss,' continued Rodriguez. 'There will be many problems facing us. We will have to take one step at a time.'

Joe said nothing. His countenance showed relief but inside his mind was racing. All his hopes and dreams could now become true. His resolve hardened. This was his one and only chance to succeed. He told himself he would grab this chance with both hands; his determination was rock solid.

'I think, to begin with, we need to establish some rules.' Rodriguez noticed Joe's silence and continued. 'I know you'll agree with me on this one. No one who works for us will be allowed to chew betel nut – either on or off duty.'

Joe nodded his agreement with enthusiasm, thinking of his brother Tony. 'You're right, my friend. Too many families have had to put up with this terrible addiction. It's the effect on wives and families as well as the men themselves that we have to consider.'

Rodriguez was not surprised by the eagerness with which Joe greeted his suggestion. 'Let's think about it from a practical point of view, too, Joe. Addicted sailors are no good to us or to our company. I think we need to agree that anyone chewing betel nut will be instantly dismissed. Anyone we hire will be paid a fair day's wage for a fair day's work.'

'Agreed!' Joe was impressed by the business-like approach of the captain, wondering if he himself would ever achieve the same level of expertise in dealing with men. He hoped at least that Pedro would develop these skills. Rodriguez Diaz would provide a fine role model for him.

Rodriguez held out a hand to help Joe to his feet. 'In that case I think the best way forward is to approach the bank. They will have advisers who can help us. I will make an appointment.'

Together they rose. Turning towards each other, they smiled and shook hands to affirm the deal that would cement their friendship and bind their two families in the fishing world that they knew best.

Three ships, locked in formation, set sale into the sunset. In the evening, with the sun swallowed by the sea gods, the wheelhouse lights show three captains to the outside crew.

The leading boat is captained by Cristiano, Rodriguez's eldest surviving boy, but a boy no more. Instead a man stands there, with pride in his countenance, the fluff on his chin turning to stubble. The ready flash of his smile is very close to the surface; confidence emanates from his easy movements. Tall for his race, he has the look of his father about him. The ship under him throbs with power, heading towards the co-ordinates marked on the map where they have all agreed to fish that night. Listening to the engine and other sounds of the ship he has heard a thousand times before, everything registers as normal. Cristiano pokes his head out of the wheelhouse. He lets his eyes become accustomed to the dark; the full moon shimmers in the night sky, dancing between shadowy clouds. Looking around at the crew and letting them know all is well, he glances at the other two fishing vessels following in his wake, and the ghostly silver shadows of their crews going about their business. To the port side, the face and torso of his best friend and confidant, Pedro, are visible in the light of the bare bulb swaying in his wheelhouse. They have grown up comfortable in each other's company. Their fathers' kindness and confidence have rubbed off on them, and they, in turn, have grown to manhood at ease with each other and the world.

Glancing to starboard, there in the glow of the light stands Antonio, the silent one, ever watchful, going about his business with a stoic acceptance; from birth, always in the background, never volunteering for anything. Cristiano frowns. Born after the death of the captain's eldest child, his brother worries him. He cannot put a finger on anything specific but the silence emanating from Antonio has somehow raised a barrier between him and the rest of the family. In his presence the atmosphere becomes wooden. The whole family tries to break his sombre moods, but to no avail. But they all still love him. After all, he is family.

Antonio has no friends. From his days at school he has been known for his fierce temper. People steer clear of him, his father making amends with the families in the village for his misdemeanours. Antonio, short and stocky, always looks for the slight in everyone, his paranoia becoming worse as he grows older. From a child, he has felt left out, ever in the shadow of his elder brother and Pedro, who always laughed and played together. Trying to include him in their games, they only made him withdraw even further into himself. He feels his life is inexplicably linked with the dead brother he has never known, linked to him through the umbilical cord of life and death. The way that his mother and father look at him makes him feel that his brother is standing right in front of him. They have no idea he feels this way. If they had they would do their utmost to dispel these thoughts from their youngest offspring.

These feelings, which started as a spark in his younger years, have grown, feeding on themselves until they have taken over all his waking hours. He even dreams about what he will do to people if they upset him. It courses through his life's blood until it consumes him. None of this shows in his eyes, however. The deadpan face never shows an inkling of what lies beyond: a pressure cooker with its lid firmly in place.

Staring out to sea, Antonio watches the moonlit silhouettes of the two ships in front of him as they shimmer and dance to the tune of the waves. He will show his brother and Pedro… some day.

Chapter Seventeen

'Right, lads!' Rodriguez rubbed his hands together, the excitement in his eyes grabbing everyone's attention. 'Joe and I have been doing some research over the last few weeks.'

'We knew there was something going on.' Cristiano acted as spokesman for them all.

Joe laughed. 'You know us, always looking for the edge against our rivals. I mean that with all good humour to our fellow fishermen.'

They shared Joe's laughter. 'Well come on, what have you come up with now?' Their appetites were whetted for whatever the news was.

Rodriguez went on. 'A few weeks ago some leaflets popped through our letterbox. The usual stuff advertising things we don't need. I threw them into the bin as usual. Well, one fluttered to the side. I picked it up to put it with the other rubbish, and the headline caught my attention: **Can you see the fish under the sea?** What's this idiot saying, I wondered and read the whole pamphlet through – seeing as I'm the only one who can read here!'

Good-humoured banter was thrown back at him. Rodriguez acknowledged it and continued. 'Anyway, after consulting Joe, we made some phone calls to the company. That's why we're sitting here today, to discuss the matter.'

'Well, what is it?' Cristiano voiced everyone's curiosity.

'A fish-finder.' Joe supplied the vital information.

'A what?'

'A fish-finder.'

The words hovered in the air for a second as they all looked at each other. What did this mean? A barrage of questions sprang from their lips.

'How does it work?'

'Where?'

'What?'

'When?'

Calming the boys down, Joe Remerez Gonzales took up the story, explaining the article which had outlined the workings of this wonderful machine. The details were vague but from what the fathers gathered, shoals of fish could be detected under the surface of the sea. The young men looked at each other, surprise showing on their eager faces.

'The thing is,' carried on Joe, 'we need one of you to go to Mumbai, which is where the company selling the machines has its base.'

Rodriguez immediately looked at his younger son. Maybe this would be a wonderful opportunity for him to visit another part of India, and perhaps help him realise what he had here with his loving family. Antonio, glancing at his father, realised his chance had come.

'I'll go, Father.' He quickly looked around at the others. Everybody nodded their heads in agreement.

'It's settled then.' Joe was eager to move the discussion on. 'The reason we want to purchase this new machine is that it will give us an advantage over our business rivals.' Not for long, he admitted, but hopefully enough time for them to make a good profit, enabling them to upgrade to modern machinery for all their boats.

The next day the final arrangements were made for Antonio to depart for Mumbai, a twelve-hour train journey. He would arrive at 21.45 and be met by Angelo, a cousin who lived in the city. The captain's family tree had many branches in both Mumbai and Delhi. Antonio felt a great deal of trepidation about the forthcoming journey because he had never been on a train before; yet at the same time, excitement made his heart pound.

On the day of departure, his father accompanied him to the station at Margao. They pulled into the station car park as an ongoing train thundered through the station, whistle blowing, wheels screaming, making the ground vibrate. Antonio felt the palms of his hands sweating.

His heart still fluttering, they left the jeep. Heading for the large entrance hall leading to the platforms, they went through into the monolithic station. Antonio could not believe the noise, hustle and human throng all around him. Porters in red tunics with bandannas round their heads hustled everyone with a suitcase. Other porters in yellow pushed very large trolleys piled up to the sky. Platforms were crowded with men, women and children, all going somewhere. Where could they all be going, Antonio wondered.

His ears buzzed with the hum of hundreds of voices speaking as one: folk shouting their farewells to friends; street vendors plying their trade up and down the platforms, crying out their age old chants. Women in strikingly coloured saris balanced baskets of fruit precariously on their heads, calling, 'Mangoes, bananas, papaya, pineapple. You buy my fruit?' Chai wallahs with thick steaming cauldrons in one hand, small plastic cups in the other, added to the throng. It was all new to Antonio's ears.

The disembodied nasal voice of the tannoy crackled into life, making Antonio jump. 'The train pulling into platform one is the Mumbai to Delhi express, stopping at every station in between.' People laughed at the irony of the announcement.

A porter in a red tunic tried to take Antonio's hold-all. Rodriguez waved him away. Putting his hand on his son's shoulder, he looked Antonio straight in the eye.

'This is your first time out in the big world, son. Don't forget, the whole family travels with you. You have your food and travelling money?'

'Yes, Father.' Antonio tried not to let anxiety show in his voice.

The train screeched to a halt alongside them, all diesel fumes and oil. The platform vibrated as they stood there waiting for the train to come to a steely shuddering stop. People alighting collided with those trying to get on. The driver's whistle spurred the frantic crowd and Antonio knew it was time.

'Good luck.' Rodriguez embraced his son as the rushing throng subsided.

Antonio grabbed the warm metal handrail to hoist himself aboard. Turning, he looked down at his father, noticing his grey beard fluffing in the breeze. 'Where am I meeting Cousin Angelo?' His mind was full of his surroundings.

'Under the station clock,' his father reminded him, 'and don't forget to ring me when you get there. I need to reassure your mother.' Wishing him well, he explained for the umpteenth time where to find the bank at which to collect the bank draft awaiting him by prior arrangement.

Antonio nodded back. His father shouted something else.

'What did you say?' Antonio leaned out of the carriage putting his hand to his ear.

Rodriguez cupped his hand around his mouth and shouted, 'Make sure you phone me after the sea trials. We're all very anxious to know the results of this wonderful new machine. Good luck, my son, take care, see you in two weeks' time.'

The noise of the train drowned his words. It shuddered and began to throb into life. Antonio hung on as they began edging away from the station. He let go with one hand to wave goodbye, then shrugged his shoulders and disappeared inside the carriage, leaving his father, still shouting, on the platform.

Chapter Eighteen

The moving giant shuddered and shook as throngs of people pushed past, entangling themselves in heavy suitcases and rucksacks. Antonio had never experienced anything like this. He stood there not knowing what to do. He decided the best thing was to wait for them all to settle down, then go and look for a seat. He squatted on the floor, holding onto the metal handrail, his body beginning to sway with the rhythm of the moving, living, breathing metal machine. Vendors passed him plying their wares. One stood over him.

'You buy my peanuts? Only two rupees.'

Antonio looked up at the man, who swayed skilfully with the train.

'Why you sit there? A little space that way.' The vendor pointed kindly down the carriage.

Antonio struggled up, still looking at the vendor. 'I've never been on a train before,' he confessed.

'Not to worry. You go that way.' The peanut seller indicated to beyond the now full carriage.

Heads popped out from some compartments, looking down the train. Some men were already standing, rubbing their bottoms; wooden seats did not seem conducive to comfortable travel. Antonio moved past them, heading along the train looking for a seat. Glancing into several compartments as he went, he saw women backing into corners trying to become invisible, covered from head to toe in rich saris, only their dark eyes visible. Their men sat opposite, pride and possessiveness of their women showing in their expressions. Antonio moved on. In another compartment a woman was pressed into the corner, her legs crossed on the seat. She cradled a baby to her breast, the child covered all over, only its feet visible. Another child, perhaps two years old, played on the dirty floor. The man with them stood up and slammed the carriage door shut. Antonio hadn't realised he'd been staring.

Moving on, he came to another compartment where several men sat in silence. He could just make out enough space for himself. 'Is this seat taken?' He politely edged inside. Two men with beady eyes looked up, moved sideways and indicated for him to squeeze in between them. Seating himself, he felt their presence and smelt the pungent aromas of curries, sweat and hard travel. He felt their movement as they tried to get comfortable. They all settled down to silence, the only noise that of the train as it throbbed its way along the steel tracks.

'Tickets, please.'

Startled, they all looked up, fumbling for their tickets. The dark-uniformed man punched them in turn, making holes in them with his steel clippers. Tiny punctures of ticket floated to the floor. Antonio in his confusion couldn't remember where he had put his. Standing up, he began to go through his pockets, searching nervously.

'Come along now.' The ticket collector's tone was impatient. 'I haven't got all day.' As Antonio emptied his last pocket, the ticket floated to the floor. Reaching down for it he stumbled to one side as the train lurched. Steadying himself, he realised he was leaning on one of his fellow passengers.

'Sorry, so sorry.' He jumped back.

'Nervous, aren't you?'

'My first time,' he confessed. 'Never been on a train before.'

'Never mind. Sit between us.'

113

Antonio sat down, relieved, opened his food tin and offered the two men a chapatti. They accepted gratefully and the taller of the two men introduced himself as Mohan.

The second smiled a greeting, 'And my name is Rajeed. Where are you going, my friend?' He munched hungrily on his chapatti.

'Only as far as Mumbai.' Antonio knew the train carried onward to other unknown stations. His mind began to race as he tried to visualise the journey ahead.

'So are we,' said the other stranger on his right, the one who had introduced himself as Mohan. 'Have you been there before?'

'No.' Antonio was becoming used to this admission. 'This is my first trip. I am quite excited.'

'Really?' The two strangers looked at each other, a look that Antonio failed to notice. 'We have been many times. We have friends there.'

Antonio began to gain confidence. 'Although this is my first visit, I hope it won't be my last.' He didn't want to appear too green behind the ears.

'What are you going for?' Mohan wiped away the remains of the chapatti from his lips and settled down to conversation.

'My family have sent me to find a company called Singh and Son. They manufacture a new machine – a fish-finder.'

Rajeed looked interested. 'How does it work?'

'We don't know yet; that's why I'm going.'

'You have a fishing boat?'

'No, three. They're deep-sea vessels with a crew of six on each. I'm one of the captains; my brothers are the other two. Our fathers run the business end.' Antonio spoke freely of his life back home, the life he thought he despised, explaining all

114

the details of the small fishing fleet he hated so much. Boasting was new to him and he liked feeling bigger than the men around him as he sat there like a preening peacock. Once again, he did not notice the glances the two men exchanged.

'My, my! A sea captain! Never been in such illustrious company before.'

Antonio's true feelings came flooding back. 'Not really. I hate it. You wouldn't understand: the smell of fish guts everywhere; the slimy decks waiting for you to slip and break an arm or leg; fish for breakfast, fish for lunch, fish for supper; the wind and the waves tearing at you day in day out. I hate it. If only I could find something different.' Innocently he told them everything about his life at home and the family business.

'How interesting.' The one called Mohan looked intently at Antonio. 'Do you know where in Mumbai this business venture is based?'

Antonio confessed that he did not.

'Well you're in luck.' Rajeed shot another unnoticed glance at his companion. 'A friend who's meeting us off the train knows Mumbai like the back of his hand. Do you realise how big the city is?'

Again Antonio had to confess ignorance.

'Then you will be surprised.'

Antonio explained that he had a cousin meeting him off the train.

'Well, my friend,' Mohan clasped the young fisherman on the shoulder, 'perhaps in the two weeks you are in town we can impress you with some of the places we know and perhaps also take you to several night-clubs where we are members. You could be our honoured guest.'

'Wonderful!' Antonio beamed in reply, feeling

more at ease with these strangers than with anyone ever before.

'Here, take our number.' With a stubby pencil, Mohan hastily scribbled down an address and phone number on a wrinkled piece of paper.

So they journeyed on through the long hours until, nearing Mumbai Central, Mohan and Rajeed stood up. Wishing Antonio well, they turned left down the corridor and were gone before the train pulled in alongside the platform.

Antonio felt good for once. Perhaps there was some fun to be had after all. He did not even consider that he had told them everything about himself, his family and his business, but of them he knew nothing.

Chapter Nineteen

The train shuddered to a halt. With a blast of the whistle, its doors burst open. A mass of people surged forward to get off, some climbing over each other, some throwing suitcases out of the windows and then madly scrambling after them through the tiny apertures. They fell onto the platform, dusted themselves off, picked up their suitcases and disappeared into the Mumbai crowds. Others, six deep, tried maniacally to leave the train through the two-foot wide carriage doors. Grunting and cursing, everyone pushed forward at once. Humans and suitcases were stuck in doorways, the shouting and swearing reaching a crescendo. With one final push, out popped bodies, suitcases and rucksacks as if a cork had been shaken out of a bottle of fizzy drink.

Antonio sat still, waiting for the crowd to subside. Other passengers in his compartment joined the throng and he saw his two new acquaintances shuffling down the corridor with the crowd. When most of the passengers were off, he decided it was time and grabbed his rucksack from the overhead rack. Suddenly the corridors became noisy once more as people swarmed onto the train, looking for seats for the onward journey to Delhi. He had left it too late. A tidal wave of humanity rushed towards him. He began to panic and could feel his temper rising as he lashed out at the oncoming throng. Forcing his way forward, he could feel hands tugging at his clothing, feet trying to trip him. He bulldozed his way through the crowd, breathing heavily, holding onto his rucksack, until he found himself standing on the the platform.

His breathing subsided and he looked around for the large station clock his father had assured him would be there. It ticked back at him, the second hand moving around the dial with an audible clunk. This was where he would meet his cousin, Angelo. He stood under the clock, rucksack at his feet, and waited. If he thought Margao station bewildering, Mumbai Central was ten, twenty times worse. It fascinated him: thousands of people rushing somewhere, trains pulling in, people boarding and alighting; above all, the never-ending noise.

He saw an empty train pull into one of the sidings. Cleaners with mops, brushes and steaming buckets of water clambered on board. He watched as piles of crumpled newspaper, tin foil and all manner of other rubbish were swept out of the carriages onto the railway line below. Street urchins gathered it all up, putting everything into their dirty sacks. Intrigued, he watched them weaving in and out of the great steel wheels, oblivious to the dangers.

He noticed a blind barber sitting on a stool, a customer in front of him all lathered up, and watched as the barber drew his cut-throat razor delicately down the side of the man's face, his left hand following the sharp blade, making sure he left no stubble. Then Antonio spotted a turbaned man with a red beard, holding a monkey on a string and playing a penny whistle. The trained monkey rolled backwards and forwards, then stood up, clapping its hands. It moved among the crowd holding a tin mug, hoping for some coins. Antonio had never expected to see sights like this, but then he didn't really know what to expect. He stood there in his peasant clothes looking every inch the village boy that he was.

'Cousin Antonio, is that you?'

Antonio looked around to see where the voice

was coming from. A smiling young man was making his way towards him. This must be Angelo.

His tall cousin towered over him and Antonio took an instant dislike to him; he always felt inferior to taller people. His uncertainties, mixed with anger, began to surface. Angelo noticed the body language and made a mental note to stay clear of this one. For now, he would act the hospitable host.

'Welcome, cousin. What do you think of our big city so far?'

Antonio bent to pick up his rucksack. 'I haven't had much time to see anything, but what I have seen amazes me – so many people.'

Angelo guided his cousin towards the exit. 'Come on then, I have a rickshaw waiting to take us home.'

Neither of them noticed that two men followed at a discreet distance behind them.

Chapter Twenty

Angelo had a one bedroom flat in the centre of the city. There, the two cousins made an awkward attempt to catch up with family gossip and business. It only took half an hour for Antonio to become morose and surly as tiredness set in and he took in the bleakness of his surroundings. His host left for work, leaving him alone in the dingy flat: stained walls, bare light bulb, no TV or radio that he could see, just a couple of greasy, stained magazines with their pages turned so many times that the corners curled upwards.

Angelo returned almost immediately, rubbing his hands apologetically. He held out a street map and key. Antonio looked at his cousin and said nothing.

'The map will help you find your way around the city and I have just had a key cut so that you can come and go as you please,' Angelo explained. 'I'm sorry for being such a poor host, but I work nights as a porter in the Taj Mahal Hotel near the Gateway of India. My hours are midnight to ten a.m., then I come home and sleep most of the day, but please feel free to come and go at your leisure. I have one day off every two weeks. Perhaps we can spend the day together then?'

'Maybe,' said Antonio. 'Maybe.' He thanked Angelo grudgingly, made an excuse and let himself out of the flat, hurried down the two flights of stairs, weaving himself between the many children playing on the landings and stairs, and out into the street. He realised he was hungry, the growling in his stomach becoming more evident. Glancing at the street map his cousin had given him, he wondered how anyone could ever find their way around in such a maze of streets. He turned the map this way and that, finally figuring that if he turned left he would be heading towards the main road. Feeling some rupees jangling in his pocket, he set off in the direction he thought he should take. A chai or food stall would suffice for his hunger. He did not see two men step from the shadows one hundred metres from the building he had just left and walk casually in his direction.

The noise of the city shocked him. He wrinkled his nose at the repugnant smells. The thought of fish odour felt familiar and pleasant up against these damp, dark fumes. Traffic whizzed by him. Buses, cars, rickshaws, all passed each other at suicidal speed. He stood there in wonder looking across the wide street: four lanes his side of the road, an island between and then another four lanes to the other side. How did people cross this dangerous place? Then he heard the traffic screeching to a halt, a red light showing. People began scurrying across the vast road. Antonio ran. He was just in time to cross with them and found himself on the other side, surrounded by taxi drivers.

'You want taxi? Very cheap.' They all pressed towards him.

He ignored them, pushing through the throng, and found himself at the mouth of a long market. Men and women, baskets and parcels on their heads, weaved in and out of the tightly packed crowds of people. Stallholders haggled with customers over fruit and vegetables; chickens, pigs and goats sat in wooden crates, all awaiting the same fate. He joined the crowds until he came to a chai stall.

He stood sipping hot tea and looked around in amazement at a butcher in the dark interior of his shop, cutting, hacking and sawing, the blood from the carcass running into the street and down a gully. Black flies nestled on the joints of meat hanging from hooks in front of his shop. Guts and the inedibles were thrown into a metal bin at the side. A small swarm of flies rose and fell. Antonio moved on down the street sipping his scalding tea. There was nothing like this in his village. Vendors tugged at his sleeve.

'You buy my goods? Very cheap.'

'Just look, please?'

'Come have coffee with me?'

'You try my shop?'

Antonio ignored them all and walked on, still unaware of the two men who followed him. Stopping at a corner, he glanced at his map, wondering where to go next. He looked about him to check where he had just been and thought he could get his bearings. More confidently he turned into another street. It seemed the same as the one he had just left – crammed full of people. A lorry was unloading its wares; skinny men, with just loin cloths wrapped around their tiny waists and circular pieces of material wrapped around their heads, waited in turn for their next load. Two men stood on the back of the lorry, loading large sacks onto the head of the waiting man. The dust from the flour sacks settled all over him, hanging off his eyebrows and down onto his shoulders, finding every crevice on his near-naked body until he resembled a powdered mannequin. As he tottered away with his huge burden, the muscles in his neck standing out like steel girders, the next man took his place.

Antonio moved on down another street, branching left and then right. He consulted his map once more. He had lost his bearings. Turning round, he tried to retrace his steps. Somehow he had missed his way. In street after street he became more and more confused. His feet were now aware of the cobbles beneath him, and the streets began to narrow. Instinct told him that he was heading out of the city. The sun vibrated off the walls as he walked through the stifling streets, the cobbles burning the soles of his shoes. He found it difficult to breathe as the sun beat down upon him like an anvil. Pungent smells, worse than anything he had ever smelt in his life, began to surround him. This was generations of grime trodden underfoot, and he gagged at the stench of rotting food, flesh and human excreta. He almost longed for the smell of fish.

As he walked on, mangy dogs with open sores began to bark at his presence. Their pus dripped onto the cobbled streets as they followed him, keeping their wary distance. Accustomed to being beaten, they lived their lives at the end of a stick. Antonio watched one creature turn on itself, snapping at its unseen tormentor, biting at its own body. Blood ran down its emaciated torso, the ticks eating him alive. Antonio had never expected anything like this.

Suddenly the buildings gave way to open spaces. In front of him now stood huts tumbling down the hillside, seeming to go on forever. In the distance the blue plastic of their roofs shimmered, the intense sunlight distorting the view.

A noise began to rumble towards him, growing louder as it came closer. The ground began to tremble and the noise grew all around him until he could not think. He fell to his knees shielding his ears. A jet skimmed overhead just yards up into the sky, the vibrations from its gigantic engine shaking his very soul. He looked up to what seemed like huge staring eyes looking down from a metal tube. Then he saw black wheels leave the body of the plane and lock into position ready for landing, then it was gone. But the blue plastic shanty town still stood there.

The smells returned to him. Piles of rubbish were strewn all around. To the side of one hill he could see people lining up and he watched as buckets were tipped over the side. In amazement he realised that this was their own waste. A river of brown liquid ran down this hill, staining and killing all vegetation on its descent; a cesspit of stagnant waste fermented at the bottom. The surface of this evil substance moved and he realised that it was alive with millions of flies.

As Antonio stood there in shock, people began to stare. The children around him stopped playing and angry dishevelled men glared at him. Women cooking on open fires, smoke billowing all around them, looked up at him. An old man began to walk towards him, his grimy hands held out, his tattered clothes hanging off his emaciated body; on shoeless feet and skinny legs he shuffled nearer, his cracked lips mouthing words that Antonio refused to hear. The beggar sidled around him, his hands still out, his one good eye pleading, his other blackened eye socket staring lifelessly, pus staining his cheek. Antonio panicked. He turned and ran, propelling himself away from this living, breathing hellhole. The dogs, growing braver now, began to snap at his heels. He lashed out with his foot, catching one on its side. The creature howled and stopped chasing. The pack let him go. With his heart pounding he ran on. A rickshaw pulled alongside him.

'You want ride?'

Antonio nodded and threw himself inside.

'Where you going?'

With his breath laboured Antonio could not answer at first. 'Do you … do you know Singh and Son, down by the docks?' He didn't wait for an answer. 'Take me there.'

He sat back into the shadows trying to regain his composure. He had never realised that people lived like that. There were millions of these wretches, it seemed. How could he have gone through life so innocent of what lay beyond his own horizons?

Chapter Twenty-one

Antonio was followed all over the city, stalked wherever he ventured, watched as he found the building of the company, Singh and Son. He was observed from the quayside as the boat left the dock, putting to sea for the fish-finder trials.

The breeze as they left the quay made a pleasant relief from the intense sun burning down on them. Antonio looked down at the squawking seabirds flying and sweeping all around them. 'No fish for you today.'

The sea was very calm as he left the side of the boat and walked to the wheelhouse. Captain Yousef Ben Ali nodded his permission for him to enter.

'Welcome aboard.' He didn't look at Antonio, just stared out at the distant horizon, concentrating on the running of his ship.   An Arab by birth, he had come to work for Mr Singh many years before, settled in Mumbai, married and never gone home again.

'Good morning.' Antonio held out his hand to Prajeed, Mr Singh's representative. He would explain the finer working of this machine.

'Right!' Prajeed switched on the machine as they left the harbour. A bright green light shone back at them from the monitor screen. 'Under this ship is an echo finder, ringing away merrily until it bounces off something ahead of us. Much the same as radar, once it finds something blocking its path it pings back and forth a few times, and then relays the message back to us via the screen. Shoals of fish show very black on the screen; other objects vary in shade. You get used to it after a little practice.' Several shades blinked onto the screen. 'Look!'

Antonio leaned forward to see where Prajeed was pointing.

'A wreck on the sea bed – top right – a fishing vessel,' Prajeed identified expertly.

The machine pinged on as they throbbed out to sea. A crew member entered, carrying three tin mugs of scalding sweet chai. Handing one each to the captain and the others he left as quietly as he had entered.

'What's that?'Antonio pointed at a large blob that appeared on the screen. The shape of the black object changed and moved just off centre.

'That,' said Prajeed, 'is a shoal of fish.'

The captain moved for the first time and stared at the screen, muttering to himself, 'Twenty degrees starboard.' He turned the wheel and the ship changed direction, heading towards the shoal. Leaving the wheelhouse for one moment, he instructed his crew to throw a small net over the side. 'Just a sample of fish so you can see how it works,' he explained to Antonio. Soon they were right over the shoal and the nets were hauled back on board with a substantial hoard struggling in the netting.

'Very impressive!' Antonio's appreciation was genuine. 'Very!'

Mr Singh's employee smiled genially. They were pleased with their success.

'It's not always as easy as this,' laughed the captain. 'Today you have brought luck with you.' He turned to the men still holding the winch with the captured fish and drew his hand across his throat. The two crew members motioned back and released the cord at the bottom of the netting. The small shoal plunged back into the water leaving several fish bouncing onto the deck.

'Those, we'll have for tea.' The captain

watched his men pick up the unlucky flapping fish and put them into a small box.

On the ship's return, monitored by the two men waiting in the shadows, Antonio's excitement was evident from his demeanour. It was a long time since he had felt any kind of enthusiasm for the business. Now he was consumed with a sense of personal achievement. He was the one with the privileged knowledge, the one in whose hands the future of the company lay, not his brother Cristiano, not Joe's son Pedro, *him*.

The telephone rang in the office. Rodriguez took the call. 'How's it going?'

'I've just left the ship. What a wonderful machine!' The grim city experiences of a few hours before were shoved to the back of Antonio's mind. 'It really works; it's amazing. I recommend we go ahead.'

'Tell me all about it, son.'

Antonio relayed everything, leaving out not one detail, his mind still fresh from the sea trial. His father seemed pleased with what he heard and gave him the go ahead to complete the deal.

Antonio returned to Mr Singh to arrange transportation by rail, accompanied by their engineer and fitter. All business done, they shook hands, and Antonio bade him farewell and strode away.

He decided to head in the general direction of the main railway station. He liked the station; it felt familiar. He remembered his experience of a couple of days earlier, his trepidation on the train journey, the hustle and bustle on the platform as he left the train, meeting Angelo under the clock. Besides, there were bars and restaurants and he was hungry.

Two days in the city had increased his confidence: he felt ready to tackle the unknown. He had some days left before his home journey. What to do? His cousin was either asleep or working. Not that he minded; he knew his mood swings made him bad company for anyone. But being used to people around him all his life made him feel rather isolated in this big city. Feeling in his back pocket for the crumpled piece of paper he had received on the train, he wondered whether to phone his two travelling companions. He remembered the ease with which he had talked to them while the journey rushed by.

Turning left into the main street for the station, he walked straight into someone. He clenched his fists – his automatic reaction to any sign of confrontation – only to find himself looking up at a smiling, familiar face. The anger left his eyes and he smiled back.

'What a coincidence,'they said simultaneously.

Antonio looked up at Mohan, whom he had first met on the train. 'I was just thinking of calling you. I have a couple of days to kill and I thought I might take you up on your invitation.'

Mohan laughed as he gave Antonio a friendly slap on the back. 'Well this is indeed a coincidence bumping into you. We've just made arrangements to join some friends for dinner tonight. Could you come?'

'Gladly.' Antonio was grateful for the offer of friendship. 'Are you sure it will be OK with your friends?'

'Of course,' Mohan reassured him. 'The more the merrier. Where are you staying?'

'Oh, not far from here.' Antonio was not exactly certain if this was true, but was pleased with his own confident display of knowledge of the city.

'Then why don't we meet at this very spot, say at eight tonight. Come in your best outfit. We'll have some fun: wine, women and song, not necessarily in that order.'

'Fine, eight o'clock it is then.' Antonio was intrigued at the prospect of a night out in the big city. The notion that he did not have a best outfit did not occur to him. He said goodbye to his new friend and, retracing his footsteps, set off back around the corner. He did not see Mohan look behind him and cross the road to join his partner at a table at the bar. He did not hear him say, 'The fish is on the line.'

Rajeed, who had watched all that had taken place, nodded and smiled.

Chapter Twenty-two

At precisely eight o'clock, Antonio, looking the best he could, duly arrived at the appointed spot. He was pleased that Mohan and Rajeed were already there waiting for him. His confidence had eroded somewhat in the intervening hours and he did not relish the prospect of waiting alone on a strange city corner. They greeted him, explaining that another friend would be joining them for a few drinks and then they would all go on to a nightclub. Crossing the road, they reached the same bar they had frequented that afternoon. There, waiting for them was another man, smartly dressed in a fully-buttoned, three-quarter length, shiny black suit, tailor made and very expensive. He proffered his hand as Mohan introduced him: 'Roshan Seth.'

Antonio's naivety exuded from him, innocence shining from his awkward demeanour. Shuffling from foot to foot and rubbing his hands together, he looked up into the other man's eyes. The penetrating stare looked straight through him. He sensed liquid evil buried deep within, dormant but none the less deadly. The smile never left Seth's face, but no warmth shone from him.

'Welcome,' he said, looking at the other two and motioning them all to sit down. 'Mohan and Rajeed have told me all about you.' The man's nonchalant attitude put Antonio more at his ease. 'Come,' said Seth, 'let's have a drink and enjoy ourselves.'

Beckoning to a waiter he ordered drinks for all, clearly in command of the people around him. With the arrival of the first drink, he raised his glass to the company, put it to his lips, tossed his head back and swallowed in one. Rajeed and Mohan followed suit. Antonio put his glass to his lips and breathed in. The fumes hit the back of his throat. He gagged and started to cough, and his eyes began to water. He tried to place his glass back on the table, spilling the drink everywhere. Laughter rang round the group.

'You've never drunk feni before?' Seth was amused.

Antonio shook his head, still trying to stop coughing.

'Never mind.' Seth waved at the waiter to bring more drinks. 'Now,' he ordered, 'hold your nose and just swallow.'

Antonio obliged. He felt the white fiery liquid hit his tonsils on the way down. His chest burned. Standing up, he began to cough. His heart stepped up a beat. More laughter. Rajeed stood up and began to slap him on the back.

Seth ordered another round. 'More feni!' He made no pretence at politeness. 'More feni!' he demanded.

Antonio sat down again and watched as his three companions downed another round. He felt all their stares penetrating him. He was determined not to be the butt of their amusement any longer; he wanted to be part of them. Stubbornly he held his breath and swallowed another drink. He felt the burning sensation run down his chest and reach his stomach. He tried not to retch. The alcohol penetrated the walls of his stomach, entered his blood stream and within seconds reached his brain. Now he liked the sensation the drink gave him. He grinned back at these three companions.

'That's better.' Seth snapped his fingers and pointed to the empty glasses. A waiter rushed over and replenished them.

'To our new friend!' Seth raised his glass in Antonio's direction. The other two just laughed, raised their glasses to their lips, tossed back their heads and swallowed. Antonio felt himself relax. He had never felt so good.

The drinks kept coming. The night drew on and stars appeared between the clouds. The moon flooded the pavement café where they sat.

'Come,' said Seth, suddenly getting to his feet, 'we must move on.' He waved a bundle of money at the waiter who hurried over, keeping his eyes on the ground. As he walked away from the café, summoning the others to follow, Seth stuffed a handful of notes in the waiter's top pocket.

Antonio quickened his pace to catch up. 'Let me pay my share of the bill,' he insisted, holding out some rupees.

'Nonsense!' Seth brushed his hand aside. 'You are my guest, so put your money away and enjoy yourself.' Striding forward, he led the three of them down side roads and alleyways until they reached a nondescript looking door with peeling paint and a heavy, dull, brass knocker. Stepping up to it, he knocked twice. A movement caught Antonio's eye as he looked at the large spyhole. After a moment the door opened on well-oiled hinges and a large man stood there. He stepped back, signalling his welcome, and they stepped into a large reception hall. When the giant closed the door, he reached for a switch and turned up the lighting. There before them was a large room, resplendent with rich furnishings. The carpet they stood on was deeply piled and as they strode across the floor they made no sound. They reached a set of double doors. The minder of the establishment flung them open.

The noise hit them full in the face. The perfume and heat reached them at the same time. Women and men were laughing together, some dancing on a minuscule dance floor, some sitting at tables, smoking. Some ladies not yet attached to clients lounged on chaises longues. Antonio took in this scene at a glance, without recognising it for what it was. Never had he experienced such splendour or such an exotic sight. His heart quickened; perspiration broke out on his forehead; excitement coursed through his veins.

Roshan Seth stepped into the room, followed by the others. Several women who were unattached got up and moved sinuously towards them, eyes and mouths smiling in welcome and expectation.

'A table for eight,' Seth demanded expansively, picking four girls to accompany them. The rest smiled politely and walked away. Antonio had never seen such beautiful young women. Glossy dark hair flowed around them; full make-up accentuated their sultry eyes. To his surprise, they were all in multi-coloured dressing gowns made of pure silk, low cut and tied at the waist. The full-length, flowing fabric swished as the girls walked across the room with the four men. He could hear the sensuous sound of silk stockings rubbing together as they passed tables. The young women's long painted nails were exquisitely manicured; their peep-toe silk slippers revealed the same colour on their elegantly pedicured toes.

Sitting down at a large round table, Antonio became tongue-tied and overwhelmed by his surroundings. The lush ambience of the establishment, not to mention the close proximity of the scantily clad and perfumed girls, undermined him. He looked at the other three men, all perfectly relaxed, ordering drinks all round and chatting amiably to the women as if they had known them all their lives. Glancing across the table, he noticed one of the girls looking at him.

Roshan Seth missed nothing. Looking around with a sardonic smile he knew the plot was thickening and he laughed – not to his companions but to himself. Touching the shoulder of the delightful young woman looking at Antonio, he indicated with his eyes for her to move around to him. Getting up, she motioned to one of the other girls to vacate her seat. She walked round the table, placed a delicate hand on Antonio's shoulder, sat down beside him and smiled. She knew her scent would assail his nostrils. She knew he would never have experienced anything like it in his short young life. She sensed his virginity with amusement. Smiling seductively, she looked deep into his eyes, anticipating the fun to come with this raw young man.

'Hello.' Her voice was husky. 'My name is Jeena.' Still smiling sweetly and catching Seth's eye, she nodded slightly. 'Do you dance?'

'I have never had the opportunity,' Antonio confessed. He could not think what to say to this beautiful creature.

'Come on,' she said, offering him her delicately manicured hand.

Rising slowly, his face bright red, he held her hand in his and followed her to the tiny dance floor. Luckily for him there was a slow number playing. As he stood there not knowing what to do, she moved closer to him. Lifting his hands with hers, she placed one around her neck, the other around her waist. When she pressed her body enticingly up to him he become rooted to the dance floor, swaying slightly from side to side. She laughed at his embarrassment.

'Relax,' she said seductively, still moving with the slow rhythm of the music. She felt his embarrassment between them; she felt the heat of his body pressed against hers; she felt his uncontrollable passion rising. Still swaying against him she felt him shudder uncontrollably. Knowing what was happening, she held him tightly until his shaking subsided. Stroking his forehead, now covered in perspiration, she whispered in his ear. 'Do not worry, my beautiful man, there is more later.'

He looked into her eyes, seeing none of the shame which he felt for himself. Feeling the warmth in his trousers as she led him from the dance floor, he asked her to return to their company and excused himself. She nodded, turned and sensuously walked away. Hurrying to the men's room, his embarrassment acute, he hoped nothing showed. He looked in the mirror as he cleaned himself, remembering her face on the dance floor. There had been no look of scorn in her eyes. He thought of her stroking his head. How was he going to go back? Surely they would point and laugh at him. The torment would be too much. Adjusting himself, he turned from the mirror just as the door opened and Rajeed strolled in nonchalantly.

'There you are Antonio, my friend. We were wondering what had become of you. Come on, we're all waiting to order some food before the real fun begins.'

Hearing no mockery in Rajeed's voice, he obliged and, leaving the gentlemen's cloakroom together, they went back to the table.

Drinks flowed freely and the food arrived on row upon row of silver platters. Mounds of saffron rice steamed up towards the ceiling. Prawns swam in ghee, garlic and ginger. Boiled lobster stared out of pink bodies and jet black eyes. Cooked crabs linked claws in defence against the forthcoming attack.

Antonio recognised the fish and rice dishes but there was much else that was new to him. He turned to Jeena and pointed at the food. 'Can you tell me what these dishes are?'

She identified for him the mounds of onion bhajees, aloo gobi, curried pork with peppers and buttered chicken. Antonio had never seen such an array. His taste buds salivated at the onrushing smells and he gradually began to relax once more, joining the others in the line to fill up his plate. He sat back next to Jeena, who looked at him kindly, and he mentally thanked her.

Filled with good food and drink, he started to laugh with the others around him and even cracked a few jokes of his own. Meanwhile the watchful eye of Seth missed nothing. The single drinks turned to bottles left on the table: red wine, white wine, scotch and vodka were strewn across the stained tablecloth. Several times Antonio reached over and poured himself a large drink not knowing or caring what it contained. Jeena never left his side.

The rest of the company were by now dancing and singing loudly. Antonio began to sway on his chair, a cue for Jeena to stand up and bid him to follow her. Feet braced apart he held onto the table trying to steady himself. The room swayed and he felt her body slip under his unsteady frame and pull him towards the stairs. Somehow he made it. Holding onto the banister, step by step they climbed the dimly lit staircase. Reaching the top and holding onto the upper rail, through bloodshot eyes he saw many corridors running adjacent to each other, disappearing into the gloom.

'Stay here.' He heard her words echo in his head as though they had come from some disembodied voice. He could not have moved even if he had wanted to. Moving from door to door she stood and listened, moving on several times until at one room she listened for a moment, knocked and entered. Returning to Antonio, she steadied him and led him forward; then, pulling him through the door, she led him to the bed. He sat down hard, directing a stupid, drunken grin at her as he fell sideways and his head bounced on the soft pillow. He disappeared between a drunken stupor and dreamless sleep, snoring immediately, with his feet still on the floor.

The tall figure of Roshan Seth, followed by Mohan and Rajeed, stood in the partly open doorway.

'Strip him!' he ordered.

His men duly moved forward and obliged. Hanging his clothes over a chair and turning his inert body onto his side, they pulled the sheet from under his naked frame and poured him into bed.

Seth stared menacingly at Jeena. 'You stay with him until morning. I want him to think he's had a wonderful time. Don't leave him or you'll have me to answer to. Is that quite clear?'

Jeena nodded her head in response. Seth turned, beckoned to his men and left, the last one closing the door behind him.

Chapter Twenty-three

Next morning, bleary-eyed, an anvil hammering in his skull, Antonio looked around at his unfamiliar surroundings, wondering where the devil he was. Looking down, he realised he was naked. Suddenly feeling another warm body lying next to him, he sat up startled. The hammer doubled its effort inside his head. He lifted the cover and looked down at the female form lying there fast asleep, also naked. Shock registered on his brain, breaking his alcoholic stupor. Rubbing his eyes vigorously, he tried to remember the night before. He recalled most of it but, try as he might, he could not remember the last few hours since midnight.

The naked figure next to him stirred and turned onto her back, glossy dark hair cascading over the pillow, her rhythmic breathing making her breasts rise and fall. Her nipples were large and dormant, dark against the olive hue of her skin. Antonio lifted the covers and looked down into the shadowy depths. There he saw the soft sheen of the woman's flat belly, and the down running from her navel to her pubic mound, very dark, curly and lush. The thighs supple, the legs lithe and long disappeared under the sheet at the bottom of the bed. He felt himself stirring, the desires of his body taking hold of him.

He had never experienced anything like this before. He reached out tentatively to touch her breast, then quickly withdrew his hand as she made a sudden movement. He had never felt anything so warm and soft in his life. The breast seemed to have a life of its own, rising and falling as she breathed. The sight of her nakedness excited him beyond control. Reaching down, he began to rub himself, still staring at her nakedness. His legs stiffened, he arched his back and his mouth opened. Throwing his head back, an unintentional sigh left his lips as he soaked the sheet beneath her. She stirred once more. Quickly coming to his senses he leapt from the bed, ashamed at what had taken place. He hastily dressed. Standing on one leg, trying to put on his sandals, he lost his balance and sat down heavily on the bed.

The woman beside him opened her eyes. Taking in the scene and shaking herself awake, she smiled. A consummate actress, she slipped easily into her role. 'Darling,' she said, raising herself on one elbow. She held out her other hand towards him, letting the cover slip so that an upturned breast became exposed, the large nipple erect. As she stared at him she could see the panic mounting in his eyes. The rabbit was ready to flee its warren.

'Darling,' she repeated, 'you were quite magnificent last night. What a man! Nobody's ever given me such pleasure before.' All the while she watched him and smiled. The confusion showed in his eyes. Sitting up, she raised her legs under the covers, clasping her hands around her knees. Still smiling, she let the sheet slip further down, exposing her other breast. She saw the change in his eyes as he watched her. To her, this pantomime was an everyday event, but she knew that he would not have had any such experiences ever before. He was too innocent to be aware of her charade. 'I thought we could breakfast together, unless you have any prior engagement.'

'No … no,' he stuttered.

'Pass me my dressing gown.' She motioned to the chair at her side of the bed. She felt him relax a little as she slipped quickly from the bed. 'Help me on with it, will you?' Now completely naked, she watched him, knowing that he missed nothing. She had a good body and was proud of it. She knew her beautiful, unblemished back, perfectly rounded buttocks and the scent of her skin would make his senses spin. Laughing, she turned around and kissed him full on the lips. He finished dressing as quickly as he could, still unable to take his eyes off her.

'Come on, let's go down for breakfast.' Taking hold of his hand, she led him out of the room.

Downstairs in the dining room several tables were laid in readiness. A few people were waiting for food, the previous heavy night's drinking showing on the blotchy faces. Women, looking thoroughly bored, sat with their customers of the previous night, waiting for them to leave, hoping that they would get some rest before the late afternoon again became alive.

Smoke fumes infiltrated the toilet sprays manfully trying to cover the previous night's heavy revelry. A background hum of vacuum cleaners sucked up cigar and cigarette ash, dog ends and food trodden into the carpet. Antonio sat at a table and Jeena reclined opposite him. He took in his surroundings, seeing only the plush red velvet curtains tied back with golden sashes, and golden coloured chairs, upholstered in rich reds. He did not notice how the half-pulled curtains kept the sunlight from showing the smoke-stained ceiling. He failed to see the torn lining at the back of the curtains, and the dimmed lighting hid from his view the once splendid but now faded red and gold flock wallpaper; rugs obscured the stained carpet. To Antonio all was magnificent: candelabra and solid silver cutlery resplendent on each table; silver salvers with all manner of breakfast dishes on tables lining a wall; waiters moving from one table to another, taking orders, delivering exotic dishes, their feet silent as they glided across thick lush carpet.

'Tell me,' said Jeena as they sat down with their coffee, 'did you enjoy the evening?'

He laughed self-consciously. 'Yes, what I can remember of it.'

Taking his hand in hers across the table and looking seductively into his eyes, she murmured, 'You were wonderful.'

The pounding of his heart was a new sensation for him. He looked at her in total admiration.

When they had eaten, she rose. 'I must get some rest now.' She led him to the exit.

'Do you think I can see you again?' Antonio asked shyly.

'Of course you can. I have to live here and the rent is quite exorbitant; my clothes and living expenses eat away at my finances quite shockingly, but my fees are reasonable and my time can be yours.' Reaching the large door, she opened it onto the outside world.

Blinking into the sharp light of the day, Antonio wished her well, turned and reluctantly walked away. As he did so he missed her expression change from one of geniality to sheer contempt. Watching his back as he sauntered down the road, she absorbed his peasant clothes, the shuffling gait of a village idiot, his unwashed body, dusty sandals and unkempt hair. She laughed.

Chapter Twenty-four

Reaching his cousin's lodgings, Antonio went round the back of the building to the standpipe. He quickly stripped down to his loincloth, stood on the concrete slab before him and let the needle of cold water splash over him and seep through his loincloth. Cupping his scrotum in his hand he wished he could remember losing his virginity. Pulling his foreskin back, he glanced down, water pouring down over his head dripping from his nose and chin and splashing onto the concrete. He did not feel any different. Drying himself on his clothing, he dressed and went round to the door of the so-called apartment. He found Angelo waiting for him. Damn, he thought, he's still up.

'Where have you been? Your father has sent you a letter. It arrived early this morning.'

Tearing it open, Antonio read:

Dear Son,

We have had a mishap. The fish-finder, which arrived two days early, was dropped on one end as it was unloaded from the train. When we opened the crate, one of the main components was damaged. I have phoned the company and you are to go along and reorder the parts. Please telephone and let us know how you get on.

Your loving Papa and family.

This brought him down to earth with a bump, from the heady heights of society back to reality. Scratching his head and reluctantly putting Jeena out of his mind, he tried to think.

'I'm off to bed. Good night – or good morning!' Angelo said with a laugh.

Clutching the letter, Antonio set off for the company. As he entered the yard he spotted Mr Singh going into his office. He managed to catch up with him just as he reached the reception area and began to explain his dilemma.

'Yes, I've spoken to your father,' Mr Singh told him. 'Please come into the office.' He looked at the invoice. 'It'll take a couple of days to get the parts from the factory. I hope this won't inconvenience you too much.'

Antonio's mind raced. Two more days in the city. He was secretly thrilled as he thought of three more nights with Jeena. 'Well, it's a bit inconvenient but it can't be helped. I do need to use the phone, though. May I?'

'Of course.'

He dialled his family's number and was relieved when his brother, Cristiano, answered.

'Antonio! Good to hear from you. How's it going?'

'Fine.' Antonio was reluctant to say too much about his visit and moved swiftly on to the business in hand. 'Sorry to hear about the accident. How did it happen?'

'Fell off the train. Too heavy for the men to manhandle it onto the platform. Father was livid. Said he'd sue the railway company. You should have seen him. The whole station came to a standstill. You could hear him shouting above the noise of the trains.' Cristiano laughed down the phone. 'Don't worry, Antonio. Once Father calmed down, about twenty miles from the station, he could laugh about it too.'

Antonio only half-listened to Cristiano's explanation. Let him talk on; it was easier that way.

'Father understands your predicament. All the necessary arrangements have been made; the bank's

144

expecting you. Well, my brother, are you enjoying the big city?'

Antonio did not want to sound too enthusiastic. 'Not much really. It's too busy and I don't know anyone here,' he lied. 'Angelo sleeps all day so to tell you the truth, I'm pretty bored.'

Cristiano seemed to accept this. 'Never mind, little brother, you'll be home soon. Everyone here sends their love.'

'Send mine back to them.' Antonio was anxious to end the conversation. They said their goodbyes and the phone line went dead. Antonio tried to hide his excitement. Three more nights to share with Jeena.

Thanking Mr Singh, he left the office for the bank. Everything was in order and all transactions went smoothly, the oiled wheels of business running like clockwork. As he left the bank his mind was racing, thinking of the night ahead with Jeena. Ah, Jeena! He would surprise her, but his clothes would not do. It had not taken him long, the night before, to realise that he had looked out of place in the luxury of his surroundings. He had some hidden money of his own; not a lot, but enough to supply him with a new suit and a silk shirt, even some new shoes. Yes, he would surprise her.

He rubbed his hands together as he walked along. Two days extra, wonderful! His mind made up, he changed direction and headed for the marketplace, looking for a clothes shop. He thought how unlike his little village it was, where there was only one tailor with his little Singer sewing machine tucked into a foot wide space piled high with material. No ready-made suit there, only made-to-order by clients when they could afford it. Here in the city it was different. He stopped in front of a shop window to admire a suit

145

on a tailor's dummy. He liked it immediately and went into the dim little shop, the musk of rolled bolts of cloth filling his nostrils.

The proprietor stepped forward from the back of the shop. 'Can I help you?' he enquired, looking at Antonio standing there in his dishevelled clothing.

'I would like to purchase a suit – the one on the mannequin in the window.'

'What size are you?'

'I'm not sure.' Antonio felt slightly embarrassed.

'And how will you be paying for your purchase, sir?'

'Why, with rupees.' He held out a small bundle of money.

'Very well.' The tailor nodded his head, at the same time whisking a cloth tape measure from his neck. Indicating for Antonio to stand still, he expertly measured him all over, writing the details on a notepad and licking the tiny stub of pencil between each measurement. 'With these measurements we can start straight away, sir. If you come back for a second fitting this afternoon we can have your suit ready in twenty-four hours.'

'No, no, you don't understand. I need it for tonight. The one in the window will do. How much?'

'But sir, we don't know if it's your size.'

'Then I would like to try it on.'

'Very well then.' He clicked his fingers and a gangly youth appeared from behind the many bolts of cloth piled high on the counter.

'Help me.' The tailor indicated the dummy. Lifting it from the window and brushing the dust from the jacket shoulders, they lowered the mannequin to the floor. Unbuttoning the jacket and removing the trousers, the proprietor shook the dust from the garments.

'I will need a shirt too,' Antonio remembered.

The shopkeeper sent the boy next door to fetch a kurta and led Antonio through to a dressing room at the back of the shop, the boy soon hard on their heels with a cream shirt over his arm. The shopkeeper told Antonio to try on the suit and said he would wait in the shop, and would adjust it if need be.

The figure that re-entered the front of the premises looked as though he had just drowned in the suit: only his fingertips appeared below the cuffs of the sleeves; the shoulders looked as if he'd forgotten to take the coat hanger out, and, because of his short stature, the coat looked far too long, leaving his short legs looking even shorter. His sandals were the only thing that fitted him.

'Wonderful!' announced the shopkeeper, edging the smirking youth out of the shop. 'Just a few adjustments needed.' He showed Antonio how he would adjust the sleeves with a few stitches. Bunching up the cloth at the back of the coat and so pulling it tighter to the chest, he led Antonio over to a half mirror at the back of the shop. As the tailor held the surplus material behind him, Antonio viewed his reflection in the mirror.

Yes, he thought, seeing the high collar of the cream kurta poking just above the collar of the suit jacket, quite elegant.

'If sir would leave it for a couple of hours, the sleeves will be adjusted and all will be well.' They settled on a price that was agreeable to both, and leaving a deposit, Antonio said he would pay the balance when he returned later to retrieve the suit.

After Antonio had left the shop, the tailor set to work. The sleeves presented no problems. The back of the jacket was another matter, however: not only did he need to cut the back but the lining also. Working against time he managed the best he could.

When Antonio returned, the garment was finished and he tried it on again. He thought he looked quite smart. He could not, at this angle, see the stitching running all the way down the back of the jacket, never intended in the original design. Antonio, perfectly happy, paid the balance and left the premises.

He decided to try and find his own way back to the nightclub. With his new suit wrapped in newspaper, tied with string and tucked firmly under his arm, he set off in the general direction he thought he should take. Not knowing the name of the place made things difficult for him; he could not even ask for directions. Fortunately, after taking a few wrong turns, he stumbled on a street he recognised from his previous visit and came across the peeling door with the large brass knocker. At last, he thought, tonight it will begin.

The minutes seemed to drag forever. The hours crawled along with the minutes. Finally the time arrived for him to leave. Standing in his new regalia Antonio felt marvellous. He would surprise Jeena. Glancing once more in the mirror, he left Angelo's flat. He walked briskly, the twilight all around him, even at this hour the streets bustling with throngs of people. The deep hum of traffic whizzed past him as he walked towards his destination.

On reaching the peeling door, he knocked loudly. Once more he saw movement behind the spy hole. The door opened slightly and the same mountain of a man spoke.

'Yes, what do you want?' His tone was not very friendly.

'I was here last night with Roshan Seth and

two friends.'

'Yes, I remember.'

Chains were released, the door swung open and the giant gestured for Antonio to enter. 'Mr. Seth and his friends are already here.' He motioned him down the large sumptuous hall.

Opening the doors, he was hit by the same familiar noise and smells as on the previous night – perfumed bodies, opium pipes, aromatic spices, the strong odour of man's presence. His sense of well-being evaporated and his confidence easily diminished, he stepped into the stuffy room feeling helpless.

Mohan came towards him through a haze of smoke and opium fumes. 'Hello, Antonio … surprised to see you. Will you join us?' Mohan took in his new attire, registering how ridiculous he looked; a stumpy penguin came to mind. 'Come on.' He grabbed Antonio by the arm and propelled him through the room towards the same table they had all occupied the night before. As they approached, Roshan Seth rose in welcome, indicating an empty chair as if they had been expecting him. Antonio sat down. Seth caught Rajeed's eye and the latter summoned a waiter.

'Drinks for our guest,' he demanded.

Antonio greeted his friends, then glanced around at the women. His heart sank. No Jeena. Another woman came and sat beside him. Smiling she placed a hand on his shoulder, but he neither saw nor felt her. He was too busy scanning the room, but Jeena was nowhere to be seen. Perhaps she would come later; after all, it was still relatively early, he reasoned.

After a few drinks, people started to head for the dance floor and others moved around the room greeting old friends. Antonio moved and went to stand next to Roshan Seth.

'Enjoying yourself?'

'Yes, but tell me, where's Jeena?'

Seth laughed. 'What am I, her keeper?'

The irony of the remark was lost on Antonio. 'No, no, but I enjoyed her company last night and would like to meet her again.'

Seth looked straight through him. 'Well if you must know, it's her night off. There are plenty of other girls here for you to enjoy. Take your pick, be my guest.' He slapped Antonio on the back, grabbed the girl next to him and disappeared into the crowd, emerging again on the dance floor dancing intimately with the tiny creature crushed in his arms.

Antonio felt deflated. All day he had waited for this moment. Despondently he sat back down. The evening began to drag. He drank no more. He just sat there, seeing nothing, feeling nothing. He did not even notice Rajeed approaching him and only vaguely heard his question.

'Are you all right?'

'No. I feel as though I've eaten something that hasn't agreed with me. Do you mind if I leave? I'm sure a good night's sleep will do me the world of good.'

Rajeed looked around for Seth. 'Feel free, but make no plans for tomorrow night. We have a private party here, and you must come. You will come, won't you?'

'Of course,' nodded Antonio.

'Then meet us at the same bar we met on the first night, same time. Good night.'

Antonio entered the starlit night still full of people; as the fresh air hit him and his lungs filled, he felt quite dizzy for some moments.

Inside the club, Mohan awaited instructions from Roshan Seth. 'Follow him home. We don't want anything happening to our plump little pigeon now.'

Mohan nodded and left. The full moon allowed him to just catch sight of Antonio as he turned the corner of the alleyway, his shadow dancing after him as he disappeared from sight.

Chapter Twenty-five

Antonio heard Angelo come in from work the next morning but did not stir. The clock crept around the dial into mid afternoon and beyond. When he finally awoke he yawned and stretched his stubby limbs. Perhaps it was still too early to get up. Rubbing his sleepy face and feeling his bladder full, he got up. He scratched his head as he relieved himself and looked out of the small stained window, noticing that the moon was rising. My god, he thought, I've slept away the day. Shaking himself dry, he retreated back into the bedroom and dressed hastily in his old clothes before going to clean his teeth, as best he could, with the water dribbling from the tap into a brown stained sink, which was the only washing facility.

Feeling pangs of hunger, he grabbed his key and let himself out. He bought some dahl and roti at a stall, not tasting one morsel; it was just fodder for his gnawing stomach. Returning to the apartment, he put on his new suit and headed for the bar. He sat down and ordered a beer. He could only see two or three people sitting at different tables, sipping their drinks. They're not here, he thought. Impatiently he kept looking up and down the street and waiting. His beer went flat in the evening heat. After an hour he decided to go home, feeling let down and angry. As he went to pay, the waiter came through the door.

'Excuse me, is your name Antonio?'

'Yes.' It was difficult to keep the aggression from his voice.

'There's a telephone message for you from Mr Mohan: he said sorry they couldn't make it, but they'll meet you at the club.'

Antonio beamed, paid for his drink and departed. This was more promising.

As he approached the bordello he saw Rajeed and Mohan entering. Quickening his step he called out, 'Hello, wait for me!'

The clubroom was empty except for the waiters scurrying around laying tables ready for the night's revels. Antonio followed Mohan and Rajeed across the room past the dance floor, and found himself in front of another door marked "Private" in gold lettering. Rajeed rapped several times with his knuckles before it was opened.

A resplendently furnished room lay before them, decorated in more reds and golds. Ceilings and walls were covered in smoky mirrors, making the reception room seem larger than it really was. Candle light reflected back, casting shadows around the room. Most of the spotlights concentrated on the roulette table as people placed their bets. The whole room crackled with excitement. The crowd stared back at their own reflections. Roshan Seth stood in the centre giving orders to a couple of perspiring waiters. Several people were hard on the heels of the three men just entering. They pushed forward, shouting their greetings, the momentum of bodies thrusting Antonio into the room.

'Ah, there you are!' Seth, looking like a giant vulture ready to pounce on its hapless victim, addressed Antonio, who looked back and smiled self-consciously, feeling distinctly out of place in these sumptuous surroundings.

Stepping forward, the vulture that was Roshan Seth placed its wings on Antonio's shoulder, led him to a seat half way down the long oblong table, ordered a drink for him, smiled and fluttered away. Attending to all his guests, he was the heart and soul of the party

153

and seemed to be everywhere at once, laughing, shaking hands and cajoling the waiters.

The powdered ladies of the bordello entered one by one, smiling their practised smiles, friends to everyone. Everybody around Antonio was laughing and drinking and having a good time, while his eyes searched for the only one he wished to see. After about thirty minutes she still had not appeared. His heart sank once more. He felt he was in a time warp, there in body only. His mind closed in on itself, protecting him from his surroundings as of old. He went onto automatic pilot, his actions disjointed from his mind. Sweat broke out on his forehead and ran down his temples. There was a barrier between himself and the other guests. With panic rising to his throat, he rose as if to flee the room. But as he turned to leave, the doorway opened and there, standing in serenity, stood Jeena, her radiant eyes glancing around the room. They settled on him and she glided across the room towards him as his heart began to pound. Stumbling slightly, he steadied himself on an upright chair.

'Hello,' she said, her voice low and husky. She took his hand in hers and made him sit, curling into a chair beside him. 'How are you?' She looked straight into his eyes. He heard nothing around him except her voice. He thought he said hello back, but to Jeena it came out as a croak.

'Get me a drink will you, darling?'

He croaked once more and turned to one of the bottles on the table, shakily pouring from it into a clean glass.

'No,' she said, 'white, please.'

In his haste to please her, he knocked some of the red wine over the table, making an embarrassing stain on the cloth. A waiter rushed forward mopping with several napkins.

'I'm sorry, please forgive me.'

'There's nothing to forgive,' Jeena laughed. The waiter poured her a glass of white wine and withdrew.

'Let's have a lovely evening and if you are a good boy, well, who knows?' She left the remark hanging. With the blood pounding in his head, he just sat there.

Excusing herself for a moment, she approached Seth. Antonio watched as they spoke in low tones, then he saw Seth turn red, speaking angrily and pointing towards him. When Jeena returned, he wanted to ask her what that had been about but figured it was none of his business. Instead they engaged in small talk, Jeena leading the conversation.

Slowly he relaxed but told himself not to drink too much. He did not want a repeat of the other night. Was it only two nights ago? It seemed longer, and a twilight world away from his family and fishing. He felt confused between his old life of family and religion and this exciting world he could never have imagined existed. People took no notice of him here. He could come and go as he wished. Nobody knew of his past. He could be himself here. With that thought his countenance changed and he let his guard down, talking more freely than he ever had. He had several more drinks and Jeena laughed and giggled at his silliest jokes, stroking the back of his neck with affection.

'Perhaps you would like to have a little gamble?'

Puzzled, he nodded.

'Have you ever gambled on roulette before?'

'No.'

'Come.' Taking his hand, she explained the playing of the game. 'You can bet on odd numbers or even numbers, fifty-fifty on red or black. The table pays out at odds of thirty-two to one from number nought to ninety or you can do split bets covering four numbers with your chip.'

'I'm sorry.' Antonio brushed his hair back nervously. 'Could you explain it once more, please? This is all new to me.'

Jeena pinched herself impatiently. Hadn't she just explained it quite clearly to the peasant? Her outward smile showed nothing of her feelings.

'I'm sorry. Split betting means you can place your chips on two squares or the centre of four, at eight to one.' She pointed to the numbered squares on the green baize table. 'You have red and black squares. You can place your bet on either red or black, betting at fifty-fifty. That means if you place your bet – for example one hundred rupees – on red, you get your original stake back plus another hundred rupees. If you put a hundred-rupee chip on one number and the white ball lands on that number, the bank pays you thirty-six to your hundred rupees. So you would collect winnings of three thousand, six hundred rupees.'

'My, what a lot of money!'

Through her smile, Jeena ground her teeth at his naivety.

'How much can I bet?' he asked.

'As little or as much as you like.'

The din grew louder as they moved in close to the table. Someone had just won. There were smiles all round as the croupier pushed a large pile of chips towards one beaming customer. Antonio felt the current of excitement radiating round the room.

'Ladies and gentlemen, place your bets please.'

Several people pushed chips onto the green chequered baize tabletop. The croupier spun the roulette wheel clockwise and placed the small white ball onto the raised edge of the spinning wheel with a much practised flick of the wrist. The ball now moved in the opposite direction from the wheel's motion.

'Last bets, please, ladies and gentlemen.'

A few people scurried forward placing chips. The first clink was heard as the white ball struck the tooth of a number, flying up once more on its circular journey. Slowing but still too quick to find a slot, onward it travelled.

'No more bets, please.'

The ball hit several more teeth. Clink, clink, clink, clink, it jumped into number seven and everyone held their breath. Someone cried out as the ball rebounded out of number seven. Antonio felt his heart miss a beat as the ball travelled over several more numbers and the wheel slowed significantly. With a life of its own, the little white ball nudged the teeth on either side of number twenty-two and stopped. Everybody breathed together, followed by one man's happy laughter. Many sighed with disappointment. 'Never mind, better luck next time,' could be heard all around. Antonio had never felt such excitement shared by so many.

'How do I make a bet?'

'Change your money into gambling chips from the croupier, then just go to the table and place your bet.'

As the whole procedure started up again, Antonio, his hand shaking, placed his modest bet on number eleven, the tension mounting as the white ball was released. He did not notice the croupier look over everybody's heads and directly at Seth, who scratched the side of his head with two fingers. A gentle pressure to the side of the table with the croupier's knee set the magnets in motion; the table was now under control. The wheel slowed and the ball jumped into number eleven. Antonio cried out as a pile of chips was pushed in his direction.

'Beginner's luck!' exclaimed Jeena as they laughed and hugged each other.

'Well done!' Seth pushed his way towards Antonio. 'Are you going to play again or just stand there congratulating yourself?'

Antonio reached across, pocketed his original stack and pushed the remaining winnings towards number thirty-two. He turned to Jeena. 'If I win we will eat and then retire.'

She squeezed his arm affectionately. Then silence prevailed. The wheel turned, the white ball danced and clinked its way round the roulette table, while Antonio's eyes never left it. Unconsciously, he clung to Jeena's arm as the ball nestled into number thirty-two. He danced with her, twirling on the spot, treading on her feet several times. Flinching, she pulled away. Clumsy oaf, she thought, smiling outwardly.

'Well I never, your luck's running high this evening. I'll tell you what! You let that lot ride and I'll match the bet. If you win I'll give you a small percentage of the club. If you lose … well, bad luck: you must pay me back.' Roshan Seth spread his hands.

Antonio was astounded. Many thoughts flew through his mind: he could move to the city, get away from the smell of rotting fish, see Jeena every day, have his own apartment. He looked at the tall figure of Roshan Seth.

'What do you mean, "match the bet"?'

'Well, I will put chips of the same value on top

of yours and if you win you get a percentage of this club.'

Antonio's thoughts swam. What had he got to lose? His original stake was safe in his pocket; if he lost he would be in just the same position as he was twenty or so minutes ago. Why not, he reasoned to himself.

'Very well.' The two men shook hands.

'Then pick a number.'

Forty-six sprang to mind, though from that moment on Antonio would not ever have been able to explain why.

'Very well then, forty-six it is.' Seth nodded to the croupier.

The wheel spun. Antonio clung to Jeena, his fate hanging before him, all his hopes and dreams wrapped up in a little white ball. The white ball realised all in a matter of seconds: clink, clink, clink, it dropped into number forty-seven.

'Well!' Roshan Seth shook his head. 'Very costly.'

Antonio watched as the croupier drew all the chips towards himself and separated them into different coloured piles, counting them. When he'd finished he looked at Seth. 'Twenty-five thousand rupees.'

'A lot of money, Antonio, how are you going to pay me?'

'What do you mean? I have lost nothing.'

Roshan Seth looked menacingly at him. Summoning Rajeed and Mohan over he spoke quietly. 'Bring him to my office. No fuss, just bring him.' He turned on his heels and walked away.

Jeena disengaged herself from him and stepped back.She watched as he was unceremoniously marched out of the room. Antonio looked back, his bewildered face shining with perspiration and astonishment. In thirty minutes he had given his naïve young life to Roshan Seth. Shoving him through the door of the office, the two men positioned themselves behind him.

'Sit down.' Seth indicated a chair in front of the large mahogany desk, the top leather bound. He began mildly enough. 'You lost the bet. I made it quite clear.'

'I don't understand. How did I lose?' Antonio was completely confused.

'You naïve fool, I made it quite clear to you: if you won you'd get a share in the club; if you lost you would pay me back my bet.'

'That's not what I understood.'

'Well it should have been. You owe me twenty- five thousand rupees. How are you going to pay me?'

'I don't know.'

'You have twenty four hours to find it. Perhaps we will come down and take one of your precious fishing boats.' Seth leaned forward. 'Do not leave town; do not even think of it. You are in debt to me for your stupidity. Now get out.' He spoke mildly but with such a threat emanating from him, Antonio had no doubt that he meant it.

Leaving the office, closely followed by Mohan, Antonio knew that either Rajeed or Mohan would become his immovable shadow, a twine of menace stitching them together. What to do? Thoughts of Jeena popped into his head and he rushed back to the private party. Laughter pounded in his ears. Scanning the room he found Jeena sitting next to a turbaned man, her delicate hand stroking the back of his neck. Their intimacy was quite apparent. Pushing through the crowds, Antonio made his way towards her. He coughed politely. The spell broken, they looked up.

'May I have a moment of your time, please, Jeena?'

'What do you want? Can't you see I'm busy?'

'Is this man bothering you?' The turbaned man rose menacingly.

Jeena placed a bejewelled hand on his immaculately tailored arm. 'No bother,' she said as she smiled at the now seated man. 'Be back in two minutes.' Rising, she beckoned Antonio to follow. He trailed after her like a beaten puppy, dishevelled and dispirited. Out in the foyer she turned on him. 'You fool!' she spat. 'How could you have been so stupid?' She lowered her voice. 'Roshan Seth never loses a bet like that. What were you thinking?'

'Only of you.' His voice cracked as he spoke.

'Me? What do you mean?'

'I thought of all that money and saw all my dreams before me, you at my side. I had to try.'

'Well, what are you going to do now?'

'I don't know. I was hoping you could lend me the money, and I would pay you back somehow.'

She laughed. 'Do you think that I could afford such a large sum?' She laughed once more. 'Don't you understand he owns me and everyone else who works here? The only way I'll ever be free is when he says so.'

A long silence followed. Antonio turned and walked across the foyer past the giant minder, opened the peeling door and stepped out into the jungle city. Jeena turned back into the room, painted a smile on her face and joined her new client.

Chapter Twenty-six

Antonio was numb. He walked the streets all day, seeing nothing, smelling nothing. He ate nothing, his hunger gone on the wings of nerves and restlessness.

Mohan and then Rajeed appeared as if in a dream, hovering around him. Lost in his own thoughts, he became more dishevelled with every stride. Hair unkempt, dark stubble sprouting on his face, he wandered on. Dusk came and went and blackness closed around him. The tentacles of dark awoke the people of the night. Mohan tapped him on the shoulder. He struggled from his shell, his mind focussing on the other man's eyes.

'Come. Roshan Seth wishes to see you.'

He nodded. Mohan and Rajeed placed themselves either side of him and, holding his elbows, guided him back towards the club. Through narrow cobbled streets they went, down dimly lit alleyways. Antonio did not know where they were and did not care. If they had tied his hands behind him and led him through the streets on a lead he would have been no more trouble.

Reaching their destination, Mohan spoke. 'We'll take him up the fire escape and use the back entrance; better not use the front with him in this state.'

They marched him up the iron staircase, one in front the other behind, and Rajeed banged on the door at the top. When it opened they led him into the office, leaving him standing in front of the big mahogany desk. Roshan Seth sat there not looking up, the tension in the room tangible, the presence of evil lurking in the air. There was silence except for the sound of

Antonio's laboured breath.

Looking up, Seth finally spoke. 'You've got my money?' It was more a statement than a question.

'No, no,' said Antonio. 'I haven't.

The evil cloak surrounding Seth darkened slowly. His black eyes stared up at Antonio.

'You look terrible. Sit down.'

Antonio sat heavily in the chair placed behind him, waves of exhaustion washing over him. Seth tapped the desktop with his fingers.

'What to do? What to do?' He turned to the two men standing at the door. 'Has he spoken to anyone?'

'No one, Mr Seth.'

'Very well then, I have a proposition to put to you, Antonio Diaz.'

'How do you know my family name?' interrupted Antonio with surprise.

'We have our methods. I know more about you and your family than you can imagine.' He left the statement for Antonio to digest for a moment, and then, snapping his fingers, he summoned Rajeed. 'Coffee and brandy for myself and him.' Seth flicked a switch and a fan began to whirr above their heads, chopping up the tension in the room.

The coffee and brandy duly arrived. Rajeed poured a large measure of brandy for Seth, serving his master first, and then handed one to Antonio. Sitting there shaking, Antonio drank deeply. The Honey Bee Brandy hit his stomach and exploded into his bloodstream. His head whirled, the tension and lack of food making him giddy. He held onto the arms of his chair and steaming black coffee was placed on the desk in front of him.

'Drink!' commanded Seth.

Antonio obediently reached for the cup and

163

drank, feeling the hot liquid slide down. It helped revive him and he sat passively resigned to his fate.

Roshan Seth spoke quietly. 'Tell me, how often do you and your company put to sea?'

Antonio leant forward. 'Why?'

'Just answer. You are in no position to ask questions. Now, once more, how often?'

'If we are off shore fishing, every night, but once a month we go long haul fishing, depending on tides and weather.'

'How long are these trips?'

'About eight to ten days.'

'I've thought about approaching your family for the money you owe me.'

Antonio stiffened. Seth nonchalantly sipped his coffee, sniffed his brandy and selected a Bolivar No 2 from a silver embossed box. He sniffed the aromatic cigar, then took from his pocket a silver snipper. He guillotined the end and dipped it in the Honey Bee, placed it in his mouth and turned to the already prepared flame Rajeed offered. Seth sucked deeply on the Bolivar. Smoke billowed out of his nostrils and mouth, travelling north towards the ceiling. The blue haze whirred around the fan in a ghostly grey embrace.

'Tell me, how would you feel about picking up some parcels for me in exchange for your debt?'

'What kind of parcels?'

'Questions, questions, questions.'

'I just wondered.'

'That's none of your business. Now, are you interested or not?'

The question seemed more like a threat. Antonio nodded.

'Very well, let me explain what I expect of you: firstly, if you let me down I will kill you or one of your precious family – and I do not make idle threats; secondly, when you pick up the packages you will deliver them to a small hotel in Panjim. You will be given a telephone number and when you have the first package you will ring it. Then and only then will you know where the hotel is. Is this clear?'

'Yes I think so.'

'When you find the hotel you will be given the name of someone staying there. You will hand the package to them, go home and wait for further instruction. The same procedure will apply for the next package except it will be a different hotel. Now repeat all this back to me.'

Antonio duly obliged.

'Very good. Now the terms of the first two packages will pay off your debt. I am not a greedy man, so let us say …' He paused. 'I will be generous to you … say … ten thousand rupees per parcel after that.'

Antonio's head spun. Ten thousand rupees. One month's wages in one day. Greed brought him back to life. He sat up straight, listening intently.

'We will need you to pick up one parcel a month for the next five months. After that we will just see, won't we?' Roshan Seth left it there.

Antonio's mind was now racing. With all that money he would be able to see Jeena. Thirty thousand rupees. He would be able to give her everything she desired. Seth rose majestically.

'Antonio, you look terrible. Come, let's get you cleaned up. Who knows, perhaps we can find someone to entertain you.' He stepped around the desk, motioning Antonio to rise. Still puffing on his cigar, he put an arm around him and they went out of the door together, followed closely by Mohan and Rajeed.

165

That night Antonio lost what he thought he had already given. Jeena handled him expertly, pleasuring him several times until he finally fell asleep exhausted across the bed. She looked down at him: hair matted, his whole body covered in sweaty hair, the sheets sticking to him, his mouth wide open, snoring. She spat at him, cursing the gods of fornication and lust. She turned, pulling the switch for the single light bulb in the shower room. Under the cold tap, she scrubbed the memory of him from her skin, but not from her mind.

Chapter Twenty-seven

Antonio telephoned his father from Mumbai Central. 'I missed the train yesterday. I'm catching the train tonight and will be arriving about ten tomorrow morning. Could you pick me up, please?' He hung up before his father could prise any more information from him and went to find his carriage.

Two minutes later, the train shuddered to life with Antonio seated on a wooden bench in third class. Vibrations ran through his buttocks and he knew he was homeward bound. Two hours later, the engine slowed and came to a halt at some obscure station. The carriage door opened and a street vendor entered, a cauldron of steaming coffee in one hand, the aroma enriching the still air, and a plastic bag of sugary doughnut-like cakes in the other.

'Coffee!...Coffee!...Coffeeeeee!' he shouted up and down the aisles. Antonio suddenly realised that he had not prepared himself for his journey. Calling the vendor over, he ordered coffee and six cakes, his stomach reminding him how hungry he was after the exertion of the previous night. Smiling at his own joke, he stood and dipped his hand into his trouser pocket, raising his eyebrows in surprise as he pulled out the gambling chips from his escapade a couple of evenings before. Had he not eaten since then? He searched his pockets twice. He had no money whatsoever. He could not believe that in all his fear and confusion he had forgotten to cash in the chips. Apologising to the vendor, he sat down heavily. His hunger would have to wait until the next day.

Hour after hour the train rumbled on through the night. Antonio's stomach rumbled along with it.

He found himself torn between two worlds. His family and familiar surroundings called to him: his mother's food, his father's reassuring arm resting on his shoulder, his brother's banter and hard play. And yet, compared to his familial duty, this new world that had thrust itself upon him, and the pleasures it offered, appealed to him.

He stirred and shifted on the uncomfortable wooden seat, the memories of the night before foremost in his mind. Thinking of Jeena, he touched himself involuntarily. He thought of the thirty thousand rupees. He could marry her and live in the city. The thought of her lying naked next to him forever filled his mind – her roundness, so soft to the touch. Blind to what was really going on around him, he became lost in the memory of her eyes.

As the express approached Margao station he leaned out of the window. With the wind rushing through his hair, he could just make out his father's battered old jeep in the station car park. As the train slowed he could see his father waiting for him. Was it only a few days ago that he'd left? He had two lives now, one a world away from the other. He must show no emotion, no tell-tale signs, nothing. Antonio retreated back into his shell.

In the hustle and bustle of people fighting their way on and off the train, Rodriguez searched for his son, finally spotting him hovering in one of the carriage doorways. He pushed his way through the throng until their eyes met briefly. He knew his son well enough to know immediately that something was wrong. 'Hello my son, how are you?' Reaching out he grabbed his shoulders and pulled him into his embrace, hugging him with love. Antonio stiffened. Was this the usual awkward and withdrawn Antonio, Rodriguez wondered, or had something happened?

He'd been very abrupt on the phone. He sighed inwardly although the smile never left his face.

'Hello, Father.'

'Is everything all right, son?'

'Why, yes.'

'Have you brought the spare part with you?'

'Of course,' came the reply. 'I'm sorry I'm a day late, but the part didn't arrive on time.'

Rodriguez knew it was a lie. His telephone call to the company the day before, when he had spoken personally to Mr Singh, had assured him that everything was on time. Being older and wiser than his son, Rodriguez let this pass. He knew time would tell and something would slip out in the end. Be patient, he told himself.

Going to the guard's van at the back of the train, they unloaded the small wooden crate plastered with "Fragile" stickers in bold lettering and Singh and Son's embossed labels.

'Father, could we go to the little station café now? I haven't eaten on the journey. I travelled without food and I forgot the few rupees I had. I left them in Angelo's apartment.'

'You must be hungry then.' Rodriguez deposited the crate on a trolley assisted by a red-coated porter complete with his inevitable strip of red material tied ceremoniously around his head. Then he headed towards the exit and out to the jeep with Antonio in tow. 'We'll stack the box in the back and then go and eat.'

When they arrived back at the village, the whole family turned out to greet them. Many questions came at Antonio all at once.

'What was the city like?'

'How big is it?'

'Did you enjoy the train?'

'How was Cousin Angelo?'

'Wait! Wait!' cried Rodriguez. 'Let the poor boy breathe. There will be plenty of time for your questions. Let him rest this afternoon. Tonight you can satisfy your curiosity. We'll have a family gathering after our meal. I'll ask Pedro and Joe to join us.'

Antonio seethed inside. He just wanted to be alone; he didn't want their stupid questions. All he could think of now was how to get back and see Jeena. Excusing himself, he went to his room, closed the door and lay on the bed. He let his mind wander back to the night before. Relaxing with his memories he slept.

Chapter Twenty-eight

Cristiano's head appeared from the engine room's hatch just as Joe hobbled down to the dock. Pedro was under the boat in dry dock, a large spanner in his hand, while Rodriguez was standing slightly to one side, directing operations. Pedro saw his father approaching.

'Hello, Papa, the new instrument is almost fitted. I think we can go for a sea trial this afternoon if you wish.'

'Excellent!' Joe looked at Rodriguez. 'I think family members only at this stage. No crew.'

Rodriguez nodded in agreement.

When the boat was re-floated and nudging the jetty, the four men prepared to set sail.

'What about Antonio?' Knowing how touchy his younger brother could be, Cristiano did not want him to feel left out.

'Leave him to rest. Besides, he's already witnessed a sea trial with Mr Singh in the big city.'

As they started the diesel engines, great puffs of smoke billowed from the exhaust above the wheelhouse. The engines warmed, settling into their familiar throb. Unfurling ropes from around the capstans, the men cast off, heading for the mouth of the estuary. They all set about familiar tasks, working as a unit. Joe steered the craft while Rodriguez fiddled with dials, then a wire, as the fish-finder sparked into life, the emerald screen blinking back at him. Joe watched their sons scurrying around on deck, tidying away loose ropes and straightening the anchor and chains. Leaving the protection of the estuary, the boat began to pitch and sway. The young men walked round the boat with an easy sailors' gait.

'Straight ahead, Captain,' said Rodriguez with a smile on his face.

Joe grinned back. 'Aye, aye, Captain.'

Time had pulled them even closer together. Soulmates. They both kept a look out for signs of weather change or other fishing vessels. The horizon kissed the sky and a few wisps of white cloud winged their way from port to starboard.

'A good sign: the wind's coming from the land,' said Rodriguez.

Birds hovered above them, looking for an easy meal. They had learned to follow the fleets, watching for discarded fish offal thrown over the side. They would dive straight down, plucking whatever they could scavenge from the sea's surface.

'Beautiful.' Pedro looked up at a black headed gull hovering above them. He tossed over the side a small dried fish that he'd found under the anchor chain, then watched as the bird folded its wings and plunged straight down. It spread its wings at the last moment, rudders down, landing gear out and splayed behind, beak thrust forward as it swooped, plucking the dead fish from the surface of the sea. With flaps down, it rose again majestically, the fish in its beak. Flicking it expertly, the bird tipped its head back and the fish disappeared down its gullet. Riding the wind once more, it waited for another. A cormorant winged its way over the surface of the sea, landing on a protruding rock, spreading its wings and allowing the sun to shine down upon it. Pedro never tired of these small wonders of nature.

Cristiano shouted to Pedro, his words lost on the wind. He motioned to him to move to the bow, and pointed down. The front of the boat turned sea water into foam while all around it was beautiful azure blue. The surface sparkled, diamond flashes winking a thousand times back at them.

'Look,' said Cristiano. There, right in front of the boat, a pod of dolphins swam. Backwards and forwards they weaved themselves up and down. Their fins broke the surface and just for an instant left foaming scars on the gleaming sea as they took turns to lead the boat. A big male leapt out of the water, grey fin and upper body, its lower belly white.

'Bottlenose,' said Pedro.

Cristiano nodded and the dolphin arched its back. The elegant creature disappeared under the surface, barely leaving a splash in its wake, allowing another, then another, to take its place. The two men laughed, enjoying the spectacle. Rarely had they the time to indulge this luxury of observing. They looked to the wheelhouse and saw their fathers' smiling faces filled with pride.

Antonio awoke, stretched his weary limbs, rubbed his hands over his face and sat up. Swinging his legs off the bed, he stood up. Still stretching he walked to the door and winced as the fierce light and heat touched him. Shading his eyes, he saw his sister Maria, child on hip, crossing in front of him from the next door bungalow where she and Pedro lived with their three sons and Joe.

'Where are all the men?'

'Out to sea, trying out that new machine of yours. I can see them, just off shore.' She pointed proudly to where the boat was just heading back into the estuary, the company flag waving in the breeze – the flag which symbolised the achievement of Joe's and Rodriguez's ambition; it symbolised, too, the union of the two families. The four years that Rodriguez had made Pedro wait for Maria had

173

seemed like forever for both of them. Now, it was as though life had never been any different.

'I think I'll go down and wait for them,' Antonio muttered.

As the craft drew alongside, he shouted to the seafarers, 'How did it go then?'

'Very well.' Pedro threw a landing rope to Antonio. 'Just as the company promised.' The powerful diesel engine died and silence settled. The boat nestled up to the jetty and Antonio waited. Jumping down, the men huddled together, talking excitedly.

'It worked!'

'We came across shoals in places we would never have fished before.'

'We couldn't believe it.'

'Tomorrow, you three can go fishing,' Rodriguez offered. 'Leave together. When you get out to sea stay in formation. The lead boat with the machine will hopefully guide you – no, not hopefully – *will* guide you to new fishing grounds. When the shoals are in range then spread out and fill your boats.'

They headed back to the huts in high sprits.

Rodriguez caught up with Antonio. 'Are you rested, son?'

'Yes, Father.'

'I know you won't like the questions the family will ask you, but please try and satisfy their curiosity. After all, not one of them has been to the big city.'

Antonio grinned back sardonically as he took his handkerchief from his pocket to mop his brow. Rodriguez saw something fall to the ground and reaching down, he picked up a twenty rupee gambling chip.

'What's this, son?'

Antonio stiffened. 'A curiosity I found in the street in Mumbai,' he lied easily. 'What is it, Father?'

Rodriguez turned the object over in his hand and gave it back to Antonio. 'I don't know, perhaps a lucky charm,' he also lied, then smiled and walked away. Antonio relaxed.

The captain's curiosity was roused. What had his son been up to? Don't jump to conclusions, he reprimanded himself. But he made a mental note of what to do. Then, putting it aside, he went home for his evening meal.

Chapter Twenty-nine

The sea began to rumble its good morning to the fishermen as they made their way towards the jetty and the waiting boats, the veil of dawn trying to push the grey mists from the sky. Nearing the quayside, they noticed the boats bobbing up and down, even in the calmness of the estuary. 'Sea's a little rough today,' someone said – a comment made just to break the silence. The other men nodded, their thoughts still wrapped in blankets from their own beds, the warmth and smells of their women still fresh.

'Right, you men, on board quickly now,' Pedro rallied. 'We'll run with the tide; it saves time and money.'

This snapped the men out of their walking dreams.

'Lively, now, hop to it!' Antonio, the harshest of the three captains bellowed down from the deck of the nearest boat, all three ships in line along the concrete jetty, the company flag flapping briskly in the dawn breeze on each one. The painted eye on the bow of each ship seemed to blink at each man in turn as they climbed aboard, each going to their allotted places, setting about their daily tasks without thinking.

'Cast off for'ard! Cast off stern!' The three captains shouted, almost in unison.

The men curled the ropes on the decking in the bow of the boats as they nudged and bobbed away from the quayside. Powerful diesel engines churned the bottom of the harbour bed to mud. Small fish darted behind the turning propellers, picking at the rich source of food disturbed from the river bed.

All three captains turned their wheels to port, heading for the mouth of the river, the three boats in line, their engines leaving white foam trailing behind. The deck hands went about their business, checking the winches attached to the netting, which was in turn attached to the windlasses at each side of the boat, the great mounds of netting carefully furled, ready to disappear down into the depths of the sea.

The deckhand cook was already fanning the charcoal burners ready for the first brew of the day. All the hands liked their first brew. Chipped enamel mugs rattled in their holders ready for the milky sweet brown chai.

One man already had his feet placed firmly in rope stirrups bolted to the stern of the boat. He leant far out over the rail, defecating into the wind. Washing himself with sea water, he deftly hopped back on board. Being a daily occurrence for all the sailors, no one took any notice.

As the boats left the safety of the estuary, the first waves hit the bows. Great mounds of spume and spray wrapped around the wheelhouses, dispersing into tiny droplets over the men in the stern.

'That'll wake them up,' Antonio laughed to himself. His strong hands kept the wheel steady, his forearms flexed to the power of the sea. Steering his boat up and over the first set of waves, he went about his captain's duties, aware of his responsibilities to his men and the company. But his mind was elsewhere, thinking of Jeena and her soft passionate embraces, her rich dark hair brushing across his face. His passion knew no bounds. Sweat broke out on his forehead. He felt his erect body brushing the wheel in front of him.

The wheelhouse door burst open. There stood the deckhand cook, a steaming mug of chai in his hand and a grin from ear to ear on his weathered face.

177

'Knock before entering!' Antonio shouted abruptly, trying to hide his embarrassment by picking some imaginary thing up from the deck. The outside dawn chill entered the small cabin, drying the tiny beads of perspiration on his forehead. 'Put that mug down and piss off.' The deckhand scurried forward nervously, spilling the hot steaming tea over the decking. 'Put it down there and get out, you clumsy bastard.' Antonio followed the man and slammed the wheelhouse door behind him, trying to hide his frustration.

'Captain's in a good mood today,' the cook commented to the rest of the crew. They all smiled wryly.

Antonio turned off the glaring, hanging light bulb and placed his hand to his brow, staring ahead through the wheelhouse glass, looking at the other two boats with him: his elder brother's boat just ahead and the other, skippered by Pedro, to starboard. He had never thought of Pedro as his friend, only as the friend and companion of Cristiano, his brother. Not even marriage to his sister had brought him any closer to Joe's son.

'Ahoy, Antonio!' came a voice from the crackling speaker to his right. 'Can you hear me?'

Antonio reached for the ship to shore radio. Pressing down the button on the handset, he lifted it to his mouth. 'Loud and clear,' he returned in clipped tones.

'Good morning, my brother,' it crackled back at him.

He resented his brother's bonhomie at this time in the morning. Why was he always so bloody cheerful?

'This new machine is great,' enthused Christiano, 'although this glaring green light's giving me a headache. Still, it's picked up a shoal of fish just off your port bow, about two hundred metres due east of you. Care to have first go?'

'Roger,' came the reply.

Antonio's boat peeled off from the formation, heading east, and Christiano saw Antonio come out of the wheelhouse, gesticulating, the crew jumping to attention, standing each side of the netting awaiting their orders. He observed Antonio giving the order to release the strong netting and the men begin working faster and faster, trying to keep up with the panning nets. As more unravelled, dragging floats and weights overboard, it seemed as though the men would be dragged over too, but expert footwork and experience kept them safe. Christiano watched as the boat slowed, dragged back by the sodden mass, and the stern dipped heavily into the sea. He smiled, glad that Antonio had got first blood. He had felt slightly guilty having the fish-finder fitted to his ship; after all, Antonio had been the firm's representative. Turning seaward once more, the two remaining boats headed towards the horizon, the green light still blinking intensely in Cristiano's cabin.

Alone at last, thought Antonio, revving the engines several more notches to compensate for the initial drag. When the nets were fully extended, he turned the wheel slightly to port, chasing the tail of the nets – not enough to entangle himself, but enough to enable him to ensnare as many fish as possible.

After several hours running with the tides and nets, he bellowed at the men to make ready. 'Have you all eaten?'

They nodded.

'Well, be ready then. Stand by for the nets.' He slowed the engine and watched as his men braced themselves, bare feet planted firmly on the decking as he engaged the winching gear. The winch motor screamed to life. He felt the boat physically slew to starboard as the heavy netting took control. He watched as the ropes connected to the winch went taut, squeezing the salt water from them, sending it dripping onto the deck. 'Careful of sea spillage,' he reminded his men. Soon the decks would be full of water, fish scales and slime.

'Winch away,' shouted his bosun.

The ship shuddered nearly to a standstill as Antonio revved the engine several notches again, keeping it on station and as steady as he could into the waves, not wanting to tip the men overboard or into the machinery. Birds appeared as if from nowhere, hovering over the sunken nets, screeching and squawking, sensing the feast ahead.

'Haul aboard!'

'Aye, aye, Captain!'

The great winches on either side of the boat's stern came to life and the stern dipped even more towards the sea's surface. The strain on the thick hemp ropes was immeasurable. Slowly the sea began to release its bounty. Trapped bodies, restricted by the nets, began to surface, their panicked splashing and struggling attracting the birds hovering above. Diving suddenly, without fear of the nets, the birds plucked their victims from the woven cages. Time and time again they nose-dived, the noise from these flying multitudes becoming deafening. Their excitement pulsated in the air, as the heaving netting began to re-enter the boat.

The men unceremoniously plucked the struggling fish from their confinement, throwing them on deck, later to be separated: sea bass, sear fish, king fish, an occasional sail fish, tuna and many mackerel and sardines.

Suddenly a dolphin and its baby appeared, trapped together. They had obviously been hunting amongst the bountiful shoals.

'Stop the winching!' shouted the bosun.

Antonio glanced back, immediately cutting the winching motor. Above the noise of the birds' feeding frenzy, the lamenting sounds of the baby dolphin could be heard mingled with its mother's helpless cries of anguish, not for its own agonies but for that of its young. All the men rushed forward, slithering over wet decking, drawing their twelve-inch knives from their sheaths. The knives, honed to a razor's edge, flashed in the sunlight. They headed for the crying dolphins. The mother saw them coming and tried to lash out with her huge tail, the wet chafing nets cutting deeper into her flesh, holding her steadfast. She gnashed her sawn teeth with frustration, the milky-eyed baby bleating helplessly at her. One of the men stripped off his T-shirt, soaked it in sea water and placed it over the mother's eyes, calming her. The other men reached her, their deadly blades held high in front of them. Watching as one, they placed their knives between the mother and the netting, and slashed, releasing the two metre long dolphin. Before she could recover, they flipped her back over the side, followed by the still bleating baby.

'Well done, men!' shouted Antonio. 'Drinks on me tonight!'

Even with Antonio's hardened exterior, the superstitions of his people ran deep within him. The men cheered him, although they had given themselves many hours' work to repair the nets. The dolphins were sacred to them; they truly believed their ancestors lived with these creatures, their guardians and eyes of this sea world.

Hauling the nets back over the sides,

separating the fish, swabbing the decks and doing all the other boring but necessary tasks took many hours. The crew looked like silver fish themselves, covered from head to toe in scales. When they finished, each man took his turn, placing feet in hemp ropes, to be helped by the others to wash himself down with sea water until the fish scales mixed with the foam at the stern. It churned and turned in the ship's wake, glinting in the moonlight, whisked away into the distant waves.

Dusk pushed on. Antonio turned on the ship's lights as his men squatted around the charcoal burner sipping chai and eating their meagre food. Tired but exhilarated and excited over the size of the catch, they knew that it would enable them to feed their families for a week or two. Steering the boat towards the co-ordinates memorised in his head, Antonio let the boat throb at half speed, hoping the crew wouldn't notice the change of direction. They were heading out to sea, not to shore.

Chapter Thirty

Sitting with his comrades, the bosun looked up at the stars. A frown creased his brow. He looked towards the wheelhouse, the bare light bulb swinging with the sway of the boat, and saw his captain's concentrated stare at the unseen horizon. He got up and walked to the cabin door, knocked tentatively and waited for permission to enter.

'What is it?'

'Excuse me, Captain, but I notice we're heading out to sea. The men thought we were on our way home, sir.'

'We soon will be, Bosun. Thought we'd try and find the other two boats before we turn back. I've just spoken to my brothers,' Antonio lied easily. 'They're not far away. Let the men rest. In an hour we'll turn for home, hopefully in convoy.'

'As you wish, Captain.'

Antonio opened the door and pointed to his personal locker. 'Take a bottle of feni and give each man a large peg. Tell them "well done". Be patient and we'll be home in good time.'

'As you wish, Captain,' the bosun repeated, unable to keep the shock from his voice. Never before had alcohol been allowed on board. It was against company policy. Joe and Rodriguez had made that clear from the day they had formed the business. It had always been adhered to until now. Still, he supposed the men deserved it, just this once. Taking the bottle, he closed the wheelhouse door behind him.

Antonio heard the men outside grumbling and then become pacified with the drink. Half an hour to go and I'll be there, he thought, as the boat rolled and

183

pitched, cutting its way forward into the distance.

He saw the light of a great ship just dipping over the horizon and knew this must be the host ship. He felt his heart begin to pound in his chest. He concentrated on the task ahead, not blinking for an instant. And then, there, right in front of him, a light pulsed on and off, on and off. Then it was gone, down into the valley of the wave. Antonio stiffened, the tension in his small cabin electrifying. He began to sweat heavily. He altered course towards his goal. There, the light rose once more riding the crest of the incoming wave.

The door burst open. 'Captain, have you seen —'

'Yes, I have.' Antonio interrupted the bosun abruptly. 'Looks like a distress beacon. Did you see that large ship?'

'No, Captain.'

'I wonder if we have a man overboard. Get the men ready with grappling hooks. I'll try to come upon it starboard. Station yourselves amidships. Don't miss it.'

'Aye, Captain.'

Antonio slammed the door as the bosun left. He could hear his shouts and the men scurrying starboard. The boat bore down quickly onto the flashing light and as they neared Antonio threw the boat into reverse, slinging the wheel hard to the right. He heard the men cheer and knew they had retrieved his prize. Once more, his man entered the wheelhouse, this time carrying a dripping yellow life jacket.

'That's all we found, Captain; nobody with it, though.'

'See if you can spot anything.'

The bosun disappeared back to his men. 'You two – one forward, one aft – and you on the port side,

184

keep your eyes peeled.' He jumped up onto the top of the cabin and switched on the powerful spotlights, traversing them slowly through three hundred and sixty degrees. Nothing. Just the lapping of the waves against the ship.

The captain's head appeared just above the cabin. 'I'll trawl back and forth; we'll run with the waves. All you men keep your eyes peeled.'

For the next hour they weaved backwards and forwards until Antonio's head appeared over the cabin once more. 'I'm afraid we've missed the poor man. Do you agree, Bosun?'

'Aye, could be anywhere, if there was anybody in the first place. Could have been an accident … slipped over the side without anyone noticing.'

Antonio didn't reply directly. 'We'll head for port,' he shouted to the crew and then turned to the bosun. 'I'll tell the police in case anyone's washed up on shore. Keep a watch until we reach the estuary though … you never know.'

He went back into the wheelhouse and altered course for home. After checking the compass once more, he knelt down to examine the life jacket, carefully deflating it with a small stab from his knife. He was surprised at how light it was. Searching carefully again he found nothing .

After checking the co-ordinates to make sure they were still on course, he examined the jacket again. Puzzled, he broke into a cold sweat. He could feel the panic rising. Had he picked up the right one? He presumed he was picking up drugs. Desperately he resumed his task, running his hands over the seams, looking for an opening. Again, nothing. He picked it up, weighing it in his hands. Nothing. Losing his temper, he threw it against the cabin wall. The collar split slightly, revealing the corner of a sealed package. Antonio leapt over to it and tore the package from the collar. A flat parcel, no bigger than a man's wallet and sealed in layers of shrink-wrap plastic nestled in his hands. What on earth was it? Was this what all the fuss was about? He turned it over again and again. The words of Seth came back to him threateningly: *When you find it, do not open it. Do you understand?* Placing the strange packet deep into his trouser pocket, he set about getting them all home safely.

As they entered the estuary, he could see the other two company boats already moored and empty, his brother and Pedro, just visible, standing on the jetty, hands on hips, patiently awaiting him. The jetty lights hung down like limpid moons.

'Where have you been?' they exploded as the third boat bumped the jetty, the men waiting to unload the fish haul already clambering aboard. Antonio relayed his story and they agreed to alert the authorities without delay. Antonio felt the small package nestling against his leg.

'You go home. We'll supervise the unloading. Go home and get some rest.'

Antonio did not argue.

He lay in his bed tossing and turning, going over the night's events. Tomorrow he would leave the village to make his phone call and receive instructions.

Cristiano, questioning the men and examining the life jacket, noticed the puncture where the knife had entered, and the loose stitching on the collar.

Chapter Thirty-one

Antonio left the village at first light. He knew he would not be missed for several hours; the families were used to him wandering off by himself. He walked into the small town seven miles away, only stopping once at a small chai stall. Several people waved to him on the way but he took no notice, heading along purposefully.

He heard the slight crackle on the long distance line and the purring ring as the call connected. After several rings an abrupt voice answered. Antonio recognised it at once. The voice became guarded when Antonio gave his name.

'You have it?'

'Yes.'

'Now listen to me carefully.' The threatening tone was always present. 'Tomorrow, go to the Phoenix Hotel, not far from your village. Do you know it?'

Antonio confirmed that he did.

'Ask for room 27. There will be someone there to receive the package.'

The line went dead before he could reply. He stood there, unconsciously rubbing the pocket containing the package. Not wanting to return home immediately, he wandered restlessly through the busy town, until he realised he had reached one of the most undesirable quarters, an area well known for gangs, drugs and prostitution. He looked around cautiously. A young girl, no more than fifteen, sidled up to him.

'Hello stranger, you here for a good time?'

He felt eyes watching him from dark corners and doorways.

'How much?' he heard himself say.

'Ninety rupees for the day, or fifty for an hour.' He looked at this young creature, the bindi between her eyes bright and colourful on her unblemished skin; he noticed the bangles and beads adorning her ankles and wrists, the delicate earrings dangling from her ears, and several studs twinkling in the sunlight, embellishing her nose. As her sari fluttered towards him in the wind, he surprised himself.

'You have a room?'

She pointed upwards. He saw girls hanging out of dark hooded windows, laughing, all dressed the same as this young nymph standing in front of him. She smiled appealingly, showing her dazzling white teeth, her eyes alight with optimistic hope.

'Lead on,' he instructed her.

They entered a dingy room. A tousled bed strewn with many cushions and bolsters, but no sheets, took up most of the space. One broken chair stood in the corner. The girl immediately twirled out of her sari and stripped; her wanton nakedness shocked Antonio. Her dark nipples thrust out on her delicate mounds. Her skin shone lustrously with youth and below her flat belly nestled a small mound of adolescent pubic hair. She stepped forward and embraced him, her small hand reaching down and cupping him. He felt himself become hard. As he threw her onto the bed, he could hear laughter and giggling through the closed door. He forced her legs apart with his knee and entered her. As soon as he felt her hot wetness engulf him, he came. Throwing himself off her, he buried his head in the cushions, trying to control his breathing.

She took a tissue from behind a cushion. 'That was wonderful. Would you like to try again?' She stroked his damp, hairy back. 'You still have most of your hour left,' she remarked dispassionately.

His glazed eyes returned to reality. He got up abruptly and hurriedly dressed. Looking down at her nakedness, he threw the fifty-rupee note on top of her and walked out of the room. As he descended the stairs two by two, he could still hear the laughter behind him.

Jeena, my Jeena, it's not the same, you are my only true love, he said to himself as he rushed through the town and back towards his village and family.

Eyes watched him everywhere he went, night and day. These eyes never slept, just doing their master's bidding. In good time they would get their rewards.

The Phoenix Hotel was full of foreign tourists. Antonio felt like a tourist himself. Although this place was only two miles from his home, it was a world away.

'Room 27?' he enquired tentatively at the reception desk.

The clerk looked at him curiously. He knew the family and their business, and he couldn't imagine what Antonio would be doing in a place like this. He dialled the room. 'Mr Antonio Diaz is at reception for you, sir.' He turned to Antonio. 'You may go up; you're expected. Up the stairs and turn left, third door along the corridor.'

Antonio moved swiftly away from the reception desk. He hadn't expected to be recognised, although he couldn't think that it mattered. He found his way up the stairs to room 27, and knocked hard. A muffled voice replied, 'Enter.'

He stepped into the room. 'Jeena!' he burst out with surprise. 'Is it really you?'

'Of course it is, you silly peasant.' The smile on

her face did not reach her eyes.

He rushed forward, grabbing both her hands in his. 'My Jeena, you look wonderful!'

And you smell of stale fish, she thought through clenched teeth and smiling lips.

'I was expecting Rajeed or Mohan, not you,' he began to burble incoherently.

Jeena heard none of it, saw only his lips moving incessantly. In her mind she heard the voice of her master, Seth: *Whatever he wants, give it to him. Do you understand?* Her mind resigned her to her mission; she became the consummate actress once more.

'Would you like a drink?' she offered. 'Scotch? Vodka?'

'Whatever.'

She broke from his grip and walked towards the drinks trolley, trying to gather her strength for the oncoming trial. 'Please, sit down.' She poured two large whiskies, offering one to Antonio. She sat in the chair farthest away from him.

'You have been well?' he asked.

She did not look at him, just turned her glass in her hands. 'Yes, thank you.'

'It seems ages since I last saw you.'

'Yes,' she replied without interest, her mind on why she was there. 'Have you got it?'

'Of course.' He fumbled in his trouser pocket, removing and offering the sealed package. She took it casually but placed it carefully in her handbag. As she sat down again he heard the swish of her silk stockings as she crossed her long elegant legs. He felt himself stirring.

'May I use your toilet? I love western bathrooms – so clean and full of the smells of soap.'

'Would you like to take a bath?'

'I'm not sure I should,' he said shyly.

'Help yourself. Seth's paying for it.'

'Do you really think it's all right?'

'Of course, go ahead.' At least it would wash some of the fish scales off him. 'Be my guest.'

The small but sophisticated room was resplendent with beautiful tiles and mirrors, a large cream tub, gold taps and luxuriously soft towels hanging on golden rails. After relieving himself, he began to run a bath, feeling the hot gushing water, revelling in the change from his normal washing routine. The communal cold water tap and a bucket, with the sun to dry him were a far cry from this luxury. On a glass shelf there were bath oils, perfumes, sachets of shampoo and small wrapped soaps with the hotel logo embossed on them. Filling the bath to the brim, he stripped off, gingerly entering the steaming tub.

Meanwhile, Jeena lifted the receiver and asked reception for an outside line to Mumbai. It rang once.

'He's delivered the package.'

'Good. Now give him his reward.'

The line went dead. She felt the sheer dread of what was to follow. Her mind and body disassociated from her actions. How many times had she done this before? She'd lost count, the faces and bodies all melted into one. The man she truly loved was married to another. Cast out from her village when her clandestine affair had been discovered, she had walked for many days, hungry and thirsty, eventually reaching the big city. Sleeping rough, usually in Mumbai Central, the same as thousands of others like her, she had been rudely shaken awake, one night, by two men. Her life as she had always known it had ended there.

Having done as Seth instructed, she paid her bill with crisp new rupee notes as a taxi waited to take her to the airport for the forty-five minute flight to Mumbai. She knew the drive would be longer than the flight and she imagined she could still smell Antonio on her, the pungency of his body hard to remove. She liberally sprayed perfume about herself to wipe out the odour of the peasant. After all, she was a city girl now.

Antonio went home, exuberant after accomplishing his first mission, and elated at meeting the love of his life again. It was a shame she had to return to the big city so soon, but he knew he would have to be stoic about that. He made sure his face gave nothing away as he reached the house and went straight to his room, his foray abroad unnoticed by his family. He went over in his mind the time he and Jeena had spent together. He was dreading the phone call he would have to make to Seth the next say, but it could not be helped. For now he felt content. In one month's time the process must begin again.

Chapter Thirty-two

'Surely there's a better way than this?' Seth shouted down the phone. In his hand was the sealed package Jeena had brought to him. 'A silly bloody package this size, why not send it by post or courier?' He turned it over as he spoke, held it to the light, his curiosity aroused.

The mild voice at the other end of the line never lost its cool. 'The post is always searched here – every package, every parcel, every letter. If a courier got stopped with one of the packages, they would know, the game would be up and as we have no diplomatic agreement between our countries, this is the safest way. My man will never let me down. As for your end, I hope everything is secure.'

Seth felt unspoken menace hanging in the moment. 'The damned sea bit gets me. Why?'

'It has directional finders, satellite homing beacons, radar, GPS – everything – and even in the unlikely circumstances of your man not picking it up, we could still track it and pick it up later. Now relax, you have your first delivery. Show that to your employers and in a few months they will have the full consignment. The money is to be transferred immediately into the numbered accounts you have already received – one package, one payment. A slight alteration with our next package: money first. Not that I don't trust you, it's how I want things arranged.'

'Are you implying that I'm not trustworthy?'

'No, no, I'm just being expedient. Let me know when the next delivery is fulfilled.'

The international line went dead.

Seth sat back, a brooding frown lowering his

brow. He was a middle man, a link in the chain between China and someone else. As such, he was being well paid not to question what he was handling, but to simply move it along the chain. He had no idea of the final destination, but he was beginning to suspect that the deal was much bigger than he had originally been led to believe. He did not dare break the seal on the package to find out what it contained – he knew his life would be forfeit – but his insatiable greed ate at him.

'Four more of these bloody things! How much could I have made if I knew what they were?' As he thumped the desk in frustration, the phone rang again. 'Yes?' he bellowed down the mouthpiece.

'Mr Seth, it's Antonio.'

'What do you want?'

'Are we safe to talk?'

Seth pressed a button on his phone. 'We are now, what do you want?'

'It's the men, Mr Seth.'

'What men?' Seth shouted impatiently.

'My … my crew. I'm afraid I can't fool them again. They would find it too suspicious.'

'I'm listening.' Seth drummed his fingers on his desk. Why couldn't the fool get to the point? He thumbed through a pile of papers. 'What do you suggest?'

'I think a bribe, bucksheesh, whatever you want to call it. Give my men enough money to keep their mouths shut.'

Seth started to take notice. This little fisherman was getting rather bold. 'How many men?'

'Six.'

'Go on.'

'Well, I figured if you give each of them the equivalent of one year's wage, they will fall in line.'

'How much?' Seth stifled a yawn, not the least bit interested in the details of peasant economics.

'Four thousand rupees each.'

'What! A total of twenty four thousand rupees! Are you taking me for a fool?' Was this really the same idiot who had stood before him, a quivering wreck, with less than a basic grasp of a roulette table?

'No, no, please listen. We have four more pick ups to make. I need the men. Without them there is no way I can complete our deal.'

'Then it can come out of your thirty thousand rupees.' Seth's tone was firm. No way was this cheeky little upstart going to get the better of him.

'It doesn't give me much incentive.'

Seth breathed in sharply, amazed at Antonio's audacity. 'You owe me, remember?'

'I know, but please be reasonable.'

'I'll think about it. Ring me back in an hour.'

Antonio rubbed his sweating palms down his trousers. Sitting on the wall outside the STD box he stared the hour away before dialling again.

'Mr Seth, it's Antonio.'

'I know who it is.' A moment of heavy silence ensued, travelling down the phone like a wave. 'How do you know you can trust these men?' Seth finally asked.

'They have been with me for years. I know my men.'

'Then you will be answerable for them. I'll give you three thousand apiece but not until the job's complete. Is that clear?'

'Mr Seth, I have to prove to them that I mean business. Could you not see your way clear to five hundred each now? That way they would know the deal was safe.'

There was a heavy pause on the line once

more. Antonio shifted from one foot to the other. The heat in the telephone box was unbearable, the fan didn't work and the midges were eating him alive. He didn't dare open the door for fear of someone overhearing the conversation.

'Very well then, you pay the men yourself for now, and I'll send the money down with a courier after the next delivery.'

'Thank you.'

'Don't let me down, or the consequences for your family will never end.'

Antonio went cold. Replacing the receiver, he realised he was shaking.

'That will be sixty-five rupees for the calls,' said the shopkeeper.

The dread at the back of his mind could not overshadow the amusement he felt at hoodwinking Seth. He laughed to himself. Two thousand rupees was plenty for each crew member, and the other six thousand he'd keep for himself and Jeena. The thought warmed him as he walked along the beach, not even hearing the sound of the lapping waves. He saw his men squatting on the sand, each shaded by a palm leaf. They were mending the cut netting, their deft sewing practised over many years. The bosun sat slightly apart, crouched under his own palm, smoking a biddi.

'Morning, Captain,' called the men.

'I've got something to say to you all.'

The men squatted in a circle, listening intently. With surprise and greed on their faces, they all nodded as Antonio outlined his version of the deal.

'Have we made a bargain then?'

'Yes!'

He was relieved at the unanimity of their enthusiasm. 'No one must know, not now, or ever. If the village came to hear, we would all be expelled, even from our families. Do you understand? Have I your word on this?' Antonio demanded.

'We swear,' they chorused.

'Swear on your ancestors and your future generations.'

'Yes, Captain, we swear.'

'Very well. You will each receive three hundred rupees after the next pick up. If any of you get drunk and start spending the money, boasting in the taverns, even in the next village, you will have me to answer to. Is that clear?'

They nodded. They knew Antonio and his fists.

'We have three weeks before the next full moon and pick up. Go about your duties as normal. We're fishing tomorrow. Get everything shipshape.'

As he walked away towards the village he could hear the men's excited babble. Inwardly he smiled.

Chapter Thirty-three

Joe and Rodriguez sat in their small office. They had been congratulating each other on another successful voyage. Their three sons were sleeping after a hard night's fishing, and now the two friends sat in silence, counting the takings from the catches. Placing the piles of rupees in the safe, Joe slammed its door. The large tumblers creaked, the lock shut and he put the key around his neck, feeling the cold steel against his hot skin. 'Let's have a brew.'

They sat opposite each other, sipping the steaming chai. Joe noticed the troubled look on his partner's face.

'What's up, my friend?'

Rodriguez looked thoughtfully across the desk. 'I'm not sure. Antonio's acting strangely ... can't quite put my finger on it, but something's up. He hasn't been the same since he returned from Mumbai.'

'He's always been a loner. You know this; you're his father.'

'I know, but something's happened.'

Joe hesitated before he continued. 'Look, Rodriguez, I've no wish to interfere, but there's something I think you should know.'

Rodriguez stared earnestly at his trusted friend and partner. 'If you know anything, please tell me.'

Joe stood up and turned away, looking out of the window. The estuary panned out before him peacefully.

'Antonio visited a lady in the Phoenix Hotel yesterday. Went up to her room, stayed several hours, and then she left to catch a flight back to Mumbai.'

'How do you know?'

'One of your distant cousins works on reception there. He recognised Antonio, told one of our fishermen and he told me. You know how our community operates, we're so tightly-knit nothing goes unnoticed.'

'Does anyone else know about it, Joe?'

'No, I told the fishing lad to keep his mouth shut. I also rang the hotel and spoke to your cousin and told him the same thing, but I'm afraid there's more.'

'Go on.' Rodriguez sat ashen-faced.

'I feel awful telling you this. I feel like a snitch in the dark.'

'Joe, you know I know differently. Please tell me.'

Joe sat down heavily. 'I went to the bar for a couple of fenis last night, just to ease my leg and eyes. You know how it is.'

Rodriguez threw him a sympathetic glance. His old friend didn't talk much about his ordeal from years before, but he knew he was often in a lot a pain.

'My usual haunt, Jack's Corner. I had a few drinks with the owner and after a while he casually mentioned Antonio making phone calls. He rang, then hung around for about an hour before ringing the same number again. Apparently he looked very flustered, paid his bill and then left. Took me several more drinks before I could prise the phone number out of him, but here it is. You know these STD phones, they record the phone numbers and every second, so they know how much to charge. He spent sixty-five rupees to call Mumbai.' Joe handed over the slip of paper with the Mumbai telephone number on it. 'It's probably a girl he's become infatuated with. You know how these things happen. She must be wealthy if she's flying to and from Mumbai. Perhaps your son

199

has hidden depths.' Joe reached over and slapped Rodriguez on the shoulder knowingly.

Rodriguez wished he could make light of the situation too. 'All the same, I think I'll phone his cousin, Angelo. Perhaps he can shed some light on the matter. I haven't told you all my side either. Antonio dropped a gambling piece the other day – a twenty-rupee chip ... told me he'd found it in Mumbai ... said he didn't know what it was. I could tell he was lying.'

Moments later, a leaden voice answered the long distance call. Rodriguez could tell that Angelo was heavy with sleep. He knew he would be surprised to hear from him, and even more surprised at his questions. He came straight to the point.

'Tell me, when Antonio stayed with you, what did you do together?'

'Nothing much; you know I work nights. He liked to be on his own anyway. I didn't have much to do with him really. You know how he is – conversation limited to good morning and good night. That's if I saw him at all. He usually left before I went to work and got home after I went to bed. By the way, the new suit he had made – should I send it down or keep it here? He did say to hang onto it for the time being, but ...'

'Antonio will tell you what he wants doing with it. Hang onto it for now, please.' Rodriguez didn't want to arouse Angelo's suspicions too much. After several minutes of family small talk he replaced the receiver and relayed their conversation to Joe.

'There you are, then. Never knew he was a one for the ladies. A dark horse, that one.'

'Nevertheless, a new suit, a gambling chip, I hope she's not leading him on.'

'By golly, I hope she is! Do the lad a world of good, seeing the bright lights of the big city and the colourful women. It will put hairs on his chest,' Joe laughed. He, of course, had never seen any of these things himself.

Rodriguez returned his laughter but was still uneasy. 'Let's not mention any of this to the family, especially his mother.'

They shared a conspiratorial roll of the eyes as they thought of how Rosa Diaz would react, then Joe turned out the light and shut the office door behind them. Rodriguez carefully placed the piece of paper with the phone number in his back pocket.

Chapter Thirty-four

The weeks sailed by with the winds and the tides until the new moon touched the midnight sky. Antonio and his crew made ready for the next rendezvous.

'Right then! Keep your eyes open! The first to spot it buys the drinks for the rest of us.' The crew all laughed. The captain was in fine fettle. 'Let go the nets. Let's hope we have a quick and heavy catch.'

As the night wore on, the men toiled, heaving the netting over the sides, filling the fish tanks, re-furling the nets, swabbing the decks, keeping the boat shipshape. The charcoal burner glowed eerily red in the moonlight, keeping them supplied with food and chai. When they had finished their chores and sat squatting on the deck sipping their tea, they heard the distant sound of a foghorn. A ghost ship moved silently across the still waters, visible only by its faint lights.

The men rose, throwing the remains of the scalding tea over the side. Antonio gunned the engine motor, heading towards the gliding lights, the same co-ordinates still fresh in his memory. The sea was calm, just a slight rise and fall as the undulating waves headed towards shore many miles away. The bosun sat on the wheelhouse roof, his unblinking eyes staring straight ahead. Suddenly he banged on the rooftop with his fist. There, straight ahead, a yellow light blinked on and off. The ghost ship disappeared over the horizon, swallowed by the vast indifferent ocean.

The chai wallah knocked on the cabin door, opened it and stepped through, the dripping life jacket hanging from his upturned hand.

Antonio took it from him carefully. 'Tell the men "well done".'

The deckhand's face broke into a broad grin and he smiled with pride for being praised.

Antonio turned the wheel to port. 'Go and tell the men to prepare for shore.' The boat left behind a luminous trail as it did an arcing u-turn, heading for home.

The next night at nine he telephoned from Jack's Corner. 'It's here.'

'Good. At noon tomorrow go to the Hotel Apollo in Colva and ask for room 211. Someone will be waiting and will have the men's deposit with them. You have done well so far.'

The line went dead.

Noon tomorrow. An eternity away. Antonio couldn't sleep. Tossing and turning in his small single bed, exotic images of Jeena kept flashing through his mind

Eventually dawn cracked the darkness, sending slivers of warmth darting across the sands. He watched the glow creep up his window, covering his room with bright light. Restless and impatient, he got up, dressed, and wandered down to the shoreline, walking towards his arranged destination, every step taking him closer to his darling love. The clock ground the time away. He had forgotten to eat, drink or bathe.

'Room 211. Please could you say that Antonio has arrived.'

The desk clerk raised a superior eyebrow. He stood there in his air-conditioned foyer, self-important in his tailored uniform with silk tie and unruffled white shirt; brass buttons shone in the spotlights. 'Are you sure you are expected?' He wrinkled his nose at this smelly individual.

'Ring 211.' Antonio could feel his anger rising.

The clerk reluctantly lifted the receiver. 'There's a gentleman here, says he's expected.' He looked at Antonio. 'Name, sir?' Antonio told him again and the clerk replaced the receiver. 'Go right up. Second floor, turn right. 211 is on your right.' The clerk prayed that he would not meet any other guests on his way up.

Antonio knocked at the door, a bunch of wild flowers he had picked hidden behind his back. He heard the muffled, 'Come in.' As he burst through the door the light in his eyes dimmed and the smile on his face disappeared.

'God, you smell horrible,' said Mohan.

'I was hoping for a bath.'

'You must be joking. Have you got the package?'

Antonio fumbled in his pocket and held it out in front of him. Mohan snatched it from his hand.

'What are you going to do with those flowers, eat them?'

Antonio dropped them on the thick carpet. 'Where's Jeena?'

'She's not available; too busy with one of Mr. Seth's special clients. Here!' Mohan tossed an envelope at him, hitting him on the chest.

'What's this?'

'Your deposit, you fool.'

In his confusion and deep disappointment, Antonio's anger got the better of him. He may only be a fisherman, but he was not a fool and no one was going to call him one. And where was Jeena? Releasing his pent-up frustration, he charged forward, butting Mohan squarely in the chest, then he jerked his head upwards, catching Mohan full in the face, breaking his nose. The charge smashed them through the bathroom door. He watched mindlessly as Mohan reeled backwards into the bath, cracking his head against the wall tiles. Antonio's clubbed fists smashed into him again and again, and he cried out angrily as he relentlessly beat him, the blood from the wounds spraying the tiles a vivid red until Mohan knew no more.

As the fog began to clear inside his head, Antonio stood there breathing heavily, staring at the creature looking back at him from the mirror. He was covered in blood. He began to recognise himself. Shaking violently, he looked down at the disfigured body lying in the tub. Its face was mashed to a bloody pulp.

'What have I done?' Panic began to set in. 'Feel for a pulse! Control yourself! Feel for a pulse, you fool!' he berated himself. He felt Mohan's heart and the beat within his chest. 'Thank God! I thought he was dead. Steady now. Think. Must phone Seth. He'll know what to do. Wait! Wash yourself first. Don't drip blood everywhere; wash yourself.' He realised he was talking out loud.

Stripping quickly, he stepped into the shower, watching the blood course its way down his body and trickle down the plughole. Towelling himself dry, he rinsed out his fishing clothes in the sink. Then, putting them back on, he dripped his way to the telephone and asked for a Mumbai number.

After several rings, he heard Seth's voice. 'Yes, who is it?'

'Mr Seth, it's Antonio. There's been a terrible accident.' His hand trembled as he held the receiver.

'What's happened?'

Antonio stumbled over the words. 'Mohan fell into the bath … He's injured himself … badly. What shall I do?'

There was a pause before Seth's reply. 'Is he dead?'

'No, I just can't get him to wake up.' He repeated his question, panic beginning to overtake him. 'What shall I do?' Everywhere he looked there was blood.

'Can you get out of the hotel? Is there a fire exit?'

'I think so.' How was he meant to know? He'd never set foot in the hotel before.

'Don't give me "think so", you idiot, go and have a look. I'll wait.'

Opening the door gingerly, Antonio peered each way down the corridor. There at the end of the hallway was a door with a metal lever arm and FIRE EXIT stamped in red lettering on it. He returned to the phone. 'Yes, Mr Seth, there's a fire exit.'

'Now listen to me very carefully. Telephone down to room service. Order something. Make sure it's delivered to the room. Take both packages. I'll make arrangements to pick up my parcel. Room service will call an ambulance. I'll take care of the rest. Just make bloody sure you're not seen as you leave the hotel, do you understand? Go home and hide the packages. Ring me tomorrow and act normal, do you hear me?'

Antonio replaced the receiver, hoping he could remember all these instructions.

He heard the noise of the siren as the ambulance screeched to a halt outside the hotel. He turned the corner and as calmly as he could, walked down to the beach and into the sea, trying to cleanse himself once more. His hands began to throb, and through the bruising, he gradually came back to life.

'Mr Seth, is everything all right?'

'All right?' Seth yelled down the phone the next day. It was time to make the peasant squirm a little. 'What on earth possessed you?'

'I'm sorry, Mr Seth. I was looking forward to seeing Jeena, and Mohan started disrespecting me once too often. I lost my temper.'

'Well you made a good job of him. It'll take him some time to recover. You realise, don't you, that he's lost his right eye and you almost killed him?' He paused, waiting for this information to sink in. That should frighten the idiot. Better not be too hard on him though; he still needed him. He smirked into the telephone. 'Oh well, perhaps it will improve his appearance. Maybe I should hire you as one of my bodyguards.' He could tell Antonio did not know how to react to this change of tone. Good. Time to get to the serious stuff.

'Do you realise you've put the whole operation under threat? Do anything like this again and you'll be in Mohan's place. You're very fortunate the police aren't looking for you; they agreed with your version of events – slipped in the bath, nasty accident. But you're five thousand rupees out of pocket. That's what it cost to clear this mess up and it will come out of your first payment. Rajeed's on his way down. Meet him at the station and give him the package. He'll be on the four fifteen from Mumbai. Don't be late.' He replaced the receiver.

'He's a wild card. Next package, you're going to meet him. I'll take no excuses this time. Hear me?'

'He makes me shudder.' Jeena put her hand up to her throat involuntarily.

'I don't care. I've been too soft on you.' Standing up quickly Seth reached over and slapped her hard across the face. 'I'm not paying you for your likes and dislikes. I'm paying you for your expertise horizontally. Now, get out.'

She turned away, masking the look of hatred in her eyes. As she closed the door behind her, she gently rubbed the angry red welt on the side of her face.

Chapter Thirty-five

Rodriguez sat smoking his pipe and staring moodily into the fire. Many thoughts were passing through his mind. Was his son having an affair with this woman? Who was she? How did they meet? Who were her family? What about the gambling chip – was she somehow connected with that? Absent-mindedly he took the piece of paper from his pocket. Should he ring the number and find out? If she answered, what would he say? He didn't even know her name. Tapping his pipe on the side of the hearth, he suddenly thought, of course, the Phoenix would know her name. His cousin would know it; it would be in the register at reception. It was a start anyway.

Rosa Diaz looked quizzically across the room at Rodriguez. 'Are you all right, my husband? You're sitting there very quietly this evening.'

He quickly pocketed the scrap of paper, which did not go unnoticed by his wife. She chose to say nothing.

'I'm sorry my darling, I've been going over the office accounts in my mind.'

'Dinner is ready. Please, let's sit together this once. You can say grace and tell me about your day.' She watched as the frown left his face and he smiled at her.

'Why, of course, that would be very nice for a change.'

Joe shuffled back from his office to the house he shared with Pedro, Maria and the children. He loved this house, a bungalow built after the marriage of the two young lovers on the strength of the profits from the prawn haul. On top of a hill near the village, with enough room for them all, it had running water and electricity – never heard of before in that area. With approval from Father Alphonso, Pedro and Maria had named the new house Holy Cross Bungalow and Rodriguez, so impressed with this building over-looking the sea, had had one built right next to it for his family.

Pedro was sitting at the table, writing up the ship's log. 'Good evening, Father.' He stood up, towering above Joe by at least a foot, his frame fit and muscular, his jet black hair shining in the firelight, his piercing green eyes, inherited from his mother, full of fun and merriment. 'Let me help you.'

Joe smiled as his son took the crutch and placed it against the wall.

'We have fish curry and rice tonight. Maria says it won't be long.'

'The fish-finder has become quite a success. Rumours abound because of the size of our catches.' They laughed, sharing the enjoyment of their latest venture. 'Have the other captains worked out what we are using?'

'Not yet, Father, and soon we'll be able to fit out our other two ships.'

'Rodriguez and I are glad you all fish together at the moment, but with all three of you fitted out you will each be independent.'

Pedro smiled wryly.

'Why are you smiling, son?'

'Antonio, ever alone, fishes alone. Cristiano and I stick together.'

'How does that work?'

'Simple, Father. When the first shoal is sighted with the machine, Antonio peels off, wishes us good hunting and off he goes … keeps in contact by radio.

He went off on his own the very first voyage and that's how it has remained. He fishes successfully and his crew seem happy; their families' bellies are full.'

Joe brooded on this information, wanting to question his son further. Was this linked to Antonio's other strange behaviour, he wondered. At that moment Pedro's children burst into the room.

'Hello Papa, hello Grandpa. Will you play with us, Grandpa?' they pleaded.

'After dinner,' Pedro commanded.

Maria walked in carrying two large steaming pots. 'Sit down, please. Children, go and play elsewhere. Shoo! Be off with you!'

The men sat opposite each other, palm leaves placed before them. Maria ladled mounds of steaming basmati rice onto the leaves, followed by hot dark fish curry. The men began to one-handedly mould the rice and curry together into bite-size chunks.

'My, this is good.' Fish sauce was running from the corner of Joe's mouth.

A smile of pleasure crept across Maria's face. 'Hush now and eat your food.'

The men began to discuss their favourite subjects: winds and tides, the repairs needed to maintain their crafts, the price of fish and everything to do with their way of life. They could hear the children playing in the yard, waiting their turn to eat.

Antonio skulked around the village, waiting for the opportunity to slip away unnoticed and walk the seven miles into town to meet Rajeed. It was not difficult and he got to the station in good time for the train. Sitting waiting, head down, quietly brooding to himself, he failed to notice people staring at his hands, which were resting in his lap. They were black, yellow and blue, with angry purple patches running between

211

his fingers. They still throbbed from the beating he had inflicted on Mohan.

He heard the train approaching the station long before it came into sight. As he stared down the track, heat waves shimmered back at him, distorting the shiny steel rails and the acacia trees surrounding them. The great train thundered into sight, all oily noise and roaring horn. Steel on steel screeched as the brakes slowed the great monster. The blackened-faced train driver hung out of his cabin, greasy ragged turban flapping. The wind tore around him and away until the train ground to a shuddering halt.

Antonio sat impassively on his bench, watching all the actions of passengers and vendors coming and going. A body blocked his view, and he looked up into the stony eyes of Rajeed.

'You have the package?'

Antonio reached into his deep trouser pockets, offering it up. Rajeed stared down at him. 'Give me one excuse and I'll kill you for what you've done to Mohan?'

Antonio's anger roused within him but he remembered Seth's words to him and just glared coldly back at Rajeed. 'If you try, I'll be ready. Don't underestimate me! It would be a pleasure to kill you for what you've done to me. If it wasn't for my need and love for Jeena, I wouldn't be in this mess.'

'You naïve fool!' Rajeed turned and clambered back on board the train, not looking back.

With those words ringing in his ears, Antonio could not shake off a feeling of foreboding. As he trudged the seven miles back to his village, he was locked in his own thoughts, as usual. Cars and lorries pounded their hooters; cyclists and pedestrians forced their way past him. He did not even notice the searing heat wafting around, stifling the very air he breathed.

Chapter Thirty-six

One week later, the ships set sail once more, all three in line as they sailed towards the mouth of the estuary and out into the open sea. The crew shouted good-humouredly to each other from one ship to another.

'Vijay, would you like me to take care of your wife if you don't come back tonight? I'm sure we'll make a lovely couple.'

'If she'd take you after me, she must be blind, my friend.'

The crews' laughter echoed and bounced off the waves, becoming lost in the wind. The three captains talked to each other on the ships' radios.

'Antonio, Pedro, be ever watchful,' Cristiano's voice echoed. 'Shore radio just warned me of a storm out to sea about one hundred miles away, heading nor' nor' west towards shore. Keep your eyes peeled. Don't wander too far, Antonio, and keep your lights on and your radio frequency open.'

'Aye, aye, Captain!' Antonio's sarcastic reply came over the radio.

About two hours later, after they had covered a distance of about twenty miles out towards the horizon, the radio crackled to life again in Antonio's cabin.

'Can you hear me, Antonio?'

He clicked the receiver button. 'Loud and clear.'

'Small shoal about half a league straight ahead. Should be enough for you.'

'Roger.' Antonio gunned his motor, leaving the other two boats behind. Half a league on, he ordered his men to pan the nets. The boat slowed as the netting dragged it back. Pedro and Cristiano's vessels sailed past, hooting their foghorns as they went.

The radio crackled again. 'Stay in touch. Just traced a large shoal about one league away off your starboard. Keep your lights on. The storm hasn't moved. Still nor' nor' west of us. Roger.'

'Good fishing. See you at dawn.'

'Keep your radio on this frequency and keep in touch. Roger and out.'

His third pick up, Antonio thought excitedly, only two to go. After this one, he would phone Jeena and ask her to meet him. Perhaps Mr Seth would send her for the package. He would ask him. He did not want another showdown like the last.

The night drew around them, masking the storm.

'Shore watch to Pedro and Antonio. Can you hear me?'

Pedro confirmed instantly that he could.

'Antonio, can you hear me?'

No reply. Only the crackle of the speaker.

'If you can hear me but can't reply, click your handset twice.' The eerie insistent crackle from the speaker droned on.

'Antonio here. Sorry, brother.'

'Why didn't you answer my call?'

'I'd just left the wheelhouse for a moment. Bosun needed my help.'

'Well, at least you're answering now. Heave to your nets. You too, Pedro. The storm's turned and is heading straight for us. Looks pretty bad.'

'How long before it hits us?' Pedro tried to keep his voice calm.

'Forty minutes at the most. If we all run for home now, we might just skirt the edge of it. Are we fit to go? Roger,' echoed from the speaker.

'I've ordered the men to hurry; the nets were three-quarters in anyway.' Pedro sounded brisk and business-like.

'I'm just hauling in,' Antonio confirmed.

'Well, hurry up. We'll untangle them on shore. Leave the fish in the nets. Roger.'

'It'll still take twenty minutes.'

'Turn away from your netting and run for home. As you refurl your nets, you should make up some time. Roger.'

Antonio fixed the wheel once more and ran to the aft deck, grabbing two axes from their holders as he went. 'Bosun!' he shouted, the sound never reaching its intended recipient. Antonio could feel the power of the waves as the gathering storm hurled towards them. The ship began to lurch up and down and side to side and he swayed with the rhythm. Walking steadily along the moving deck, he bellowed again. This time the bosun heard his captain, though the winds were getting fiercer as the moments passed.

Cupping his hand to the bosun's ear, he shouted, 'We're going to cut loose the nets – you port, me starboard. We haven't got time to haul them back in.'

'But Captain, the catch is huge.'

'Don't argue with me, do as you're told. We'll just have time to run with this wind to our rendezvous point. We are not missing that, do you hear me?'

'Aye, Captain.'

'Now go! We must cut together, or the ship could slur into the waves and be swamped. Is that clear?'

The first storm wave hit the bow, reaching out with its cold fist and covering the whole ship in water. Both in their positions, legs splayed wide, axes high above them, they felt the boat shudder with the weight. The others sailors, seeing what was about to happen, braced themselves. Antonio gave the signal and they brought their axes down together, cutting through the hemp ropes. The boat leapt forward with the loss of the drag. Antonio rushed for the wheelhouse, unleashed the wheel and fought the waves. Turning the wheel, his powerful body willed the ship to run with the wind.

The bosun gathered the crew behind the wheelhouse. 'Hold on, men!' he shouted, nestling in the lee of the cabin, shielding his men from the worst of the storm.

'What's your position?' bellowed Cristiano from the speaker. 'Have you hauled in your nets?'

'Negative. We've had to sever and abandon them. We're trying to keep our nose into the waves. The storm's growing with every minute.'

'What's your position?'

'We're on the edge. It looks mighty black from here.'

'What are your options?'

'Not good. I feel our best chance is to ride it out. No good trying to turn, the waves would swamp us. It's all I can do to hold the bloody boat into the waves.'

'It should blow itself out in an hour or two. You hold on, my brother. I'll radio you every half hour. Good luck. Over and out.'

A giant wave rushed at them. The boat met the challenge, riding up the side of the watery mountain. As it reached the crest, Antonio saw the flashing yellow beacon not too far away. He banged on the glass window behind him and the bosun looked up from his protective haven. Antonio beckoned him and the bosun gingerly edged his way around the cabin, holding onto the brass handrail. He entered the wheelhouse just as another giant wave burst over the boat. The water pushed him forward into the cabin, sending him sprawling along the floor and following him in, slushing violently around the small wheelhouse.

Antonio left the wheel for a split second, putting all his weight and shoulder behind the door, slamming it shut. Turning, he grabbed the wheel just before it began to spin out of control. Looking down at the floundering bosun, he shouted above the roar, 'Beacon's dead ahead. Same co-ordinates as before.'

The bosun picked himself up from his watery landing. 'How are you going to retrieve it this time, Captain?'

'I'm not. You are.'

'How? It's blowing a gale force eleven out there.'

'Three of you can tie yourselves together. When you reach the gunnels the other two can follow. Use a grappling hook or gaff – whatever. We don't have long. This storm's worsening. Now go!'

Reluctantly the man left the relative safety of the cabin, retracing his footsteps back to his men.

'You there, and you – sorry, no time to ask for volunteers – lash yourselves together and follow me.' He didn't wait for an answer. Judging between the waves, he slid and slewed his way to the gunnels, the waves breaking violently all around him. The cold wind tried to tear the clothes from his body, and the noise was deafening. As he looked out beyond the ship his heart missed a beat. The sea rose all around them. Millions of tons of water towered above them. He watched as the white spume at the tops of the waves detached itself and raced off into the wind. Glancing back he saw the white trail as the engines worked overtime trying to keep them into the waves. His men slithered towards him, lashed together, the cord holding them as one person.

'Lash yourself to us, Bosun; three strengths are better than one.'

'No! I have to reach out and grab the beacon when we come upon it. Pass me that gaff and hold onto me. There, look!'

They all looked up at the blinking yellow eye high above them, sliding straight for them down a mountainous wave.

'Steady, men!'

The light raced at them, smashing into the side of the boat.

'Ready!'

The light began to move down and away from the boat. The two crew held their comrade by his trousers as he reached out, just snaring the lifejacket with the gaff.

'Steady!' he shouted into the wind. 'Steady!' His arm went taut as he snared his goal, pulling it towards himself.

He did not hear the anguished cries of his men, their warning lost to the wind as he hung out of the boat. The sea gods had decided his fate and a lesser wave crept along the vessel and plucked him over the side. His two shipmates held onto him, fighting his weight as they followed him over. The rope between them snared on the gunnels, leaving them dangling right out and over the side. The next wave picked them up and threw them back on board. Their ancestors did not need them just yet. Scrambling to their feet, they looked at the torn trousers they held in their hands.

'Man overboard! Man overboard!'

They could see the bosun desperately holding

on. At the last moment fortune appeared to favour him, lifting him back towards the boat.

'Get a grappling hook, quick!'

A third crew member scrambled into one of the waterproof lockers, reaching out in desperation. His hand closed around the four-pronged hook and a thirty-foot piece of strong rope.

'Hurry, he could be washed away from us at any moment!'

Slipping and sliding back to the side, they steadied each other. The bosun extended his arm towards them. Waves were washing over him every few seconds. One of the men threw the hook towards him. It arced outwards. Finding its mark, it dug into the life jacket, bursting the bosun's only form of support. They heard the whooshing sound as the air escaped from the lifesaver.

'He can't swim!'

The bosun scrambled desperately for the hemp rope, just feeling his fingertips on it. Then it was gone. Quickly they hauled it in. Up it came, with the grappling hook.

'Throw it again!' one cried desperately.

In his eagerness to save his comrade, he threw it too far, completely missing their target. A huge wave crashed down on the bosun, forcing him under. He thrashed his arms up and down, trying to regain the surface. His head appeared briefly. Another wave broke over him, pushing him further from the ship. Both men reached out for him, willing him back towards them. The life jacket, all torn and tangled strings, wrapped itself around him. The sea gods' fingers reached out for him, pulling him down into the abyss. They saw his wide-eyed terror as he disappeared for the last time. They did not see him helplessly sucking sea water into his lungs; they did not see him silently choking. All the crew saw was the flashing yellow light as it followed him into the depths.

The two men struggled to the cabin door, pushing their way in.

'Did you get it?'

'Bosun ...' they stammered.

'Speak up! What about the bosun?'

'He's gone.'

'Where, you idiot? Speak plainly now!'

'Lost overboard, Captain,' the other man answered.

'Overboard?' Antonio stared at them.

The two blurted out their story, one filling in what the other left out. Antonio stood there in silence, in shock himself, wondering what to do. His selfish thoughts came to the surface.

'Did you get the jacket?'

'It went down with him,' they explained again. 'It all happened so quickly. One minute he was there, the next – nothing.'

All Antonio could think of was the package and what he was going to tell Seth. Surely this was not the end? They would just have to wait another month. It couldn't make that much difference.

He forced his attention back to his men. 'Let's get our stories straight. He was washed overboard by a freak wave. You tried to save him, but he was washed away. Is that clear? Stick to this story and all will be well.'

Another great wave crashed into the boat, bringing his attention back to the task in hand. Steadying the boat up into the waves once more, he grabbed the microphone. Clicking down on the receiver he gave the distress signal.

'Mayday! Mayday! Man overboard!'

The receiver crackled. Nothing. He tried again. Then he heard his brother's anxious voice.

'Receiving you. What happened? Are you all right? Over.'

'I'm fine, lost our bosun, washed overboard.' He was surprised how little emotion he felt. He had known this man for years, knew his wife and children, watched as they grew up. He felt nothing.

'Is everyone else OK? Over.'

'Yes, storm's still heavy, wind's running about thirty knots, but the boat's holding well – as long as the engine holds up.'

'Could we find him when the storm dies down?'

'No chance. The crew watched him go down, said he sunk like a stone – couldn't swim.'

'We'll have to tell his family. That's not going to be a pleasant task. Storm should break in about an hour. I'll radio you again. Good luck, brother. Over and out.'

The line went dead.

The storm eventually released the ship from its grasp. Tired and weary, Antonio turned the boat for home. The crew stoically went about their duties. They knew the bosun's fate could at any time be their own. They prayed in their minds to the gods of fate, the superstitions of their trade holding them in pitiable fear.

Their captain eased the boat alongside the jetty. The men sat in silence, knowing what was to come. People from the quayside clambered aboard, a thousand unanswered questions pummelling their ears. A police sergeant took a statement from Antonio.

After a while, the battered sailors trundled slowly towards their meagre dwellings, seeking comfort from their women and the open fires in their hearths. Wearily they collapsed in their cots, falling into nightmarish dreams.

Chapter Thirty-seven

'Mr Seth, we lost the package and a good man last night.'

'What do you mean you lost the package? How?' Shock registered in Seth's voice. Antonio explained patiently, going over details as Seth cross-examined him.

'I don't believe this! It had everything fitted to it: GPS, radar, lights – every tracking device man has invented. It's impossible for this to happen. How could you lose it? You couldn't have.'

'We didn't lose it. It sunk.'

'Impossible!'

'Mr Seth, the men tried everything to retrieve it, and the man hanging onto it for dear life. Surely we can run again, it's only another month.'

'You just don't understand, do you, you moronic imbecile! … I'll have to make some phone calls. Stay where you are. Phone me in two hours.'

Two hours later, the phone only rang once before it was picked up.

'You'll have to come to Mumbai. We need to speak to you here.'

'That's impossible, Mr Seth. How would I explain my absence? Everyone would know something was up. Anyway, I haven't got the money.'

'You mention money at this juncture?' A sarcastic laugh burst down the phone, making Antonio's ears ring. 'You get here, do you hear me? I don't care how you do it, just get here.'

'No. I'm sorry, but my family would never forgive me if they found out. No.'

The line went silent for what seemed like an

eternity. 'Are you still there, Mr Seth?'

'Talk to no one. You will hear from me.' The line went dead.

All it would take was one more trip. What was the matter with the man? Antonio wandered off in the general direction of his favourite little seafront restaurant where one of the waitresses had a saucy wiggle.

Roshan Seth paced back and forth in his office. He was in too deep to pull out. His debts were mounting astronomically. The contact sending the packages was waiting for payment for the third drop. The consortium was waiting for delivery, the money already dispatched. Once more, he wondered about the real market value of this project and what the whole consignment was worth. He also worried about how the contact in China would react to the loss of this package?

The phone rang, startling him. Rushing to his desk he snatched the receiver from its cradle. He heard the long distance click as the call connected. He heard the calm voice at the other end of the line.

'Is that you, Seth?'

'Yes.'

'You left an urgent message for me to call. I expressly forbade you to ring me, unless we have an emergency.'

'Believe me, we have an emergency. Are we free to speak?' The scramble button on his phone was already depressed.

'We are clear. Tell me the problem.'

Seth relayed the news, answered the questions, the counter-questions, the recriminations, the debate.

'I'll check for any satellite sightings,' the cold, calm voice finally stated at the other end. 'If we're being double-crossed, I'll know.'

The international line died. Seth replaced the receiver. He felt his designer silk shirt sticking to his perspiring torso. His hand trembled as it left the receiver.

Antonio wandered back to the village, where preparations for the funeral were taking place despite the absence of a body. The bosun's wife was inconsolable in her sorrow. The black kohl of her eyes ran down her cheeks, giving her the eerie look of a mannequin doll. She tore at her hair, pulling out great chunks at the roots as she staggered around the village in her grief. The other women, her relations among them, followed her around, their combined wailing not helping matters.

The men squatted in small groups, silently smoking their cob pipes and biddis, reflecting on their small community's sorrow. It could be any one of them next. No children played, no dogs barked, not a cat could be found; they all sensed the gravity of the situation. The empty coffin would be buried that afternoon, as was the custom.

Antonio squatted with the men of his family, head bowed. It was funny really, how you could work with a man for so long and never know his name. He realised he had only ever known him as "Bosun". His silent thoughts wished the man a seat among the sea gods: *May you have prime fish and a pick of the mermaids. If all is well send a message with the dolphins.*

The phone shrilled in Roshan Seth's office once more. He depressed the scrambler button. A disjointed voice sounded far away.

'Something is not quite right.'
'What do you mean?'

'The satellite signal disappeared from the monitoring screen at precisely 3.35a.m. your time. I don't understand. It could not just disappear. It had too much equipment on board. Something would have surfaced – GPS reader, homing device, bleeper – something would have survived.'

'What do you want me to do?'

'I have spoken to the people your end. They want that package. They want you to go and interrogate that little fisherman friend of yours. See if he had other ideas. Or may I say, with a word of warning, we all hope your own ambitions haven't outgrown your usefulness.'

Seth spluttered down the phone. 'No, no, believe me, I have your best interests in mind. I wouldn't do anything like that.'

'Time will tell, my friend. Time will tell.'

The line died in Seth's hand. His anger rose. 'Mohan! Rajeed!' he bellowed through the closed door.

They both shuffled in and stood passively awaiting their orders. Mohan's face was still an angry purple and yellow, his missing eye covered with a leather patch, the other side of his face angrily swollen. Several of his teeth were still loose in his gums. He couldn't eat properly and he had not slept well since his beating. His temper flared at the slightest provocation.

'We're going to see our little friend in Goa.' Seth saw Mohan's good eye light up in anticipation. 'Seems something is not quite right. Three flights a.s.a.p.! No, wait, make that four; we'll take him a little sweetener.'

Mohan grinned through clenched teeth and pain.

The funeral took place as the custom dictated. Father Alphonso led the procession from the church to the grave site.

These wailing women! thought Antonio, as their tears coursed down their faces. Where does it all come from? Isn't there enough salt water in the sea?

After the burial the dead man's wife was led away by her relatives. The rest of the village split into reflective groups, entered their dwellings and remained in mourning. Maria and her mother served their men hot chai, each lost in their own thoughts.

Joe broke the silence. 'Why was the bosun away from the protection of the wheelhouse?'

Antonio looked up, startled. 'What did you say, sir?'

'Why was the bosun by the gunnels, the most dangerous place to be?'

All the men looked directly at Antonio, who squirmed in his seat trying to think of an answer.

'I don't know. I was doing my best not to lose the ship; we'd already lost the nets. I honestly don't know. You'll have to ask the men. Perhaps he was being sick.' He knew this was a ridiculously stupid and lame answer, and wished he'd kept his mouth shut.

Seth's party booked into the Phoenix Hotel, not far from Antonio's village.

'Tomorrow we'll visit our little fishing friend and see what he's been up to.'

Mohan and Rajeed patted their heavily laden pockets and smiled. Jeena sat on the sofa, watching these dangerous men, wishing she knew what was going on.

Chapter Thirty-eight

The next day at dawn, news reached the village that the cast off netting had been seen floating aimlessly about fifteen miles out. Cristiano called his brother and Pedro together. 'I think we should go now and retrieve it.' The others nodded their agreement.

Joe stretched, scratching the scars on his face absentmindedly. 'You know, I think I could do with a trip myself. Don't see why we should disturb the men today. It is Sunday.'

Rodriguez laughed. 'What you mean is you don't fancy leaving all those fish out there to waste, you old rogue.'

They all laughed.

'Count me in,' he continued. 'I could do with the wind in my face for a change.' He turned to Cristiano. 'Have you got the co-ordinates?'

'As good as they could give me, allowing for wind and tide. I think we have a good chance of saving the nets.'

'Antonio, we'll take your boat. Go and refuel.' Rodriguez naturally took the lead. 'If we're lucky, your nets can go straight on board. Pedro, tell the men to stay with their families. Joe, organise some food from our women; we might be gone some time. The estuary is full; the gods are on our side. Let's hurry now.'

Joe shuffled towards the kitchen. He could already smell cooking. Maria stood with the children playing happily around her feet.

'You heard the conversation?'

'Of course. The food should be ready before you leave. It will be cold when you eat it, but that can't be helped.'

'It will still be as delicious as always.'

Maria smiled to herself. Joe was always complimentary and kind. When he was around her she sensed his need for female company, his old losses very near the surface. She looked on him as a daughter would, rather than a daughter-in-law.

With the boat made ready, they all clambered on board, the older men acting as crew. Casting off the mooring ropes, Rodriguez and Joe stood in the stern, feeling the wind as it coursed through their hair.

'My, this feels good. Reminds me of times gone by.'

'Do you miss this, Joe, my friend?'

'Sometimes – times like this – but not the heavy waves and cold winds.'

'Look at the boys working together,' Rodriguez observed. 'We've waited many years for such a moment as this: our fine sons, our grandchildren, the business running smoothly. Our lives are complete.'

'Not quite.' Joe looked at his friend with his good eye.

'What do you mean?'

Joe leaned forward so as not to shout. 'Maria's pregnant again. Pedro only told me this morning. Keep it to yourself for now.' He raised his finger to his lips.

Rodriguez smiled. 'Congratulations. We'll drink to the baby's health tonight.'

'Birds!' Cristiano shouted, pointing ahead. All five men searched the skyline. Diving birds this far out could only mean one of two things: a shoal or the nets.

'Steady as she goes,' ordered Rodriguez. 'Let's not get tangled. Half ahead and keep a lookout; there could be large predators feasting unseen. All hands to grappling hooks. And keep your hands on the surfaces.'

Sure enough, right in front of them the stagnant nets rose up and down with the waves. The birds hovered above them, screeching their protests. The sea lay deathly quiet on the swell, just the breathing of the ocean. Gently the men reached over and ensnared the net. The many fish, trapped but still alive, splashed their presence. Tentatively, the men began to draw the heavy mesh towards them. Trapped air bubbles rose from the deep. Hand over hand, they began to pull the heavy mass towards the prow, while Rodriguez and Pedro waited to lash the tangled mesh as best they could to the winding gear. The motor whined in neutral. Cristiano suddenly stopped dead, still peering down into the moving waters. A slight reflection deep down had caught his attention. He did not take his eyes from the surface.

'Let go netting! Stand back!' he shouted to Antonio who took the order and complied.

An almighty roar disrupted the surface. A great shark's mouth opened and closed on a trapped sea bass weighing about twenty pounds. Blood whooshed up from the stricken fish, splashing the deck. Most of the large fish disappeared down the shark's gullet. Some netting became entangled on its teeth. As the great fish re-entered the sea, the whole edifice moved with it. Realising its trapped predicament, it began to struggle, turning the sea to foam, thrashing backwards and forwards. The men in the boat watched with fascination. Joe went white, remembering his ordeal of years before. The instinctive hunter finally let go and disappeared back beneath the waves. All was silent once more.

'Well, that was interesting.' Pedro tried to make light of the situation.

They all laughed, mostly with relief, and agreed to try again. They attached the nets to starboard and the windlasses brought the whole lot on board, yard by yard. They separated the dead fish from the living and threw them back overboard. The cries and screeches from the birds as they gorged themselves were deafening. The men took no notice as they sorted the different fish into separate tanks.

Maria watched as the ship cleared the estuary and sailed out of sight, then turned and gathered her children, all dressed in their Sunday best, she herself in a long dress she kept just for their church outings. Already the organ had begun to play. The hymn warmed her as she steered the children into the church, nodding to the neighbours as she ushered her little ones towards their usual pew.

All around her, voices rose in song. The men were in their best outfits, women in the colourful dresses of the region or saris, boys in crisp white shirts and black shorts, and girls in frilly dresses with puffed sleeves. The altar burned brightly with tallow candles, the statue of the Madonna and Child looking down on them all. The priest in his Sunday vestments stood in the pulpit, his hands either side of a huge bible, already open. The organ grew silent and the incense burners were waved side to side by robed altar servers. The choir waited patiently. The priest raised his hands. 'Let us pray.' The whole congregation knelt, bowing their heads. The children giggled.

'Mohan and Rajeed, you've been following Antonio for weeks. Go down to the village. All the fools will be in their church by now. Search his room thoroughly, even if you have to tear the place apart. I want that package.'

Mohan and Rajeed entered the deserted village. A few dogs barked, keeping their distance. The two men went straight to Antonio's room.

'It's locked.'

'Well kick it down.'

Rajeed kicked at the lock with his foot. The door swung back, cracking on the back wall. They entered, trying to adjust their eyes to the gloomy interior.

'Start with that cupboard by the wall. I'll check out the bed,' suggested Mohan.

Slowly and methodically they took the room apart, leaving nothing unturned or unbroken. The interior of the mattress spilled from its casing, swelling over the sides of the bed and onto the floor; cupboard doors hung off broken hinges; slivers of glass cascaded across the floor. All Antonio's everyday things lay strewn around. Nothing.

Mohan scratched his head. 'There's got to be something. Start again. If we go back empty handed Seth will kill us.'

Maria opened her eyes right in the middle of the prayers. Had she taken the cauldron off the fire? Earlier on she'd been boiling the children's clothes. If that boiled dry, not only would the clothes be ruined, but it could set the house alight. Had she taken it off? She really couldn't remember. Turning to her praying neighbour, she nudged her in the ribs. 'I have to leave. I'll explain later.' The woman nodded. 'Stay here,' Maria said softly to her sons. 'Stay with Aunty.'

The boys, kneeling with hands placed firmly together in front of them, turned their heads and opened one eye, looking at the other woman. She nodded towards them reassuringly. Maria stood up and side-stepped her way out of the pew. She looked at Father Alphonso, who quizzically returned her look, bent her knee and crossed herself, turned and left. Hurriedly she ran through the village, taking the door key from round her neck as she went.

Opening the door, she saw the cauldron sitting on the floor next to the fire. Silly woman, she berated herself, hands on hips. Now she remembered: she'd taken it off just before they left for church, not wanting to scald the children. What with the men putting to sea, it must have gone clean out of her mind. She would have to explain to Father Alphonso later.

She sat down at the kitchen table. How quiet it was – no screaming, playing children, no husband, no father-in-law. She sat there, enjoying the silence, so rare in her life. Perhaps she would make some sweets for the boys. She rubbed her tummy, the little life inside her warming her.

A muffled crash reached her through the wall. A dog barked its warning. What on earth was that, she wondered, as the wind carried gruff male voices towards her. She heard another crash and more harsh words. Her curiosity roused, she stood and looked out of the window. The door to Antonio's room swung half off its hinge. A figure moved across the doorway. Who's that?

She left the sanctuary of her own home, moving stealthily towards the noise. Reaching the entrance she peered inside, shielding and squinting her eyes in the dark interior. A man, his back to the door, knife in hand, slashed at the mattress. Maria unconsciously moved forward, trying to pierce the gloom. Someone else entered from another room and saw the figure in the doorway, hand raised and silhouetted in the harsh light.

'Mohan, watch out!'

Mohan turned on his blind side, half seeing

something in the doorway. He reached into his pocket and, still turning, fired instinctively. The roar of the gun in the confined space was deafening. Cordite smoke billowed from it, making them cough. The figure in the doorway moved towards them, hands held out in front. Defensively, Mohan fired again, stopping the figure in its tracks.

'Who is it?'

'It's a woman.' The shock registered in Rajeed's voice.

Maria could not move. She felt the warmth running down her thighs. Everything seemed to be happening in slow motion. 'My baby, please God, not my baby,' she whispered anxiously. She felt no pain. 'Why can't I move? What do you want?'

Blood began to ooze between her breasts. It was as if she'd been punched. She reached up, tracing the outline of the small hole, and felt the stickiness on her hand as she moved it away and put it up to her face. A pool of blood formed at her feet and a red tentacle trickled towards the two men. She coughed. Blood ran down her chin. She began to tremble uncontrollably as she sank to the floor. 'My best dress ruined ... My poor children ... I must get back ... the sweets will burn ...'

'What have you done?' screamed Rajeed. His eyes darted around wildly in case they had been seen. Someone must have heard the shot.

'It's your fault! You warned me! You made me fire! Why did you make me fire?'

'I didn't. I was just warning you. Let's get out of here.' He tugged frantically at the floundering Mohan, who in their haste to escape, trod on the prostrate figure on the floor.

Inside the church, the two shots had stopped the congregation in mid-verse. The people began to murmur in their confusion. What was that? It sounded like gunfire. Father Alphonso hesitated and then took control.

'We'll go and have a look. Ladies and children stay here. You men, come with me.'

They burst through the church entrance, the intensity of the sun hitting them. Shading their eyes, they just had time to see two men running from the village.

Chapter Thirty-nine

Mohan and Rajeed burst into the hotel room. 'Mr Seth!'

Seth was furious. He sat up in bed, pushing Jeena roughly to one side. 'Get out!' He stopped to take in the complete panic in the other two and calmed his tone a little. 'What's happened?' He got out of bed not bothering to conceal his nakedness and lit one of his huge cigars. Jeena was forgotten.

'There's been a terrible accident, Mr Seth. One of the villagers is dead.'

Seth looked at them and could now see the blood on their clothes. 'What's happened?' he repeated more urgently.

'Mohan accidentally shot one of the villagers.'

'And you came straight to me? In that state? You fools! Why don't you just point a gun straight at my head, you blithering idiots? Get out!' He snatched up his wallet from the bedside cabinet, pulling out a wad of notes, not stopping to count them. 'Here, take this and hide until dark. Then make your way back to Mumbai. Don't talk to anyone, do you hear me? Now get out and get rid of those guns.'

The police, only a few buildings away from the hotel, took a call from the receptionist.

'I'm sorry to trouble you, Sergeant, but two of our guests have just dashed up to their rooms covered in blood. I thought you should know.'

'I wonder if this is related to the call I've just had from the parish priest. Seems there's been an incident in the village. The doctor's on his way now, and I've sent one of my men to investigate. I'll be with you in a couple of minutes.'

The receptionist heard the sergeant's shouts to his corporal, then the line went dead.

Mohan and Rajeed changed quickly, stuffing their stained clothing and guns into an overnight bag. Closing their room door quietly, they dashed down the stairs, colliding with the two police officers making their way up.

'Are you in a rush, gentlemen?' The sergeant and his corporal turned the men expertly around, painfully forcing an arm up each of their backs. 'Now stand still; we wouldn't like to hurt you.' The sergeant yanked Rajeed's arm even further upwards. 'I believe there are four of you. Where are the other two?'

'Room 234.' The receptionist, hovering at the bottom of the staircase, provided the information.

'Thank you. Now lead on.'

The police shoved them roughly up the stairs. With the room still unlocked, they entered quickly. Pushing Seth's two henchmen towards the middle, the two officers drew their guns. Seth and Jeena sat on the sofa, their dressing gowns pulled tightly around them, shock evident on their faces.

'What is the meaning of this, Sergeant?'

'Sorry to bother you, sir, but it seems you may have answers to some questions that I won't have until my man and the doctor get here from the village. If you will get dressed and follow us, I'm sure we can clear this up without much inconvenience to you both.'

Turning around he pointed his gun at the two accomplices. 'Corporal, 'cuff them, and take them to the station. Separate them. I want them in different cells. Don't let them speak to each other.'

He turned back to Seth. 'Now then, if you and your lady will get dressed, we will follow them.'

'Is this necessary, Sergeant? My wife and I are going nowhere.' Seth was thinking hard and desperately now. 'If you give us a little time, I'm sure we can clear this whole thing up.'

A thousand rupee note fluttered from Seth's pocket as he stood up and walked towards the bathroom. He looked down at it, feigning surprise. 'Is that yours, Sergeant? It seems you must have dropped it when you pulled your gun.'

'My, my, perhaps I did. Well, if you give me your word you won't leave the hotel, then I'm sure we can clear this up with my officer, sir.' The sergeant tucked the note into his pocket.

'I hope you can, Sergeant. If you do there will be ten more of those waiting in reception.'

'Did I hear you say fifteen, sir?'

'You surely did.'

'Thank you, sir. I hope you have a pleasant flight. Oh, by the way, I will take your details from reception. Good day to you both.' The sergeant and his corporal turned and left.

Silence ran through the village. A shock wave of grief surrounded the people. How could this happen here? Another death in Rodriguez's family. What had they done to deserve this? Rosa Diaz squatted next to her daughter's body, rocking backwards and forwards, tears streaming down her face. No sound came from her open mouth as the doctor tried to coax her away. The doorway was full of curious villagers as Father Alphonso issued Maria the last rites.

'Now, out you go. Please, go home.' The policeman tried to usher them away. The ambulance siren wailed as it turned into the village, stopping outside the hut. Entering with a stretcher, the paramedics tried to remove Maria's body.

'You're not taking my baby! Leave her alone!'
Rosa threw herself across the body, refusing to move.
She screamed at the top of her voice, her anguished
cries heard throughout the village, 'Leave her alone!
Leave her alone!'

The doctor took a syringe from his bag and
carefully placed the needle into a bottle of tranquiliser.
He siphoned off enough to calm her, squirted some of
the liquid into the air to remove any trapped bubbles,
and quickly plunged the needle into her outstretched
arm. The narcotic reacted almost immediately and he
felt her relax over the body, her head to one side.

'Help me remove her,' he instructed the
ambulance crew. 'Place her over there. I'll take care of
her. Now, take the body to the hospital. I want a full
autopsy. Tell them I'll be along later.'

Chapter Forty

Antonio's boat pulled alongside the jetty.

'Strange.' Cristiano spoke for them all. 'Where is everyone? The dock is deserted.'

Manhandling the fish themselves, they stacked them on blocks of ice, all the time aware of the uneasy silence. They finished their task, covering the fish with crushed ice and hessian sacks, then made their way back to the village. All was quiet. Something was wrong. The community was always full of noise and playful children. A village elder stepped out from the first building and came and stood in front of them.

'What's the matter, venerable father?' Joe asked for all of them.

'Pedro, your wife is dead.' He did not know how to say the words kindly.

Pedro stood dumbfounded. 'Don't be silly, I only left her this morning. Of course she's not.'

The wizened old man stepped forward and placed his hand on Pedro's shoulder. 'I'm sorry, my dear friend, and for you, Rodriguez Diaz.'

'How can this be? What's happened?' Joe spoke for his son and his friend as they stood in bewildered silence.

The old man, sticking to his directness, looked Joe straight in the eye. 'We believe she was shot.'

'Shot? What do you mean, shot? Who would do such a thing to such a sweet girl?'

'The police are here. The doctor's at the hospital now. We'll know in a short while.'

Pedro dropped the fish he was carrying. 'No! This can't be true! How can that be? I only left her this morning.' He stumbled into the village. 'Where is she?' His voice broke and tears began to stream down his face. 'No! Not my Maria! Please!'

Rodriguez's mind could not take in the enormity of the few words spoken. So final: *Maria is dead.* 'No, it can't be true!' He staggered forward, not feeling Joe supporting him. Involuntary tears welled up. He swallowed hard but they ran down his cheeks. His heart pounded in his chest.

Joe stumbled, his own emotions surfacing. It took all his strength to stop his friend from falling. Tears flowed from his good eye, sobs escaped from his lips. Who would do such a thing to his beautiful daughter-in-law? 'Come, my friend,' he said between clenched teeth, 'we must think of the boys.'

Rodriguez stopped swaying. 'The children. What will become of them with no mother?' He felt the same feeling he had had when he lost his son. The memory had been pushed to the back of his being, but now it resurfaced. He felt himself going mad. He could not make it this time. Where would he find the strength? It was too much for one man to bear. Age reached up for him and pulled him to the ground.

'Father, tell me it's not true, please, tell me it's not true.' Tears flooded from Cristiano's eyes. 'Not my baby sister.' He sat down heavily, his whole body in denial. The most beautiful person in the whole world, taken from them. Why would God allow such a thing? Perhaps she was too good for this world … so final, never to speak to her, or laugh with her again. Never to watch her, hands on hips, scolding the children, or see her hair blowing in the breeze as she waited by the jetty, waving as the boats came to rest. A deep sob left his chest. He placed his hands over his face and rocked back and forth, crying brokenly.

Joe heard Pedro's anguished cries from the village. He walked with leaden feet towards the sounds. His son would need him more than ever now.

'Where's her mother?' he asked the old man as they shuffled along.

'The doctor gave her something. He said she'd sleep at least until morning. It's a heavenly relief. She was hysterical.'

Cristiano and Rodriguez helped each other towards their own dwelling. Through his grief Cristiano knew they must be strong for the sake of his mother and the children.

Antonio, deathly white, stood rooted to the spot. Who would have done this to his family? Mr Seth would not do this. It was only one drop lost and they could make that up. No, this must have been robbers and bandits, come to rob the village. Not unknown. He'd phone Mr Seth in the morning. He'd know what to do. Why would anyone want to hurt his sister? She was too good to be harmed. 'I'll go for a walk and everything will be all right,' he said aloud to himself. 'Yes, that's a good idea.' Rubbing his hands together he began to walk away from the village. 'Everything will be all right tomorrow,' he repeated.

'I'm afraid she was shot in the stomach and in the chest. Went clean through her heart. Death would have been almost instantaneous. Dead before she hit the ground, poor thing.'

The chief of police took notes. 'When can we have the bullets for forensic reports? We've got two men locked up, two guns with fingerprints all over them and two shots fired from one of them, plus a suitcase full of bloodstained clothes. We hope to match that with the woman's blood type. If we match the riffling on the bullets, those bastards will swing, mark my words.'

'Are the family very close?'

'Yes, from what the priest tells me. I've only been here a couple of years myself. Came down from Delhi – climate's better.'

Maria's body lay on the mortuary's marble slab, waiting to enter the large filing cabinet of death. A label tied around her toe let the technicians know who she was.

'Put her in D92,' the coroner instructed. 'She'll be in there quite some time. It's a murder investigation. It'll be quite a while before the family can bury this one.'

The tray to the oversized cabinet closed on smooth rollers. Maria's body was cooled to a temperature that would prevent decomposition.

'Enter this one in the file, will you? I'm going home. If I 'm late again I'll be in trouble. Good night. See you tomorrow.'

No one in the village slept that night. Father Alphonso opened the church. Men, women and children knelt in the darkness, seeking solace from their spiritual centre. The priest blessed everyone and cried along with them. Nothing like this had ever happened before. It would be a long time, if ever, before the village could forget.

Chapter Forty-one

Rodriguez recovered sufficiently to help carry his wife to their bed. She did not stir, safe in her drug-induced state, the bliss of oblivion.

'If only it were me.' He sat down next to the bed, absently stroking her hair. Tears rained from him, soaking his bare chest. He stared at the empty wall opposite, seeing nothing, feeling everything. Time crept around slowly. He nodded off fitfully, waking with a start now and again. Remembering his agonies, he tried to disappear back into his nightmarish dreams.

Dawn woke him once more and he rubbed his sore eyes, forcing himself into consciousness. Glancing down at his wife, he tenderly covered her with their blanket. He tried to stand but his limbs would not respond. Rubbing and kneading his legs vigorously, he felt the blood pumping life back into them. Eventually he could stand up. Painful pins and needles tingled his feet and toes. Placing the kettle on the glowing embers, he stared into the fire, reliving the horrors of the day before.

Rosa screamed herself awake and he rushed over to her side. She was inconsolable. Great sobs tore themselves from her chest. 'My baby! My baby!' She rose, staring around the room with sightless eyes. She crashed into the furniture, cracking her shins on the bed. Nothing could stop her. She tore out her hair as her great cries of anguish pierced the air. Her deafening screams bounced off the walls. She dug her nails deep into her cheeks and the blood ran down to drip off her chin. Rodriguez grabbed hold of her. It took all his strength to hold her to him. She hit her head repeatedly against his chest as she cried herself out. He felt her go limp in his arms, her oblivion a blessed relief. He placed her back on the bed, at first recoiling from the pungent odours as he realised she had lost control of her bodily functions. Gently he removed her wet and stained undergarments, throwing them into a plastic bucket. He washed her and ran a comb through the ends of her shiny hair, remembering how beautiful she had been when they first met. He recalled their wedding day and the moment she lifted her veil. The depth and twinkle in her eyes had taken his breath away. After their first fumbling together, his own urgent need overriding hers, she had calmed him, teaching him the less urgent, greater pleasure. Their mutual shyness slowly turned to deep love and the miracle of their first born and then their other children. Their love grew deeper with every passing year. And now this.

Covering her with the blanket, he cried with dry sobs. It was as if there was no moisture left in his body. Leaving her to her restless dreams, he shuffled from the room. Every muscle, every bone in his body ached. Tomorrow things would be better, he told himself. He did not eat or drink that day, just sat there getting older by the hour. He heard her cry in the darkness but was too weary to move. 'Tomorrow, my darling, things will be all right.' He rested his head on his chest. His body could take no more and entered that place between sleep and death.

He woke with a start, the sunlight beaming through the window straight into his eyes. Again his exhausted body screamed its protest as he moved. Pain wracked him as he stood up, the dizziness almost making him fall. He grabbed the table for support. Groaning with effort he willed himself forward. 'I'm coming, my love, I'm coming.'

As he looked down at his wife, he realised she had not moved. She still lay on her back, the blood on her cheeks dried to a dark red.

In the kitchen he poured some water into a bowl and took a clean cloth from a cupboard. He spilled some of the water onto the floor as he sat down heavily next to his wife. Dabbing gently at the scratch marks on her cheeks, he consoled her. 'There, my darling, we'll clean you up before I make some chai. Would you like some?'

She did not move. Not even an eyelash flickered. The water in the bowl turned a pinkish red and once more he staggered to his feet.

'I'll be back in a minute. We'll have some hot chai. That will make you feel better.'

Cristiano entered looking dishevelled, his swollen, red-rimmed eyes telling their own story. 'How are you, Papa?'

His father didn't answer the question directly, he just sighed, 'Your mother's still sleeping.'

Cristiano glanced through the open door, noticing the angry red welts on his mother's cheeks. 'What happened?'

'She went into hysterics last night. I held her until she calmed down. She's been asleep ever since … can't seem to wake her.'

Cristiano went into the bedroom and sat by his mother, stroking her arm affectionately. 'Wake up Mother, we all need you. Come back to us for Father's sake.'

She did not move.

That afternoon the doctor came and examined her thoroughly. Holding his stethoscope to her chest, he heard the regular beat of her heart. 'Has she eaten?'

'Not since our daughter's death.'

'Give her time. She's in deep shock. If there's no change by tomorrow, I'll put her on a drip feed.'

Day after day and well into the nights, Rodriguez nursed her. He talked to her of their past life together and their shared happiness, hoping something would reach her inner mind and she would come back to him. He watched as she grew as thin as the mattress beneath her. Family and villagers came each day, sometimes bringing fruit and small gifts with them. They tried to encourage her by talking of the life she was familiar with. Still she did not move, except for the regular beat of her heart and the movement of her chest up and down.

'If she's no better tomorrow, I think she should be moved to hospital,' the doctor finally decided.

Rodriguez nodded resignedly.

That night he lay in a deep sleep next to her. She suddenly opened her eyes and looked at him. 'My beautiful husband.' She turned, cuddling up to him. He unconsciously put his arms around her, pulling her close to him. A deep sigh left his throat and a smile curled his lips as he felt her familiar warmth next to him. He slept deeply for the first time since their shared tragedy.

Waking slowly in the morning warmth, his wife still folded in his arms, he reached up, stroking her forehead. She was cold. Sudden realisation dawned. He embraced her even harder, rocking backwards and forwards as the tears flowed and great sobs of sorrow left him. As he cried out, many of the villagers dropped to their knees, crossed themselves and prayed.

Rodriguez Diaz turned completely grey overnight. His wife was buried before her own child.

Chapter Forty-two

Joe Remerez Gonzales sat on his balcony staring out to sea for hours on end while his son Pedro drank himself to sleep every night. Nothing, not even the children, could console him for the loss of his true love and soul mate. Childhood shyness had grown and blossomed into a deep love and friendship. She was all he had ever known, all he ever wanted to know, a perfect wife and mother. Neighbours helped them with the washing and cooking, but Pedro noticed none of this. His weight loss turned him into an emaciated skeleton. The company ships lay idle in their moorings.

Antonio walked up and down the beach, his hair down to his shoulders, his beard an uncontrollable bushy mess. He talked aloud to himself incessantly, bunching his fists and smashing them against his breast. The whole village thought he had gone mad.

'Mr Seth would not do this to me ... Why hasn't he been in touch? ... What about my Jeena, what's happened to her? ... It's not my fault my sister's dead ... Where's Mother? I miss her cooking ... Why are all the family so quiet? You would think someone died.' He stopped walking. 'That was funny.' He began to laugh. He lay on the sand and laughed, rolling onto his back, waving his arms up and down, and kicking his legs at the same time. His laughter grew hysterical. Foaming at the mouth, he spat sideways, almost choking.

The local children watched him in awe and terror. Their mothers had told them if they did not go to sleep at night, Antonio would get them. They ran back home, nervous and giggling.

'I'll phone Mr Seth tomorrow; he'll know what to do.' Antonio repeated the phrase over and over, like a mantra.

Cristiano knew he had to pull himself together and cast off his mourning for the sake of the family and the business. He sat down next to his father, both warming themselves in the rising sun. 'Father, we have to talk.'

'Go ahead my son, what have you to say?'

'I know how deeply hurt you are, Father, as I am.'

Rodriguez placed his hand on his son's knee. 'Speak.'

'The family ships are idle. Weed is growing on the hulls of the crafts. The letters and bills are mounting up. Our competitors are stealing our fishing grounds and our men. It can't go on.'

'Son, I'm too old and tired to fight any more. What do you propose?'

'If I can motivate Pedro and Antonio, perhaps you would permit me to run the company for us?'

'If Joe agrees, and I can't think why he shouldn't, you have my blessing.' Rodriguez spoke with little enthusiasm, at the same time realising that his older son had the strength for all of them. He prayed he would be successful.

Joe readily agreed. Perhaps this was what his son needed. The salt wind in his face would be something to give him back his dignity and purpose in life. This was the opportunity he had been hoping for to snap Pedro out of his terrible depression.

That night, hollow-eyed, Pedro poured his first drink.

'Before you drink yourself into a stupor, I need

to talk to you, son, if you are capable of listening to me.'

Pedro put his drink on to the table. 'What do you wish to say, Father?'

'I think you should start looking after your own family now and stop feeling sorry for yourself.'

'What do you mean, feeling sorry for myself?'

'You're wallowing in grief and guilt because you weren't there to save Maria. It's not your fault you weren't there; it's not your fault, my son.'

'I should have been here.' The tears welled in Pedro's eyes. 'I should have been here.'

'How were you supposed to know, son? She was in the wrong place at the wrong time. It could have been any one of the village women.'

Pedro banged the table with his fist. His drink fell over, spilling onto the table and dripping off the edge. 'But it wasn't, was it? It was my Maria.' It was the first time he had spoken her name in weeks. All the hurt and self-loathing burst out of him. He could not control himself any longer. Great sobs and tears ran down his cheeks. 'What do I do Father, what do I do?' His whole body was wracked with grief.

Joe rushed over and held his son. Tears welled up in his eyes as he remembered his own losses: his beautiful wife, snubbed out giving life; their darling daughter taken back, moments after being born, forever cradled in his lost love's arms.

'You have her little ones to look after now. Your sons need you more than ever. How will they get on if they don't see their father tall and strong? Be strong for them, my son. Let it out, it's the only way.'

Pedro cried it all out.

'Let's have a peg or two in her memory,' Joe said with tears on his cheeks. Then they cried together, Pedro for his loss and Joe for his long past lost loves.

Finally, Pedro spoke. 'Do you remember when I approached Rodriguez about taking Maria for my wife and he told me I would have to wait four years? At that time it seemed forever.'

They both laughed, still stained with tears. There had been so many moments of happiness and pleasure. They both drank themselves to sleep that night, but the next morning Pedro washed and shaved, and, although still painfully thin, he met with Cristiano.

His father hobbled onto the balcony, taking his usual place.

'I've spoken to Cristiano, Father. Tomorrow we're hiring back our crews. We're going to get the boats shipshape and ready for sea.'

Joe smiled to himself. At long last his son was on the mend.

'Can't find Antonio though. He seems to have disappeared … hasn't been seen for days. Nobody in the village has seen him either.'

Chapter Forty-three

The police officer who had interviewed Mohan and Rajeed requested a visit with the two heads of the respective families. They retired to the company office.

'Please be seated.' Rodriguez sat behind his desk and indicated a chair opposite for the visitor.

Placing his cane on the office desk, the uniformed man broke the silence. 'Well, gentlemen,' he looked directly at Rodriguez, 'it seems your son got himself embroiled in quite a mess. After interrogating the two suspects for several days, we've come to the conclusion that there's more than just these two involved, but at the moment we haven't broken them.'

Joe looked at Rodriguez and became their spokesman. 'I'm sorry, Officer, could we start from the beginning? We haven't a clue what's been going on.'

The officer crossed his legs, twirling his hat on his lap. 'I'm sorry, gentlemen, but it seems your son Antonio got himself involved with some shady characters from Mumbai. Apparently he was picking up something for them on his fishing trips. We haven't established what exactly, but we will. The police in Mumbai are on the lookout for him … he was seen boarding the train. It will only be a matter of time before we pick him up. In the meantime, we wish to interrogate his crew. My men are rounding them up as we speak.

'I'm sorry for your bereavement. I'm sure you and your sons have had enough at the present.'

With this statement left open, the police officer rose, ready to leave. Rodriguez immediately stood up to show him out.

'If your son telephones or tries to contact you,' the officer added, 'I hope you won't do anything foolish. Please keep me informed of any future news. I bid you two gentlemen good day.' Placing his cap on his head and his swagger stick under his arm, he turned and walked through the door Rodriguez held open for him.

Rodriguez returned to his chair and the two partners looked at each other. Joe spoke first, feeling the hurt emanating from his friend.

'I'm afraid everything is falling into place.'

Rodriguez shook his head in disbelief. To find one of his sons had turned bad on top of everything else that had happened was almost unbearable. How could Antonio do this to his own family? Didn't they love him enough? Why had he dishonoured them? 'If they find him, I'll kill him with my bare hands.'

Joe squeezed his friend's shoulder. 'I'll tell Pedro and Cristiano when they get back to shore this evening. You have enough on your shoulders at the moment.'

He watched Rodriguez physically shrink into his chair. He looked grey and bent with weariness. Only forty-nine years had passed in his life, yet his spirit had resigned. He could not cope. The fire had been beaten out of him by losses too great to bear.

A brown envelope dropped through the prison warder's door just as he was preparing himself for night duty. He turned the envelope over in his hand: no address, no stamp. Using his finger as a paper knife, he poked it through the top opening. Inside he saw three crisp one thousand rupee notes. A small square of paper accompanied them. His curiosity aroused, he removed the piece of paper and read: *Stay away from cells 24 and 48 tonight and you will receive the same again with our thanks*.

This was more money than he had ever seen at one time. His heart fluttered. He could pay off all his creditors and still have some left over for some pleasures at his local brothel. He went to work that night with a light step and a smile on his face.

All the cells were closed and barred, the landing lights dimmed to just a glow. The inmates slept. Some snored, some tossed and turned restlessly. Two figures moved silently down the corridor, looking at the numbers on the doors. The cells they were looking for were both on the same landing. Stopping outside number twenty four, one of the men peered through the peephole, checking that the occupant was asleep. Stealthily he inserted the home-made key in the cell door and turned it slowly. The clunk of the tumbler releasing the lock sounded inordinately loud in the still night. They both waited, holding their breath. Nothing stirred. Slowly they slid back the door, the rollers hissing as it opened. Again they paused. They could hear the sound of the man sleeping on the wooden palliasse. He stirred and turned onto his back, coughing once.

Signalling to each other, they entered the small cell. One went to the head of the bed, the other level with the man's thighs. With a look acknowledging they were both ready, they pounced. One grabbed the pillow from under the sleeping man's head, forcing it over his face; the other straddled the now struggling form, while the glint of a blade shone in the dim light. Placing the point just under the ribcage he thrust it violently upwards. The long knife felt no resistance, slicing into the prisoner's heart, killing him instantly. Replacing the pillow under the dead man's head, they re-locked the door and headed down the corridor looking for cell forty eight.

The police officer paid his second visit to the Diaz company office. This time Cristiano opened the door and stared at him with surprise.

'Do you want to come in?'

The officer stepped over the threshold and removed his peaked cap. 'I'm here on an official visit. I won't waste your time, but I'm afraid our investigation has come to a dead end.'

'Why?' Cristiano's surprise was evident in his voice.

'Our two prime suspects have been murdered.' Not waiting for a response, the officer carried on. 'They were murdered in their cells under our very noses. I'm afraid we now have no further leads. In fact, we've been told from higher up to drop the investigation and unless we find your brother, or he turns up here, we'll have to do just that.'

He barely waited for a reply. He stood up, placing his cap under his arm, shook Cristiano's hand and left quickly. Cristiano stood alone in shock. How many more people would be murdered before this sordid affair ran its course?

Chapter Forty-four

Antonio retraced his steps back to Mumbai. This time people steered clear of him. Muttering to himself, he was the picture of a lost soul looking for peace. Although used to seeing poor souls such as him every day of their lives, people just did not want the genie inside him rubbing off on them. He had no difficulty finding a seat on the train as everyone moved away from him.

He rocked back and forth, mumbling to himself. He did not eat or drink on the long journey. On reaching Mumbai he left the station and wandered through the streets in the general direction of the bordello. Horns blasted all around him, cars screeched past, raised voices cursed him, fists banged on the sides of vehicles. Nothing moved him. He trundled on, totally impervious.

Eventually, he found himself standing outside the familiar peeling door with the great brass knocker. He banged twice. The square spyhole opened and the giant's face peered through.

'Go away,' he boomed. 'We don't give to beggars here.'

As the man went to close the shutter, Antonio spoke. 'Mr Seth.' The man hesitated. 'Tell Mr Seth that Antonio the fisherman is here.'

The spyhole opened once more and the big man stared intently at the beggar standing in front of him. 'Wait here.' He slammed the shutter.

'He's here? You two, go and bring him up the back staircase,' Seth commanded.

His two new bodyguards left the room,

returning a few minutes later manhandling Antonio through to the office.

'My, what a disgusting state you're in. You look awful and you stink.'

Antonio stood motionless, saying nothing.

'What do you want? Speak up or I'll have my men throw you out.'

Antonio hesitated.

'Speak up, man.'

'Why haven't you been in touch? We had a deal. You were going to pay me when all the packages were collected. I tried to phone you but you wouldn't take my calls. Then the operator said you were no longer available on this number.'

'Are you really that stupid, you imbecilic moron? Did you think I would be in touch after what happened in your village? I barely got out with my skin attached, let alone Jeena's … cost me a fortune.'

He did not tell him – why should he? – that the man in China had reimbursed him for expenses incurred so far. Why he had done this was a mystery to Seth, but what did he care? The man had promised to be in touch in the future.

'What do you want from me?'

'I just wondered when we will resume our deal.'

Seth laughed, nearly choking on his whisky. 'Our deal with you is finished. Over! Or do you wish me to put it in writing?'

'What do you mean, finished? There are still three more parcels to go.'

'You've cost me two good men, and that stupid woman got in the way.'

'What do you mean, "that woman"?'

'The wretched woman who got in Mohan and Rajeed's way.'

Realisation exploded in Antonio's skull. *They killed my sister. She's dead because of all this – because of me! I helped kill my own sister and mother?* His brain would not accept it. No, no, this could not be! How could this be his fault? All he wanted was to pick up the packages and to live the rest of his life with Jeena. How did it come to this?

'It's your fault we are in this position,' Seth droned on. 'Why did you keep the package? More money? Did you think the people concerned would give in to your demands? They sent us down to get it from you. They knew you still had it. But it's no use now. What you have is useless without the knowledge to put it all together. It's not worth a rupee. You tried to blackmail the wrong people. They will come after you, mark my words. It's not over yet.'

Antonio heard nothing of this. It wasn't his fault the bloody bosun missed the package. If it hadn't been for him everything would be all right. A pox on him and all his family! Desperately he rocked backwards and forwards, rubbing his hands together.

'Where's Jeena?' he blurted out.

Seth pressed a button on his desk and a servant entered. 'Get Jeena! I don't care whether she's asleep or with a client, bring her immediately.'

The moment she entered the room, rubbing her eyes and clad in a bright dressing gown and fluffy slippers, Jeena's instincts made her wary. What did Seth expect from her this time? She sensed the potentially dangerous atmosphere in the office. 'I was sleeping,' she said irritably.

Seth wasn't interested. 'Don't you recognise your sweetheart?' he asked.

'What's he doing here?'

'Wants to run away with you, marry you and live happily ever after.'

Seth's taunts rang in her ears and the two bodyguards laughed.

'Don't listen, Jeena! Come away with me. I love you,' Antonio broke in angrily.

The silence hung heavily around them. She placed her hands on her hips and faced him.

'Do you really think I could live with a peasant like you, end up eating fish all day and smelling like you? What on earth gave you the idea that I'm remotely interested in you? Look around you, you fool. Do you think I would leave all this to live in a stinking fishing village?' She laughed loudly.

'But I love you, Jeena.'

'No you don't. You take lust for love, and greed above everything else. If you hadn't been so greedy wouldn't that woman in your village still be alive? Wouldn't that man you buried recently still be alive?'

And wouldn't my mother still be alive? he heard echoing inside his head. It *was* all his fault. His family, his father – he had destroyed them all. The shock of this realisation hit him with such force he collapsed, senseless, on the floor. Seth walked over to him and poured his decanter of whisky over his face. Antonio spluttered back to consciousness.

'Take him out of here.' He looked down at Antonio. 'You pathetic creature, if I ever set eyes on you again you're a dead man. Now get him out of here.'

His men dragged him down the back stairs and threw him onto the pavement. He made no protest, his whole being possessed by thoughts of his mother and sister and all the other people he had involved in his petty, greedy ambition. He dragged himself away, heading nowhere.

He wandered around the city, eventually

finding a dark, quiet corner in a deserted alley. Saliva dribbled from the corner of his mouth, running onto the cobbles beneath him. Every now and then an anguished cry escaped his lips, echoing from the darkness as he lay there consumed with guilt, hatred and self-pity.

He began mumbling to himself again. 'Why me? All my life people have picked on me. Even at school I had to protect myself. They're all out to get me. But they won't. I won't let them. I'll hide. I'll make myself invisible. Nobody will find me.' He began to chew his nails. 'Yes, that's good. If I lie here for another day people won't find me. I'll hide in the city and only come out at night. If they come after me, I'll pretend it's not me. Yes, that's good.'

A dog barked in the distance and Antonio curled his fists into hammers and bared his teeth. A deep growl left his throat. 'Let them come. I'll be ready for them. I'll get them before they get me.'

A cat arched its back and hissed, mesmerised by the crazed pair of eyes staring from the dark corner.

'Come here, little person, and I'll kiss you with my teeth.' A shrill laugh left the confines of darkness.

The cat spat and hissed as it moved away from the evil thing in the shadows. It jumped up on the wall, tail held high. The thing in the corner fell silent once more.

For three days Antonio did not move, lying in his own mess. No food or water passed his lips. The sun beat down relentlessly. The early hours were bone marrow cold. The third dawn arrived and reluctantly he opened his eyes. He crawled on all fours, leaving dark stains where he had lain. He no longer belonged to the human race. He resembled a creature of the night. His gods had passed him by. Hunger gnawed at his belly; thirst drove him further into insanity. He could smell water ahead of him and found an open gully running with waste water; on hands and knees, he lapped it up like a dog.

He took to wandering the streets at night, finding scraps of food wherever he could. He competed with the rats and dogs for his survival. His hair grew matted and greasy. His skin became sallow and grey. No water touched his body. His teeth were blackened, his finger and toe nails broken and yellow. What remained of his clothes hung ragged and torn off his emaciated body which was infested with lice and ticks. He scratched himself incessantly until he bled. At night the mosquitoes nourished themselves on his open sores. The stench emanating from him was so nauseous that anyone nearing him gagged. He lived with the underbelly of the city.

On certain days he became quite lucid, remembering his part in the three deaths. The guilt forced him back into madness. Other tramps and beggars avoided him and eventually dogs too gave him a wide, wary berth. Fighting a pack of dogs for scraps of food, one day, he managed to grab one of the dogs and strangle it. He tore the poor creature limb from limb and ate it.

He travelled the cesspits, the great rubbish dumps, deserted food markets – anywhere he could find a morsel of food. His mad bulbous eyes protruded from their sockets and he talked to himself constantly, always mumbling about the three lost women that he had to find.

'Cristiano, I have to try and find him.'

Christiano, as tall, proud and strong as Rodriguez used to be, turned and faced his ageing father. 'I knew you would, but please don't tax yourself too much. You haven't fully recovered yet.'

'And I don't think I ever will. Can you arrange accommodation with Cousin Angelo? If I don't try I know I'll never rest in my grave.'

'Don't talk like that, Father, you have years to go yet.'

Two days later, Cristiano drove his father to the station in the battered old jeep. He waved him off on his long journey. I hope he doesn't find him after the damage he's done to the family, he thought.

Theirs wasn't the only family that had been affected. The crew from Antonio's ship had been discretely asked to leave the village, taking their families with them. The women shamefully trailed behind the men, a few meagre bundles of clothes and pots balanced precariously on their heads. The men held their heads down in shame. The children cried and waved to their friends as they left. Father Alphonso gave them absolution and a blessing for their journey. With nowhere to go they knew their times would be hard. Some would end up digging roads for a pittance and their wives breaking up granite ready for the foundations or surfaces. None of them would know where the next meagre meal would come from.

All this ran through Cristiano's mind as he drove back. Pedro had been growing quieter by the day, but as always did his work well. Joe still sat on the balcony staring out to sea. Cristiano knew he was the one keeping the company going and the mantle rested easily on his shoulders. He had hired a captain for Antonio's boat, a big gruff man, but fair to his men. The new crew settled into village life, taking over the quarters of the banished men.

For days, Rodriguez wandered the streets of Mumbai

showing complete strangers a photo of his son, looking for a lead, any lead, to his whereabouts. He put posters on lampposts and trees – anywhere with passing people.

One day, a creature stared out at him from a great mound of refuse. The eyes, looking straight at him, touched his soul and unsettled him. Abruptly he walked on, crossing himself. The creature slithered down the pile of rubbish, a rotten piece of meat between his teeth.

For three weeks Rodriguez trudged the streets to no avail. Every now and then he stumbled across the same poor creature he had encountered before. Every time they met, the poor thing would bare his teeth at him and shy away, slinking under a building, or disappearing down a narrow, dark alleyway.

Finally, a flash flood washed away most of the posters and Rodriguez headed home a broken man. He sat on the train remonstrating with himself: if only he could have found him, perhaps he could have got to the bottom of it all, found out where he had gone wrong and put things right, just so his beloved wife could rest in her grave. 'I won't be long now, my love,' he told her. 'I'll be with you soon.'

He could not stop the tears and his eyes became red-rimmed as silent sobs choked in his chest.

Chapter Forty-five

The phone rang in the sumptuous office twenty floors up, overlooking the fume-filled city of Bangalore.

'Yes this is Vikram Ghosh. How can I help you?'

There was a slight delay as the words rushing at the speed of light reached the man in China. Then he spoke. 'I now have a solution to our problem: thanks to our American friends, the way is now open and the other parcels will arrive overland. Luckily the third package was replaceable. You will receive them in the next three weeks. I hope this is satisfactory to you.'

'There will be no more mishaps and the arrangement will remain the same.'

The silence remained for exactly two seconds then China spoke. 'Have all the loose ends been tied up?'

'Almost.' The man in Bangalore looked down out of his window at all the people scurrying, ant-like, below. 'Monies have been reimbursed, dispelling all anxieties. Everything is falling nicely into place. You will receive the next payment after the first consignment arrives and all the loose cannons have fired. Do I make myself clear? If we have any more mishaps our tentacles are very long, you have my word.'

China replaced his receiver and Vikram Ghosh pressed an internal button on his desk. A small, slim man, dressed entirely in black, silently entered the office. The soft carpet deadened the sound of his shiny shoes on platform soles at least four inches thick, giving him stature he did not possess. His dark suit was well tailored, the creases of his trousers razor sharp. His movements were slow and methodical, giving the impression of cold calculation. His skin was slightly paler than was normal for his caste, hands as sleek as a girl's, hair coiffured, teeth brilliant white. His eyes were jet black and iced. Coldness rose from the depth of his being. He personified menace as he stood awaiting his orders.

'It is time to cauterise the loose ends,' said Ghosh. 'Take two of your best men with you. No telephone calls. Report back to me in three days.'

The small man left as silently as he had entered.

He checked the luminous dial on his wristwatch: 3a.m, the most vulnerable time for man, his instincts lost in slumber.

Three men moved like a single shadow and with little effort picked the back door lock. Taking the stairs two at a time, they tried several doors, peering inside as they moved down the corridor. Eventually, they came across the room they were looking for and stealthily entered, waiting for their eyes to become accustomed to the gloom. All three put on surgical gloves. The small man removed a leather wallet, specially designed to carry medical equipment, from his inside pocket. Removing a large syringe and needle, he checked the liquid inside, indicating to his accomplices to hold the man firmly.

Two lovers lay on the bed completely naked, their feet still entwined. Their breathing was easy and regular; the man's arms were flung above his head in abandonment.

The small man, nostrils flaring as he took in the repugnant aroma of lovemaking, plunged the needle deep into the man's armpit, squirting the

265

deadly liquid in one smooth action. The man's eyes opened in shock. The other two men held him down with a vice-like grip, one with a hand on his shoulder and a hand over his mouth, the other with both hands holding his hips. In vain, he tried to rise. The man with the syringe stepped back, fascinated, watching him die. His pitiful struggles weakened. His face went red. His eyes began to push out of their sockets. The veins on his neck and forehead protruded, looking as if they would explode. He tried to open his mouth but nothing came out. With one last convulsion he lay still, all life gone.

The woman turned onto her back and relaxed, unwittingly exposing herself as her legs fell apart. The leader shuddered at her open body as he indicated to his two men to take up similar positions around her. He refilled the syringe, not bothering to let the air bubble escape from the needle, and reached down, hovering just over her inner thighs. Her labia were still slightly open from lovemaking and he plunged the needle violently in between the lips. She jumped with the sudden intense pain, but the two men held her in their steel grip while the leader emptied the lethal dose into the wall of her vagina. Placing his rubber gloved hand over her mouth, he looked deep into her shocked eyes and smiled as her lights went dim. She struggled no more.

After turning on the gas supply of the small, unlit fire, the men left as silently as they had arrived, leaving no trace of their presence.

Next morning the waiter took Seth his usual cup of coffee. He knocked and waited for the customary summons from within. He knocked once more, thinking Mr Seth must still be asleep or in the shower. He knocked a third time, more loudly. It was then that he noticed the smell of gas. Putting the tray

266

down, he peered though the keyhole. The curtains were still drawn, making it impossible to see anything, but the distinct whiff of gas caused him to straighten and hurry down to report to the concierge.

With Seth's two bodyguards trailing behind, the manager returned with the waiter.

'Haven't I got enough to do without this?' he complained, knocking on the door vigorously. 'Mr Seth, your coffee, sir! Mr Seth!' He banged again. No answer. He took the master key from the chain hanging from his pocket and inserted it into the lock. As he opened the door the strong smell of gas enveloped them all.

'Oh my god!' The manager placed his handkerchief over his nose and mouth, entered and quickly turned off the gas fire. 'Get the window open, *now!*' he ordered the waiter as he rushed over to the two prostrate bodies on the bed. The waiter pulled back the curtains, exposing the two naked bodies to the sunlight, and flung open the window. The manager then turned to the open-mouthed waiter. 'Go and call the police and an ambulance! Move, man!'

Giving him a push, he then turned his attention to the two bodyguards who were looking on in disbelief. 'Stand at the door and stop anyone from coming in. We don't want this turning into a side show for our other guests. I'll go down and wait for the ambulance.'

By the time the police and ambulance arrived, the smell of gas was almost gone. After questioning everyone, the officials concluded that the deaths were suicide or accidental, caused by carbon monoxide poisoning. They found no suspicious circumstances.

In Mumbai, a creature of the night burrowed into the piles of rubbish, forming a makeshift nest. Ever on the move he was as quiet as his shadow. He imagined himself in perpetual hell, the demons of his mind pouring boiling sunlight over his emaciated skin, while hunger gnawed forever at his belly. The waste from his body ran down his legs and dripped off his ankles.

Antonio would not make old bones.

Chapter Forty-six

Nothing could ever be the same again, even though the villagers went about their business: children played and attended school; mothers worked together, cooking or doing their washing at the river bank; the fishing boats came and went. Cristiano put to sea with Pedro and the new captain, all three boats fitted out with the fish-finders. In the evenings he managed their paper work and banking. Life went on. It had to. Weeks turned into months and Joe still sat on his stool staring out to sea, while Pedro seemed to withdraw even further into himself.

As the anniversary of Maria's death drew near, Pedro approached Cristiano. 'Can we talk?'

'Of course, let's go into the office.'

Side by side, they strolled into the building.

'Coffee?'

Pedro nodded. They sat opposite each other, the silence palpable. Pedro cleared his throat.

'How are we doing?'

'Very well,' replied his partner. 'Why do you ask?'

Pedro fidgeted in his chair. 'Can you afford to buy me out?'

'What!' exclaimed Cristiano, completely astonished. 'Buy you out? For heaven's sake, why?'

'I can't settle … too many memories. I need a fresh start.'

'But what about your sons and Joe, let alone my father? Have you thought about this?'

'Every waking moment of every day. The memories are too strong. I can't get Maria out of my mind. There's too much here. In the house are her pots and pans, her chair by the fire. I go to bed at night exhausted and can't sleep; every time I close my eyes I can still smell her sweet fragrance, still feel her soft hair against my face and her warm body next to mine. She's everywhere, haunting me. Joe does his best, and you and Rodriguez have been a tower of strength to me. The village couldn't have done more and Father Alphonso has listened to me for hours. But it's gone beyond grief: this hurt never leaves me.

'So I've decided to leave and live a simple life. I'm going back to my father's old village. I'll teach my sons what that long lost old man taught my father many years ago – things that I had forgotten until lately. It will make them hardy and ready for anything life throws at them. It will teach them that nature is the best provider, and that money only buys things – not happiness. That old man taught my father more than I realised.'

Cristiano sat stunned. 'That was some speech. I'm glad you got it off your chest, but what about your sons' schooling?'

'They can read and write. What more do they need? They have not yet learned how to survive. They have not felt their instincts honed for everything nature can throw at them. The sea wind in their hair, the salt smarting their eyes, the thrill of catching their own supper: you know of these things, Cristiano, but they have been spoiled.'

'But your old village is deserted.' Cristiano looked for an excuse to break his friend down. He would be such a loss.

'Can you buy me out?' Pedro repeated the question flatly, his voice resonating with determination.

'Yes, yes, of course we can. What will you do with the money?'

'Invest it for my children's and grandchildren's futures. You must swear to me you won't tell. I don't want my sons to know. I don't want them growing up soft bellied. I'll tell them when the time comes.'

'Well that's settled then. I'll have the papers drawn up by our advocate. It will take time, Pedro.' In the time lapse maybe he could talk Pedro around. It was the mad idea of a desperate man.

Pedro felt relieved. Now they would have to break the news to their respective fathers. Leaving the office they remained silent, reflecting on their own thoughts.

Joe remained sitting on the balcony. Pedro sat next to him saying nothing, happy as they were in each other's company. After a while, Pedro coughed.

'May I speak with you, Father?'

Joe did not answer at once. Turning, he put both hands on Pedro's shoulders and looked straight into his only son's eyes. 'When do you want to leave, son?'

Pedro looked startled. 'How did you know?'

'You are my flesh and blood. I've watched your suffering all these months, seen how uncomfortable you've become. I've sat through your silences. I've heard you cry in the night.' Joe let go of his son. 'I have only one thing to ask of you: let me come with you.'

This time Pedro put his hands on Joe's shoulders. 'You wily old devil. You're so much wiser than we give you credit for. I had no way of approaching you over my dilemma. I've paced the decks trying to find a way to tell you, but you knew all the time.'

They smiled at each other, revelling in each other's warmth.

'Papa, how do I tell the boys?'

Joe scratched his chin, his one eye sparkling. 'Make it into an adventure when you tell them, and promise that they will visit their friends at least once a month. It's important for them to bond with others of their kind. That way they won't feel too lonely and isolated. When will we leave?'

'After I've concluded our business dealings with Cristiano and Rodriguez.'

'When we are ready,' said Joe thoughtfully, 'I'll ask the reverend father for his blessing.'

Next morning Joe knocked on Rodriguez's door.

'Come in, come in, my dear friend.'

Stepping over the threshold, Joe noticed, not for the first time, how empty the place seemed now that his old friend's wife had gone.

'I hear you're on the move. I will dearly miss you, my old friend. Cristiano told me all about his meeting with Pedro. I knew you wouldn't be left behind.'

Joe looked at his companion: he had aged twenty years in just one; his hair was completely white and his muscles sagged under his robes. Joe watched as he shuffled across the room, and then painfully eased himself into his chair.

'Sit, my friend, sit. Let's smoke a cob pipe together.'

They sat by the cold hearth, contemplating their past. They had smoked many pipes together in happier times: the formation of their company, the union of their children, the birth of their grandchildren. Now it had all come to this. Rodriguez sucked strongly on his pipe. The tobacco crackled and burned; the strong, thick, grey smoke idled up to the ceiling, staining it a smoky yellow.

Joe's gaze followed the line of smoke. 'I'm

going to take my old boat and nets if you don't object.'

'Would you take some advice from a fished out old crock such as me?'

'Of course.' Joe banged his pipe on the side of the hearth, watching the embers fall to the floor and burn themselves out.

'Pedro should keep one third of the business and become our sleeping partner. That way, you'll get your dividend at the end of each year. After all, it is still our company. Pedro is young and impetuous. Who knows what the future holds? Who knows how the youngsters will grow up?' he added with sadness in his voice.

'You speak wisely for one so old.' Joe hugged his friend good-humouredly. 'It's a wise move, a good plan. I'll put it to Pedro.'

Pedro left his father in charge of his sons. He felt nothing as he entered their old village, the place he had spent the first eleven formative years of his life. He remembered how hard their lives had been, his papa always protecting him. He could not remember many people. They had been virtual outsiders here. Still, it was a good place to bring the boys. He looked over the village, abandoned for the past decade since the easy living in the towns and city had tempted the people with television adverts and pulled them away with material thoughts.

Standing in the middle of the ghost town triggered an old bad memory. His mind clicked a photographic image of four older boys taunting him.

'Where's your mummy? Your papa's not here to protect you now, is he?'

Tears of frustration run down his cheeks. With fists clenched he charges at one of the taller boys, blind fury driving him on. Losing his footing on uneven ground he falls into the dust. The four tormentors, seeing their chance, jump on him together, kicking and punching his prostrate figure. He puts his arms over his head as the blows rain down on his body. Shouts from the older men drive the boys away, laughing as they run.

Pedro snapped back to the present, driving this bad memory back to where it belonged – in the past. He replaced it with more pleasant thoughts as he walked through the village towards the shoreline.

His father's smiling face beams down from their little vessel; he holds a string of fish in one hand, a large sea bass in the other. 'Tonight, my son, we will eat well!'
  He hugs his father with pride, the waves washing around them as they stand in the surf.

A lone seagull winged past him, its cry piercing the warm air like a lament. He stood there as the waves lapped against his feet. One day they'll realise what they have here, he thought. The one thing materialism does not teach is self reliance. You lose your independence working for others in order to possess material things, which mean nothing in the end.
  Leaving the village he walked inland a little, noticing how the paddy fields had been abandoned to the birds. Egrets and jackdaws, buzzards and pied kingfishers now ruled here. The weeds grew tall and strong. They would have a lot of work to do but hard work never killed anybody.
  Over the next few days Pedro erected a temporary shelter on the beach, all bamboo poles, palm fronds and blue plastic sheeting. This would be their home until they built their new place. He was determined his boys would help with everything:

their new house, the rice fields, and the maintenance of the small craft – every bit of their future lives. The boys would know how to make, mend, sow and harvest. The land and sea would be their teachers.

On the day of their departure, Joe and Pedro went through the village, door to door, giving everyone sweets as was the custom. Although saying goodbye was hard, everyone accepted their going with stoic good humour and the boys were looking forward to their new adventure. Only Rodriguez and Cristiano were sad.

'Goodbye old friend.' Rodriguez looked unhappily at Joe.

'This isn't goodbye, we're only a few miles away, we'll be in touch. But I know what you mean.' Joe hugged his friend and a tear fell from his good eye. 'I've got a bit of sand in my eye.' He blew his nose and tried to swallow the lump in his throat.

'Take care of our grandsons,' Rodriguez replied.

Joe knew then that his old friend would not see another Christmas. He felt privileged to have known such an honourable man. He remembered with gratitude the life and self respect that Rodriguez had given him. He recalled the pride they shared, seeing their ocean going trawlers rounding the headland for the first time with their painted flags and their three sons at the helm. They had laughed then as they had seen the machine of life turning, churning out another cycle. The laughter had grown and grown, bellowing from them until it made them cough and splutter, tears running down their faces. Now the tears were for a different reason. 'Goodbye, old friend.' He turned and hobbled away.

Cristiano and Pedro embraced. 'Don't phone,

write to me; it will give me something to read on the dark evenings.'

'It's about time, Cristiano, that you found yourself a wife. You must, for your father's sake, keep such an honourable bloodline alive.'

Cristiano smiled. 'There's time yet, my friend, there's time yet.'

Pedro laughed and embraced his friend again.

Joe turned and looked out to sea and the continuous presence of time, grinding ever onward, never still.

Coming soon …

Don't miss
Dark Horizons,
the sequel to **Distant Horizons.**

Eric Charles Bartholomew started writing when he was sixty years old (it's never too late), having worked in the city of London and abroad for over forty years, including five years lecturing in his chosen profession. The part he enjoyed the most was the travel. Luckily for him, his wife Mary also enjoys travel. Their first trip covered India, Sri Lanka and the Maldives. They fell in love with India and went back many times, eventually living there for several years. They have also travelled to Egypt, Africa, China, Outer Mongolia, Thailand, America, Europe and many other destinations, meeting wonderful fellow travellers, sharing their highs and lows, and swapping exaggerated stories over a glass or two of arak or feni.

Eric and Mary have been married for over forty years, and they have three children and two grandchildren. They live on a narrow boat, with no fixed abode, going wherever life takes them.

To learn more about Eric or to contact him, visit
www.distant-horizons.org